RICHARD ROSEN

SATURDAY NIGHT DEAD

AN ONYX BOOK

NEW AMERICAN LIBRARY

NAL BOOKS ARE AVAILABLE AT QUANTITY DISCOUNTS WHEN USED TO PROMOTE PRODUCTS OR SERVICES. FOR INFORMATION PLEASE WRITE TO PREMIUM MARKETING DIVISION, NEW AMERICAN LIBRARY, 1633 BROADWAY, NEW YORK, NEW YORK 10019.

ONYX TRADEMARK REG. U.S. PAT. OFF. AND FOREIGN COUNTRIES
REGISTERED TRADEMARK—MARCA REGISTRADA
HECHO EN DRESDEN, TN, USA

SIGNET, SIGNET CLASSIC, MENTOR, ONYX, PLUME, MERIDIAN and NAL BOOKS are published by New American Library, a division of Penguin Books USA Inc., 1633 Broadway, New York, New York 10019

First Signet Printing, June, 1989

1 2 3 4 5 6 7 8 9

PRINTED IN THE UNITED STATES OF AMERICA

to Mac

LAST LAUGHS

Executive Producer
ROY GANZ

Producer
Leo Rhoades

Director
Ralph Morello

Head Writer
Joey Hanes

Writers
Karen Baldwin
Marty Beaver
Chuck Causey
Curt Geller
Dickie Nacke
Barry Sondell
Rick Vergaard

Cast
Tom Angel
Eddie Colasono
Ron Fellows
Nancy Pildone
Candee Wersch
Rob Whent

Featured Players
Brenda J. Johnson
Jimmy Lanahan

Musical Director
Nash Fieldman

Production Designers
Miles Papierniak
Gloria Sams

Costume Designer
Deborah Shibko

Makeup Supervisor
Celeste Temkin

1

Harvey Blissberg stood in the doorway of the Ninth Avenue bar, watching the man who had been watched by millions the night before as he flied out to end the World Series. It was less than sixteen hours since the New York Mets had beaten the Boston Red Sox in the seventh game of the Series, and less than two since Harvey had taken the Pan Am shuttle down from the city of the losing team to the city of the winning team.

In the brown light of the bar a fly orbited Dave Kasick's head like a little loud planet. He was oblivious to it behind his designer sunglasses. Harvey was certain that even the detonation of a hand grenade at Dave Kasick's feet would have occurred well below his threshold of awareness.

Travel bag in hand, Harvey walked slowly toward Kasick's booth, took the bench opposite him, and counted five empty tumblers on the table. A grizzled piece of lime lay in the bottom of each of them. The ice cubes in three of the glasses were still in various stages of decomposition, indicating the furious rate at which Kasick had been absorbing his favorite fluid, Stolichnaya vodka. Kasick's large hand enclosed a sixth, half-filled tumbler. Given his present condition, there was little prospect of the glass reaching his mouth any time in the near future.

When Harvey leaned over and removed the sunglasses, Kasick's eyes were closed. The bender had rubbed all the handsomeness off his face. Harvey knew from experience what would be required. He gently removed the active vodka-and-lime from Kasick's hand and poured it over his head. Kasick seemed not to notice. Harvey took Kasick's nose between two knuckles and pulled it to within a few inches of his own. Kasick's left eyelid twitched slightly.

"Batter up!" Harvey yelled in Kasick's face.

One of the few other patrons in the bar, a man in only marginally better condition than Kasick, lifted his head at a nearby table and inquired, "What inning is it?"

Harvey released Kasick's nose.

Kasick slowly smacked his lips twice. "I—" he managed to say before the effort exhausted him.

Harvey laid his chin in his right palm. "Yes, Dave?"

"I . . . am . . ."—he opened his right eye—". . . *faced.* I . . . am *completely* . . . faced. And it is . . . is *sho* unlike me." He was wearing a slice of lime on his head.

"No, Dave. This is just like you."

Kasick's head teetered on his neck, dropped forward against his chest, and popped up. "And who are you?"

"Take a guess, Dave."

"I'll need"—he closed his eyes to reflect—"a clue." His breath was quite bad.

"A clue," Harvey said. "All right, Dave. Several years ago this man was your roommate on the Boston Red Sox, the team for which you still play. It was his honor to rescue you several times from the brink of personal degradation in dives around the American League."

"I'm . . . afraid . . . I'm afraid I'll need . . . more'n that."

"The first name is Harvey."

Kasick shook his head. "Thash not a whole lot to go on."

"I'm being careful not to make it too easy."

"Then jush give me the lash name."

"Dave, that'd give it away."

"Hey, let me be the judge. Wha's your lash name?"

"Blissberg."

Kasick rubbed his two day's growth of beard. Between the stubble and the sunglasses, he would have gone unrecognized. "Let me take a shot in the dark," Kasick said. "Your name's *Harvey* Blishberg."

"You're getting warmer."

Kasick slammed his hand on the table, knocking over two of the six glasses. "Harvey Blishberg! So! And how is your large and exquisite pershon?"

"Fine, thank you."

"Okay," Kasick said. "Now who am *I*?"

"Oh, Dave, I knew it would come to this."

"Well, damn it," he said with great urgency, "who *am* I?"

Harvey sighed. "You're Dave Kasick, Dave. You play the outfield for the Boston Red Sox. You're one of America's most popular athletes."

"Tell me more."

"You hit thirty-four home runs this past season. Your gilded tongue and your ebullient personality have made you a favorite of post-game interviewers and lady baseball fans everywhere. You're an alcoholic."

"You know, this pershon . . . shounds . . . shounds vaguely familiar . . . to me."

"Well, you think about it for a moment."

Harvey got up, went to the bar, and asked the bartender for a pitcher of ice water and a towel. "How long has he been here?" he asked.

The bartender consulted a watch halfway up his forearm. "Let's see. He was here when I started my shift. So I'd say he's going on eight hours." He bent down to fill a pitcher with ice.

"Don't you have a policy about how much a guy can drink in this place before you kick him out?"

"Sure, we got a policy," the bartender said, sliding the fluted plastic pitcher across the scarred bar. "If a guy's braindead, that's it. We cut him off. No more to drink. That's the policy. Don't matter how much he kicks and screams." He handed Harvey two bar towels.

"You know," Harvey said, "if more bars in New York cared as much about their customers as this place, I think we'd see a real significant drop in the city's alcoholism rate. Thanks for the water."

As Harvey approached the table, Kasick was saying, "Hey, tell me more about thish Dave Kasick. I shwear to God I know him."

"I'll tell you more about him in a minute," Harvey said. "First I want to get that piece of lime off the top of your head." He stood behind Kasick and poured the contents of the pitcher over him.

Kasick's body barely registered the event. When the pitcher was empty and Harvey had taken his seat across from him, Kasick blew some ice water at him and said, "Well, tell me, did you get that piece of lime off my head?"

"You're a dickhead, Dave," Harvey said, whipping the two towels at him. They hit him in the chest and dropped in his lap.

"You know this guy you were talking about, Harvey? Well, I've got to confess something to you." His dark hair hung down his forehead in spikes. The gray buckling linoleum around his chair was flooded.

"What's that, Dave?"

He wiped his face. "You're not going to believe what I'm about to tell you."

"Try me."

"I think that guy is—are you ready for this, Harvey?"

"I'll brace myself, Dave."

"Well, I think that guy is me." He covered his eyes with his right hand. There was a blood blister on the tip of his middle finger. "Now I feel like—I—I'm having a vision that I've just played in . . . a World Series. Am I right?"

"Correct."

"And we lost the Series, am I right?"

"Right again."

"We lost it in seven, am I right?"

"Yes."

"How'd I do, Harvey? It'll come back to me soon, but I think I'd like to know now."

"You did just fine, Dave. You hit two-seventy-three and played the outfield with much grace and aplomb. In game six you even threw out a runner at home."

"Well, that's good to know." Harvey could tell how far Kasick was from sobriety by the fact that the movements of his mouth were still badly coordinated with his speech. "How'd you find me?" Kasick asked. There was more jaw action than the words warranted.

"I assumed you'd be in one of the sinkholes on Ninth Avenue you used to drag me to when we were in town playing the Yankees. Your taste in bars, Dave—must be something in your steel-town background."

Kasick pondered this information with the false gravity of the drunk. "I had a fine upbringing. But *why'd* you find me?"

"Roy Ganz asked me to."

"Who's that?"

"For God's sake, Dave, sober up."

"Can't, Harvey."

Harvey sighed. "Ganz is executive producer of 'Last Laughs.' "

Kasick squeezed his eyes shut for a moment. "Wait— why'd this person ask you to find me?"

"Do you mean why did Roy Ganz want you found, or why'd he ask *me* to find you?"

Kasick clutched the edge of the table with both hands. "Give me both barrels, Harvey. I can take it."

"Roy Ganz wanted me to find you because you agreed to guest-host the show this Saturday night. But, as I understand it, you didn't show up because, apparently, you were busy getting completely faced, you dickhead. So Roy Ganz's people called your agent, who told them he had no idea where you were, but that I might."

"You?"

"I'm your former roomie and drinking buddy, Dave. And, as you may know, since I left the game you still play so admirably, I've been making my living as a private detective."

Kasick licked his lips contemplatively. "It's coming back, coming back, coming back to me," he mumbled. "This show you're talking about—I believe there was . . . there was some talk about my being on the show."

"Not talk, Dave. You and your agent agreed to it."

"But it's a, if I'm not mistaken, a *live* show, Harvey.

In front of many, many million Americans. No can do."

"I've come to take you back, Dave."

Dave fished an ice cube out of a glass and lobbed it into his mouth. "No, Harvey, I'm not going!"

"Yes, you are."

"I've got stage fright." He broke the ice cube between his teeth.

Harvey patted the breast of his mountain parka. "You're not going to make me use my tranquilizer gun on you, are you, Dave? You know, if I have to, I will. If it's necessary, I'll return you to Roy Ganz with a tag in your ear."

"You wouldn't."

"If I don't bring you back, I don't get paid. I took the case on contingency," he lied.

"They're *paying* you? To bring me in? How much are they paying you?"

"Two grand if I bring you back today."

"Bounty hunter," Kasick said. "That's all I'm worth? Two lousy grand?" He reached into his pants pocket and brought out a stack of bills folded in half. He dealt out twelve one-hundred dollar bills on the table in front of Harvey, and then slapped down three twenties. "There we go—what's that? Two grand?"

"Twelve sixty."

"Okay. I'll write you a check for the rest." He pushed the money at Harvey. "Just please don't take me back."

Harvey put his hand over the bills and pushed them back across the table. "Let's go, Dave."

"Harvey, I can't go ahead with it."

"For God's sake, be a big boy. You're an MVP."

"Huh?"

"Dave, you're a shoo-in for American League MVP this year. So act like one. You know, Roy Ganz probably could've had any New York Met he wanted for the show this week. But he wanted you, Dave. You're hot shit. You're somewhere between a cultural icon and a national treasure." Kasick's role as TV spokesman for a popular motor oil had as much to do with his current crest of celebrity as his baseball career.

"M . . . V . . P . . . M . . . V . . . P," Kasick said slowly, with a little lopsided smile. "Most Vicious Prick in the league?"

"Let's go," Harvey said, unable to contain a grin.

Kasick was busy thinking. "Much Vanity on Parade?"

"Let's go, Dave." He stood.

"More Vodka, Please."

"I'm giving you ten seconds to stand up, Dave. Unassisted." Harvey was not smiling now.

"Me Vacate Premises?"

Harvey looked down at his former roommate. "Must Vamoose, Pardner," he said. "Me Very Pissed."

—— **2** ——

Harvey pushed a damp Dave Kasick into a cab on Ninth Avenue, got in after him, and directed the driver to the offices of "Last Laughs" in midtown Manhattan. He thought it wiser to produce Kasick as soon as possible, even in this sad and fragrant state, than to waste another hour making him presentable at his hotel. Harvey was also eager to conclude the transaction and make the six o'clock shuttle back to Boston.

"More Vodka, Please," Kasick said while the taxi idled in rush hour traffic on Forty-second Street.

"Be quiet, Dave." Harvey rolled down the window another few inches.

"Championship ring would've been nice," Kasick murmured.

"You almost had it."

"I don't believe in almost, Harvey."

"Well, it'll have to do for now," Harvey said. Although he and Mickey Slavin had watched grimly on TV back in their Cambridge home as the Red Sox surrendered to their ancient curse and pissed away late-inning leads, the Series had been an exhilarating dose of miraculous occurrences that, when over, moved Mickey to mutter something about "a major spiritual experience." The games had left them with the impression that baseball was less a metaphor for life than life a metaphor for baseball. At the very least, the games had forced them both to abandon the customary cynicism of their respective roles—Harvey as a former major leaguer, she as Boston's only female television sports reporter.

The security woman at the Art Deco elevators in the ANC network building lobby did not believe that the derelict clutching Harvey's arm could be in any way associated with "Last Laughs." She agreed to let the two of them pass only after calling up to the twenty-fourth floor.

At the bank of elevators on the twenty-fourth, they were met by a young woman in green suede pumps and matching jade earrings. "How nice to meet you," she said to Kasick, who didn't answer because he was busy wiping some residue from his mouth with a corner of his denim jacket. "I'm glad you're all right."

"You have an extremely generous concept of all right," Harvey said, still discreetly supporting Kasick with a finger through one of the back belt loops of his jeans.

"And you must be Harvey Blissberg," the woman said. "I'm Paula Coles, the talent coordinator."

"Pleased to meet you."

"Thanks for finding him."

"My pleasure."

Kasick suddenly started rotating his head.

"Well," Coles added with a worried expression, "we've got four days to get him ready to perform live sketches on national TV."

"Oh, I believe he's ready now," Harvey said. "Provided you've got a lot of sketches involving a thirty-two-year-old ballplayer with delirium tremens."

She glanced at Harvey, as if to say, Nice try, but why don't you leave the comedy here to us.

"Many Vile Projects," Kasick mumbled.

She turned to Harvey again. "What'd he say?"

"He said, 'Many Vile Projects.' "

"Well," she said, lightly clapping her hands. "There's a shower in the executive men's room. I don't think Roy wants to see him like this. I want to get him cleaned up for the writers' meeting at six. I'll have wardrobe send up some fresh clothes for him."

"Sixteen-and-a-half, thirty-five," Kasick said. His eyes were closed.

"Now what's he saying?" Coles said.

"I believe he's telling you his shirt size."

Coles swiftly led them down a carpeted corridor, past white walls covered with framed vintage movie posters. She turned Kasick over to a young, casually dressed man with scarlet-framed glasses, and guided Harvey toward an open area, where several women were on the phones at their desks.

"Wait here just a moment," she said. "Roy wanted to see you. I'll make sure he's free. Of course"—she smiled wearily—"he's never free, so what I really mean is I'll see whether this is one of those moments when he can be deceived into thinking he's free to see you."

She headed for a closed door at the far end of the open area, leaving Harvey standing awkwardly between a desk and a rubber plant in the offices of the comedy show that had, as the critics were fond of saying, reflected and defined a generation. Harvey, like so many others in his generation, remembered the show's first broadcast back in the mid-seventies, an event that now belonged in the Baby Boom's canon of historical moments. You remembered exactly where you were for the assassination of one Kennedy, possibly both; the first time you heard the Beatles' "I Wanna Hold Your Hand"; Martin Luther King's assassination; the killings at Kent State; the secret bombing of Cambodia; Nixon's resignation. And you remembered where you were the night that a dapper twenty-eight-year-old former television child-actor named Roy Ganz suddenly appeared on your set after the local evening news. He was standing behind a butcher's block holding a meat cleaver.

"Hello," he had said dryly into the camera, "my name is Roy Ganz and I'm the producer of the new network comedy you are about to see. It will be performed live, which makes me very nervous. But we're the generation that likes to take chances. That's why we're doing the show, and that's why you're watching it. I hope you like it. In fact, I *really* hope you like it. Because if it doesn't work, if the next sixty minutes don't prove to be funny, I will reappear at the end of the show and chop off my pinkie with this meat cleaver. That's right—I will dismember myself on national television as a token of how seriously I take this new enterprise. I will also be dismembering myself so that nothing that the network executives have in store for me if I fail can really hurt me. So remember: if you enjoy the show, I won't have to mutilate myself—it's that simple. Remember: my pinkie is in your hands. The choice is yours. Thank you and welcome to 'Last Laughs.' "

During the seven years that Ganz had produced "Last Laughs," other networks had tried unsuccessfully to imitate his formula. It was widely believed that he possessed an alchemical touch for combining unknown improvisational actors with the countless other, and sometimes ineffable, elements of television comedy production. Some fifteen million Americans had tuned in weekly. Harvey used to watch the show on the road in his hotel room, and had even spearheaded, during one rain delay in Baltimore, a dugout contest to determine which teammate could do the best impersonation of original cast member Warren Howard's much imitated impersonation of a stoned Abraham Lincoln delivering the Gettysburg Address. During those seven years under Ganz, the show had launched several suddenly famous cast members on movie careers, most of which wobbled and exploded like inferior NASA missiles once they entered Hollywood's atmosphere. The fact that original "Last Laughs" cast members like Claire Strawbridge and Tony Rocchio never truly thrived outside Ganz's protective custody was taken as further proof of his genius.

After seven years, though, the party was over. Every postmortem on Ganz's regime that Harvey had ever read concluded that the mood had begun to turn a little ugly by the show's third season, although there was some difference of opinion as to why. The show itself had not completely lost its sparkle, even toward the end of the Ganz era, but it was rotting within. The humor's original varnish had started to wear away, revealing middle-class snobbishness underneath. Some observers blamed the widely publicized drug use for the show's decline. Some favored the too-much-too-soon theory of self-destruction, while others speculated that the moment in history that had made Ganz's triumph possible in the first place—a unique crossing of social, political, and cultural forces—had simply passed.

The show's ratings settled downward at a level that network executives still found tolerable, but that an exhausted Roy Ganz took as one of several signs that he should get out while the getting was gracious. In a *New York Times* interview at the time—like many of the show's fans, Harvey had monitored the program's fortunes like a favorite stock, had read what he could about the intriguing Ganz—the producer had remarked that, after seven years, watching the show sometimes seemed to him like looking at a photocopy of the original. And so at thirty-five Ganz had disappeared with his golden name into that entertainment industry ether of development deals, television pilots, and screenplay projects that evaporated somewhere between pitch and production. For several years Ganz wandered in the West Coast world of costly near-misses and elaborate failures; meanwhile, "Last Laughs" survived under far less inspired leadership, pumping out fainter and fainter Xeroxes of that first, vivid, Ganz-inspired image.

Then, three months before, the network had lured Ganz back as executive producer to rejuvenate "Last Laughs." Most of the publicity had concerned how much money it had cost the network to rebag such big game. For the most part, the press had greeted his return as messianic. But they had treated the show roughly. On the shuttle down from Boston, Harvey had read the *Globe*'s television critic's denunciation. Something about "the Emperor's New Jokes" and reaching new depths of tastelessness in last week's sketch portraying the Kennedy brothers as gay: one of the generation's dynasties violating another. But however bad "Last Laughs" might be at the moment, Roy Ganz was unmarked. You felt that his present would always be adequately illuminated by his past. Roy Ganz still glowed.

Paula Coles was at Harvey's side. "Roy would like to see you," she said.

Harvey's stomach fluttered, and it took him an instant to identify the feeling. It was what a baseball fan felt, pen in hand, tentatively approaching a favorite player in the parking lot after the game; what he had felt years ago waiting for the Red Sox of the early sixties outside Fenway Park. It was the slight dizziness experienced in the face of celebrity. Harvey was a Roy Ganz fan. He fell in step behind Coles.

The sputtering of a commercial popcorn machine in one corner of the open area caught Harvey's attention. Exploded kernels were dripping softly over the edge of its metal pan. It was the only detail that might have distinguished the scene from a secretarial pool at an insurance agency.

"I don't get it," Harvey said to Coles. "I expected to see a bunch of writers furiously smoking cigarettes and shouting gags at each other."

"They're over in the writers' wing," she said, walking ahead.

"Got to segregate these creative types, huh?"

"You must be thinking of the old days. I was an intern back then, with the drugs and the fist fights and the pet iguanas and all that. Sometimes I think the only thing that's left from those days is the hours. I think most of the writing still gets done after midnight." She stopped at the door of a corner office. "Right in there."

When Harvey entered, Roy Ganz turned briefly to him from his perch on the edge of his carved oak desk and said, "Come in. I'll be right with you," before returning his blue eyes to a man sunk deeply in a wing chair. Harvey could only see a bit of flannel cowboy shirt. "I want to be sure you understand me, Leo," Ganz said.

Harvey's first impression was that Ganz did not seem so much to be wearing his clothes—red-and-white striped shirt, pleated pants with gray suspenders, fashionable high-topped black lace-up shoes—as displaying them. His shirt was so heavily starched that it hardly changed its contours when Ganz reached into a small wicker basket of popcorn on his desk and placed a single kernel on his tongue. His face possessed a corresponding wrinklelessness. Behind him on the desk stood a row of unopened one-liter bottles of Diet Coke.

"The last thing is Alex's agent called me today," Ganz was saying to the person secreted in the wing chair. "Alex is worried about hosting the show. He's worried about the bad reviews, and he wonders if hosting the show can do anything for his career. Leo, it's your job as producer to allay his fears. I want you to convince him that hosting the show will help his career, to say nothing of improving his chances for happiness in this life. And as executive producer, Leo, it's my job"—Ganz smiled condescendingly—"to take the credit when you get Alex on the show."

Ganz turned toward a large bulletin board on the far wall of his office. Colored index cards in a row across the top were hand-printed in green ink with the show dates for the season. Vertically, underneath the dates, were index cards inscribed with the names of that week's guest host, featured musical act, and stand-up comic. Under "November 1," the three cards read "DAVE KASICK"; "BASKET CASE"; and "JULES THE BARBARIAN." Under "November 15," the next scheduled show, the name of "ALEX RIND," the movie actor, was written in blue ink.

"As you can see, Leo, Alex's name is now in blue ink. Blue, as we know, stands for 'tentatively scheduled.' Blue is also for how sad we'll be if he declines our invitation to participate in the renaissance of 'Last Laughs.' You must make it your business to change the color of the ink on that card from blue to green. Green for 'booked.' Green for money, which is what the network makes more of when the ratings go up, which is what the ratings are sure to do that week if Alex hosts the show. Green is also"—that quick, imperious smile again—"for the envy others will feel toward me because I have so capable a producer as Leo Rhoades. *Comprende?*"

Leo Rhoades rose out of the wing chair. He was a large, unkempt man in his thirties with a low forehead and a pale, unbaked loaf of a face. On it, his small features seemed lost. He was out-of-focus compared to Ganz's clarity. He said, "I'll give him a call this evening, Roy." Rhoades's flannel shirt billowed, and the cuffs of his corduroys failed to meet the tops of his unpromising brown shoes by at least three inches.

Ganz reached behind him for another kernel of popcorn and chewed it meditatively. "Leo, I want you to be charming, giving, and enthusiastic with Alex."

Rhoades looked uncomfortably at Harvey for an instant. "No, no, no, I will, Roy," he said, punctuating the sentence with a beeping sound that came from the back of his throat.

"I want you to suck up to him, Leo."

"I understand."

Ganz hopped off his desk. He was much shorter than Rhoades. "I'm not sure you do, Leo, so let me put it to you this way: after you've talked to him, I want to smell ass-hole on your breath."

Rhoades moved toward the door. Ganz advanced a few steps and said, "Leo, this is Harvey Blissberg, who's been good enough to find Kasick for us."

"Good," Rhoades said, shaking Harvey's hand distractedly.

Ganz stood in the middle of the office's peach carpet and said, "Harvey's also been good enough not to have heard anything that we've just said, and to remember even less."

Harvey smiled stiffly. If Ganz hadn't wanted him to hear official business, why had he allowed him in his office with Rhoades still there? Just to treat Harvey to a demonstration of the Ganz style?

Once Rhoades had left, Ganz motioned Harvey to the wing chair and sat down behind his desk, where he promptly unscrewed the cap from a bottle of Diet Coke and poured a glass. He had pretty, even, crisp features; the only evidence of his real age were the bursts of poorly trimmed hair in his child-sized nostrils. "When I think of the things I put in my system the last time I occupied this office," he said after a polite sip. "So what's the story with Dave?"

"Stage fright," Harvey said. Through the window behind Ganz's head, he saw the lights of midtown, whole blankets of them. The top of the Empire State Building was lit blue and orange in honor of the Mets' World Series Championship.

"It happens. Where'd you find him?"

"Where people with stage fright go," Harvey said.

"Is it likely to happen again this week?"

"The drinking?"

Ganz tasted his Diet Coke. "I remember when Craig Barton spent most of the week before the show in a stupor. We were pumping black coffee into him right up until air time. If Kasick likes to drink, that's not my business. But putting a show on the air this Saturday is. So my question is whether it's likely to happen again."

"You want my honest opinion?"

"I'd value it considerably more than the alternative."

"Yes, I think it's likely to happen again."

"I want to get this straight," Ganz said. "You think it's likely that between now and Saturday night Kasick might disappear to a watering hole again without leaving a forwarding address?"

As Harvey nodded, the door to Ganz's office opened and a middle-aged woman poked her head in. "Roy, the writers are all waiting outside your office for the six o'clock. When shall I tell them you'll be ready?"

"I'll just be a few more minutes," Ganz said. "And see if you can get Kasick toweled off and in here too. Paula put him in the shower ten minutes ago."

"Will do," the woman said.

"One other thing, Tina. Change my reservation at Balfrey's to nine-thirty and make it for three. I'd like Harvey here to join us."

Tina withdrew and Ganz placed a small hand on top of a stack of stapled scripts on his desk. "Harvey," he said, and paused to let the confidential tone communicate itself. "I'd like to hire you from this moment until twelve-thirty A.M. Sunday as Dave's escort."

"You mean his baby-sitter?"

"As you wish."

"Well, it's not the wish I had in mind."

"Well, how can I make the proposition more attractive to you?" Ganz compressed his sandy eyebrows in an expression of sincerity. He was boyish even at his most businesslike. Harvey was too young to have watched him in "My Baby Brother" in the mid-fifties, but he remembered from a rerun or two the cute belligerence still apparent in Ganz's features.

"Let me think for a moment about my obligations in Boston." Harvey would have to postpone a meeting with some local officials about establishing a new antidrug campaign in Boston's suburban schools. A woman in Weston wanted him to determine whether her daughter was living with an ex-con in New Hampshire. He would miss Mickey's birthday, which would be a serious, but not fatal, breach of decorum. Besides, she had been working hard on her documentary for Channel 7, editing late, imposing on him the occasional hardship of falling asleep clutching a pillow instead of what he had referred to recently in her presence, and with surprising impunity, as her "tawny body."

Roy Ganz mentioned a figure. It was surprisingly large.

"Of course," Ganz said, "I realize you wouldn't be doing it for the money. The main appeal of my proposal is that it gives you a chance to watch how a successful live network comedy show operates."

Harvey detected the arch note in Ganz's voice, and matched it—"You took the words right out of my mouth"—but Ganz was absolutely right. Harvey would be flattered to be part of Ganz's clubhouse for a few days.

Ganz awarded Harvey a smile. "Well, I can see we have a deal. I'll have Tina book you a room at the Boswell House, where"—he impersonated "Last Laughs" announcer Geoffrey Doone—"guests of 'Last Laughs' stay in exchange for this promotional consideration."

Ganz reached over his desk and shook Harvey's hand. "You're welcome to stay for the writers' meeting," he said, and punched his intercom. "Tina, send them in, please." He reclined in his chair and said to Harvey, "As you may know, I cleaned creative house when I came back this fall. New cast, new writers. I didn't want to be reminded that there was a time when I wasn't here. Leo and I hand-picked the comedy writers who are about to walk into my office. So, presumably, they are among the funniest individuals you would ever want to meet." He flashed his smile. "Presumably. Why don't you make yourself comfortable on one of the couches."

As Harvey settled into a blazingly white couch at the far end of Ganz's long office, the door opened and a group of seven men and one woman quietly filed in. Leo Rhoades took the wing chair again, pushing it against the wall. The others deployed themselves on the two long couches and a pair of velvet tub chairs. What they had in common was their race—Caucasian—and their style of dress, which erred on the negligent side of casual. Harvey didn't know what he had expected. The smirk of the perpetually amused? A small brand on their forehead indicating that they had passed inspection as worthy of Roy Ganz's comic standards?

Two of them—one fat, one lean—seemed to be in their twenties. Leo Rhoades, the woman, and two other men looked to be in their thirties. One had crossed the great divide into his forties. And the last and best-dressed of them—he wore a navy blazer and slacks with running shoes—had to be pushing sixty. They sat expectantly, some of them with legal pads on their laps, while Roy Ganz thumbed through scripts on his desk.

"The gentleman you don't recognize," Ganz finally said, "or perhaps you do, is Harvey Blissberg. I've retained him to keep an eye on Dave Kasick, who, you may now know, is at last among us." He cast a glance at the door. "Well, he's on the premises."

The writer sitting next to Harvey on the couch leaned toward him and whispered, "I saw you beat the Angels a few years ago in Anaheim with a bases-loaded triple."

"I think I remember that one." Harvey smiled.

"Let's just wait another minute for Dave," Ganz said.

As if on cue, the door opened and Kasick stepped uncertainly into the room. He was wearing a fresh shirt and pants and he was freshly shaved and had combed his wet hair back from his forehead. He surveyed the room from the door and smiled sheepishly. "Here I am," he said. "I hope that if any of you are Mets fans, you'll just be real sensitive to my feelings at this difficult time."

Everyone in the room except Harvey and Ganz started to applaud, which caused Kasick to break into that large grin he sometimes adopted while rounding the bases after a home run. He came across the room and sat on the arm of the couch next to Harvey.

"Well," Ganz said. "Now that we've gotten that out of the way."

Harvey looked up at Kasick. "How's it going, Champ?"

Kasick bent down and put his mouth close to Harvey's ear. "Me," he said softly, "Vastly imProved."

3

"Let me tell you where I'm at," Roy Ganz began, inspecting his cuticles.

Among the writers in his office, there was the nervous collective shifting of those about to be judged. Next to Harvey, Kasick struck an absurd pose of serene sobriety that was belied by a trembling lower lip.

"This is show number four coming up," Ganz said. "As you know, the first one had an eleven rating, with a thirty-two share. These numbers, because they eclipsed last year's best numbers, have allowed me, for one thing, to become arrogant again." He offered the assembled his ironic smile. "Naturally, I ignored the generally vicious reviews of the first show, as well as the generally less vicious, but still quite damning, press on the second and third shows. The reason I was able to do this is because I know from experience that, in the case of a program like ours, advertised as the *new* 'Last Laughs,' it takes the press a while to overcome its reflexive tendency to exercise its encyclopedic knowledge of negative modifiers. I think the sketch about the gay Kennedys did a lot for us, the proof of which is that the critics universally singled it out as tasteless. As for the critics calling the show 'sophomoric' and 'tasteless,' " Ganz said, pausing to sip his Diet Coke, "well, that says less about our work than the conditions of their arteries."

A few feet from Harvey, a sallow, trimly bearded

man in his thirties covered his face with his hand in a private gesture of despair.

Ganz dropped his voice into a lower, foreshadowing register. "Now the ratings slipped some for the second and third shows, and I'm willing to live with that for now. In the second show a couple of sketches got lost in the control booth; changes we made between dress and air weren't communicated to them. In the third, some of the cast seemed to have misplaced their talent for reading cue cards. What we ended up with was a lot of eye cheat, and some pretty mediocre performances. But I can live with it." He sampled his Diet Coke again.

"Here's what I can't live with. A couple of the guest hosts we'd planned on are now bowing out, and their agents say it's because of the writing on this show." He scanned the staff portentously. "I'm telling you this so you won't hear it first from someone else. Although some of you, I'm sure, will be hearing it from your agents."

Harvey thought Ganz had the demeanor of an extremely articulate executioner. Most of the writers were now too nervous even to shift. Except for the older man, who kept plunging what looked like an orange toothpick between his teeth, they sat motionlessly, looking down, like a classroom of contrite seventh graders who had completely misunderstood the assignment.

Ganz gave them a moment to reckon with their chagrin. "I sense—no, I've observed," he said, "a lot of cheap hysterical criticism of the show around the office. This is not only counterproductive, but immature, since you ought to be criticizing yourselves. I mean that in the very best sense. You were all hired because you represent competence at various shadings of comedy writing. We are paying you to do what you have already proved you do so well. If the writing is not up to the quality I expect, it's not for lack of talent. Partly, it's because some of you have never written for a live comedy show and are trying to get the hang of what works: namely, small, short, bright pieces that show off the cast. I am not looking for long sketches where you build on the premise with endless variations that may be ingenious, but which bore the audience, which got the idea in the first thirty seconds."

Ganz's ritual was transparent. Harvey had spent enough time in his life being chewed out by coaches at all levels of organized baseball. His eye caught a photocopied *New York Times* article lying on the coffee table; the headline read: GANZ REDUX: "LAST LAUGHS" LINES UP FRESH FACES, NEW WRITERS.

". . . Ten, twelve years ago," Ganz was now saying, "it was sufficient just to get a new kind of humor on network television. By now viewers have been inoculated *against* a lot of what worked for us. Now the humor's got to be the best of its kind. It's got to be"—he looked directly at Leo Rhoades, the producer— "bright. I don't want pieces that could go on other comedy shows. I just want pieces that could only go on *this* show. . . ."

Harvey reached over and picked up the photocopied article. It had appeared on the morning of "Last Laughs" 's first show of the season three weeks before. Harvey read: Forty-year-old Roy Ganz, known as "The Miniature Man" in the mid-fifties when he played Jimmie Bolling on the sit-com "My Baby Brother," is the big man the network is counting on to restore "Last Laughs" to its former glory and high ratings. He has hired as his producer Leo Rhoades, who worked under Mr. Ganz as a writer during the show's early years. But with few exceptions, Mr. Ganz is relying on new personnel, new cast members, and new writers to turn the trick.

The only cast member with extensive television or movie acting experience is 34-year-old Rob Whent, best known for his infectiously funny performance in the movie "One at a Time, Please." Tom Angel and Ron Fellows, both 28 years old, join the cast after spending several years with Warm Front, the Los Angeles comedy troupe they helped to found. Nancy Pildone, 26, a New Jersey native, was discovered over the summer at a Manhattan comedy club by Ganz and producer Leo Rhoades, who also plucked 24-year-old Candee Wersch from relative obscurity, in her case a small improvisational comedy troupe in Detroit. The last of the regular cast members to be chosen was 15-year-old Eddie Colasono, a Brooklyn teenager who has made a name for himself as perhaps the youngest working stand-up comic in the business, and also by appearing in several national television commercials. Rounding out the cast are two featured players, who will be used mostly in supporting roles for sketches: 29-year-old Brenda J. Johnson, and 31-year-old Jimmy Lanahan.

"We didn't want to go back to the same old well and come up with known actors," Mr. Ganz said. "I always saw the essence of this show as freshness and spontaneity, so over the summer we scoured several cities for what we considered to be the brightest unknown talent."

The writing staff combines newcomers to network comedy with a few veterans as ballast. Mr. Ganz has brought back "The Grand Old Man of Gags," Marty Beaver, an elder statesman of network comedy shows and sit-coms who worked under Mr. Ganz in "Last Laughs" 's first incarnation. . . .

Harvey looked at Beaver sitting in his navy blazer and running shoes, placidly working his orange toothpick around his gums. He wore his rust-colored hair in an eccentric pompadour.

Harvey read on:

. . . Head writer Joey Hanes is a holdover from last year's show, where he held the same position—that of coordinating the staff's senses of humor and subduing their worst excesses. Perhaps the most excessive sense of humor Mr. Hanes will be called upon to control belongs to veteran "Last Laughs" writer Barry Sondell, the reclusive comic who penned some of the original show's blackest sketches, such as "The Tap-Dancing Coroner," and a skit about a day care center for the children of heroin addicts.

Mr. Ganz has imported Curtis Geller, a "joke doctor" from the West Coast with a reputation for invaluable, and usually uncredited, fine-tuning

of comedy scripts; Karen Baldwin, a stand-up co-
medienne who specializes in character sketches;
and Dickie Nacke, a screenwriter. In addition,
Mr. Ganz has hired two young writers in their
twenties: Chuck Causey and Rick Vergaard.

Harvey glanced up from the article and surveyed the
room. It was easy enough to pick out Karen Baldwin.
She had a soft, malleable face, and was sucking so
hard on her lower lip that Harvey had the momentary
vision of her sucking in and consuming her entire face.
The two youngsters, Causey and Vergaard, sat side by
side on the carpet near the base of Ganz's desk. As for
which of the others was Joey Hanes, Curt Geller,
Barry Sondell, or Dickie Nacke, Harvey could not
tell. One of them was missing, since the article mentioned eight writers, and there were, besides Harvey,
Dave Kasick, Roy Ganz, and Leo Rhoades, only seven
others in the room. Harvey guessed that the missing
person was the "reclusive comic," Barry Sondell.

"So who's working on what?" Ganz was saying.

One of the writers in his thirties, a black-haired man
whose pleasant face was interrupted by a wide slash of
mustache, leaned forward on the other sofa. With his
fist, he stroked the tie carelessly knotted over his
aging shirt.

"Yes, Joey?" Ganz said to him. "Your body language indicates you wish to speak."

"I've been working with Vergaard on a sketch about
international terrorists at home. You know, what the
dinner table conversation is like when your dad plants
bombs for a living."

"Oh, yeah?" said the writer who looked to be in his
forties. "Like 'C'mon, son, what do you say you and
me go down to the basement after dinner and we'll
fool around with some plastic explosives? Hey, how
would that be?' "

There was a ruffle of laughter in the room, which
Joey Hanes ignored. Harvey perked up; it was sinking
in that what was batted around here would end up on
national television in a few days.

"It's almost done," Hanes continued. "All it needs is a couple of major rewrites."

Rick Vergaard, the skinnier of the two kids sitting on the carpet, turned toward Hanes. "And some jokes in it to make it funny."

"Yeah," Hanes said, now looking at Ganz, "but other than that, and the fact that we don't know how to end it, it's just about perfect."

Ganz flexed his lips. "Well, make sure you get Candee in the sketch. She's going to be light in the show, I have a feeling." He turned to Leo Rhoades. "Unless you can rewrite the triples-bar sketch to get her in."

"I'm working on it, Roy," Rhoades said. "But the triples-bar is too much like Barry's sketch on the two amnesiacs in love, which I thought you wanted to get in the show this week."

"I do, if I can figure out a way to get it by Standards and Practices. Sondell's gone right to the edge again with this one. By the way, Leo, when's the last time Barry was in the office?"

"I saw him once. Weeks ago."

Ganz ran a thumb under a gray suspender. "Do you think, considering all the money we're paying him, that he could make an appearance up here once in a while? Just as a courtesy?"

"Roy," Rhoades said, "you've known him longer than I have. He's allergic to human contact."

"So be it," Ganz said with resignation, but was promptly agitated by another thought. "Has Barry been producing?"

"In a manner of speaking," Rhoades said.

"Leo, is he *producing?*"

Rhoades rearranged his large body in the wing chair. "Well, most of what he's been submitting—by courier, of course—is—well, ill-suited to the show."

"You mean it's material the critics could call 'tasteless' with some justification?" Ganz said.

"I doubt it would meet the standards for mail-order pornography." Rhoades began laughing at his own line. It began with a series of beeps in the base of his throat, like an engine gruffly turning over in cold weather. Then his laugh caught, ignited, sputtered, spewed, erupted, and sustained itself for a good ten seconds.

Most of the people in the room joined in the laughter, although not as demonically; it would have been rude to strand Rhoades on the island of his own self-amusement. Ganz, however, remained expressionless, as did Marty Beaver, who was quietly excavating a shard of his lunch from between two teeth.

"All right, all right," Ganz said, gesturing with hands raised. "What have we got cooking for Dave? We need ideas where we can use Dave as himself."

Next to Harvey, Kasick's head, which for the last few minutes had been gradually falling toward his chest, jerked to attention. Above Kasick's right eye, the one Harvey could see, was a crooked scar shaped like Cape Cod. Harvey remembered watching the head-first slide five years ago that was responsible for it.

The fortyish writer said, "What about a sketch featuring Dave at home—you know, here's one of baseball's great players, and he keeps fumbling things, lacks all physical coordination—you know, he's incompetent." He had the jarring combination of a youthful face and a thinning crown on which his sparse, curly hair now sat like a collection of dustballs. He wore a heavy gold I.D. bracelet, an ornamental anachronism in the largely younger group.

"I don't think so, Dickie," Ganz said. "Unless you can tell me if it goes somewhere interesting from there. It's a pretty well-worn premise."

"Besides," Leo Rhoades said curtly, peering around the side of the wing chair, "it's the same premise as the thing Joey and Rick are working on: terrorists at home."

"Oh, well," Dickie said. Harvey consulted the *New York Times* article. Dickie Nacke, the screenwriter.

"C'mon," Ganz said. "What else've we got?"

"Something in a locker room?" said Chuck Causey, the other kid in his twenties sitting on the carpet. He was as chubby as Vergaard was thin.

"Drugs," Rhoades announced. "All the players are pissing in jars for their urinalysis before the game.

Only when Dave returns from the bathroom, his urine's got all kinds of pills and joints and syringes floating in it."

This got some laughter, punctuated by a voice saying, "I won't do it." It was Kasick. Harvey wasn't sure whether Kasick's protest referred only to the suggestion of a sketch that would portray him as a drug abuser or to doing the show at all.

"How about the first female major leaguer?" said the only woman in the room, Karen Baldwin. "We could do something about her and her teammates in the locker room before her first game. Dave could be showing her—"

"Sounds like something from 'The Carol Burnett Show.' " Rhoades cut her off and beeped, like a car signaling all other drivers to move to the side. Harvey was surprised by this show of force. Alone with Ganz before, Rhoades had been submissive. Baldwin's face crumbled.

"Now," Rhoades said, "I can see a sketch about a female TV sports reporter trying to get into the locker room after the game." The engine of his hysterical laughter was already turning over in his throat. "I see Candee in this sketch, Roy. The team tries to keep her out because they know she's, like, incredibly voyeuristic. *Beep, beep.* She digs cock. That's why she chose this line of work. *Beep, beep.* So she finally gets her way and bursts into the locker room and when the ballplayers see her—most of them are just wearing towels—they all get as far away from her as they can because—*beep*—they know what she's really interested in. But she manages to convince Dave to consent to an interview, and Dave's standing there in his towel answering some meaningless questions about the game, and all the while Candee's motioning her cameraman to pan down to his crotch, because she wants to get it on videotape, and her hand's already moving slowly toward Dave's towel, and then suddenly she whips off his towel—with his back turned to the audience, of course—and she takes a look as he tries to cover up, and she says, 'Now I know why you're the Most Valuable Player in the American League.' *Beep, beep, hee,*

hee, hee, haw, haw, haw, HAW, HAW." Rhoades exploded in mirth.

Chuck Causey was laughing, but without conviction. Dickie Nacke was chuckling. Marty Beaver's head was bobbing in a soundless imitation of someone laughing. Karen Baldwin seemed to be slipping into autism. Rick Vergaard's smirk had congealed on his face. Head writer Joey Hanes looked impassive. "Joke Doctor" Curt Geller, whom Harvey had now identified by a process of elimination, had removed his wire-rimmed glasses and was rubbing his eyes. Ganz was smiling at Rhoades, but it was hard to say whether it indicated enjoyment or merely tolerance.

Rhoades was still laughing, but winding down. "The longest dick in the American League," he said. *"Beep beep."*

When Rhoades's laughter had exhausted itself, the silence revealed to Harvey another sound closer at hand, a loud rhythmic breathing. He looked at Kasick.

The guest host for Saturday night's show was snoring softly, his chin against his massive chest.

4

At eight o'clock Roy Ganz adjourned the writers' conference, and Harvey escorted Dave Kasick to the office in the writers' wing reserved for guest hosts. Kasick resumed his nap in the armchair by the window. Outside the office door Harvey could already hear the typewriters starting up down the hall. He sat at the desk and called Mickey Slavin at her television station in Boston.

After titillating her with a brief account of the writers' conference, he explained that he had signed up to baby-sit Kasick until Saturday night.

"I was kind of looking forward to seeing some foliage this weekend."

"I'm sorry, Mick. You could always fly down here for a couple of days."

"Oh, yeah, I understand the midtown foliage is at its peak right now."

"We could watch the traffic lights turn color on Avenue of the Americas."

"So, Bliss." She sighed. "All you have to do is watch Kasick and make sure he doesn't hit the bottle?"

"That, and change his diaper."

"I feel kind of sorry for you."

"I know," Harvey said. "It's hard finding Pampers for two-hundred-pounders."

When he got off the phone, he looked at Kasick, who now appeared to be in REM sleep. Harvey watched

Kasick's eyeballs roll around under his lids. Then the phone rang, and Harvey picked it up.

"Mr. Kasick?" the woman's voice said.

"I'm afraid Mr. Kasick's busy. This is Harvey Blissberg."

"Oh. Hi. This is Tina, Roy's secretary. Roy wanted me to remind the two of you about dinner. He'd like you to come by his office at eight-forty-five."

"I think that'd be fine. I don't know what kind of place we're going to, but neither of us is wearing a jacket or tie."

"No problem," she said. "I'll just make sure Roy isn't either."

Harvey left Kasick's office and wandered down the corridor to the bright fluorescently lit reception area of the writers' wing. Four of the writers were lounging on the two battered couches, deep in conversation. Harvey recognized Karen Baldwin, Dickie Nacke, and the two youngsters, Chuck Causey and Rick Vergaard. A liver-and-white springer spaniel was asleep at Nacke's feet. The long table in the reception area was covered with unemptied foil ashtrays, opened soda and beer cans, crumpled tortilla chip bags, and stray script pages. A cirrus cloud of cigarette smoke hung over the room. The whole scene had the bleak quality of college sophomores taking a study break in the dorm's common room.

As Harvey passed by, Karen Baldwin was saying, "I mean, how can you argue with the fact that Leo's dominating the show? Why the hell'd they hire all of us if we can't get any of our scripts on the show? Leo and Roy went out and bought all of us at high prices and then basically they're just storing us here in the writers' wing. These guys are like antique collectors. I feel like some dusty, once-valuable thing."

"I think," Dickie Nacke said, "that Marty Beaver is the only writer here you could accurately call an antique." He patted his dome. "Of course, I'm well on my way."

Baldwin, ignoring him, lurched forward on the couch. "Okay," she said intensely, "here's the archetypal Leo Rhoades sketch: 'Honey, did you put the homosexual snake out in the yard? Gee, I hope it's not in the toilet!' " She lowered her voice: " 'I put it out, dear. But what do you want me to do with this cripple in the living room?' "

"I like it, I like it," Vergaard laughed. "But c'mon, where's the gastrointestinal distress? There's always gastrointestinal distress in a Leo sketch. Or an eating disorder."

"I put a toilet in there," Baldwin protested. "Give me some credit."

"All right," Causey said, "but you forgot to put in any sex. C'mon, there isn't even any leering."

" 'Dear,' " she said in a soprano, " 'what do you want me to do with this *naked* cripple in the living room?' "

"That's better," Causey said.

Harvey walked to the bulletin board near the receptionist's desk and pretended to study the posted production schedule for that week.

"You know, it drives me crazy," Baldwin went on. "I've been a stand-up comic for ten years, and I've never made this kind of money, but at least I had control over my work. Christ, here they pay you all this money, and you have no control at all. I've had one line on the first three shows."

"Yeah? Which one?" Causey asked.

"Oh, some line I threw out at a meeting that ended up buried in Leo and Joey's sketch about the nymphomaniacs' convention."

"A classic," Nacke said, his I.D. bracelet clanking against the tabletop as he reached for a can of ginger ale.

Baldwin turned to him. "Dickie, your ideas get trashed as much as anybody's here—"

"Thank you, I'm flattered."

"—and you don't seem to mind so much. So what's the secret to your equanimity?"

"You forgot that I spent the last few years writing screenplays," Nacke said evenly. "I'm used to making a lot of money and having no control. I'm a wealthy man and I've never had a screenplay produced, and I kind of like it that way."

"You like it that way?" Baldwin said. "I mean, don't you feel kind of—of—insubstantial? I mean, all that work and the public's never seen it?"

"Oh, c'mon, Karen," Nacke said. "You're talking like an *artist*." The word disagreed with him and he made a dyspeptic expression.

"I guess it'd be a mistake to consider you one," she said.

"I'd be a fool to. I arrange words for people who can't do it themselves but have money to spend on those who can. And then I rearrange those words, and I keep rearranging them until everybody's happy. And between rearrangements, I just keep going to the bank." With a finger Nacke referred to the gray hairs highlighting his temple. "Now, granted, maybe it's given me a few of these, but at my age, who's to say I wouldn't have them anyway?"

Rick Vergaard pulled his thin legs up and crossed them on the couch. "But didn't you take this job with the expectation of, you know, getting your stuff on the air?"

"No," Nacke said. "That would have been naïve."

"Dickie," Baldwin said, chewing her gum furiously, "I can't believe you're as cynical as you're pretending."

"Well, I'm not. I'm more cynical than I'm pretending."

"Wait a second," Vergaard said. "That sketch you wrote about the crazed puppy killer was great—"

"A little off-color," Nacke conceded.

"Well," Vergaard went on, "I thought it was great because it was so completely absurd. I mean, it took the idea of lovable puppies and violated it so thoroughly that it totally transcended bad taste."

"I don't know if it transcended it, or, you know, embodied it," Nacke said. "Actually, I thought it was just the kind of bad taste that Leo would go for. I thought it would hit him right smack in his vulgarity."

"So why didn't it make the show?" Vergaard said. "I mean, it probably got the biggest laugh at read-through so far. Everyone loved it."

"Yeah, how come it didn't make the show?" Baldwin asked.

"Leo didn't like it," Nacke said.

"But it was funny."

"Well, I guess Leo didn't think it was funny enough."

"Didn't you ask him why he didn't like it?" Baldwin said.

"Karen, has it ever done any good to ask Leo why something you wrote didn't make the show, or even make read-through?"

She stopped chewing her gum. "Well, no. His response is always, 'I didn't think it was funny,' and then he immediately starts to tell you about some idea of his he thinks is hilarious. The experience is so depressing. Sometimes my paycheck doesn't even make a dent in my despair."

"Then there you have it," Nacke said, cracking the knuckles of his right hand, one by one. "I avoid Leo. My policy is to write, to submit what I write, and to shut up."

There was silence for a moment. Baldwin, Causey, and Vergaard seemed to be considering the merits of Nacke's policy.

"Do you think Ganz really goes for Leo's humor?" Causey asked of no one in particular. "I only have dim memories of the old 'Last Laughs,' but the humor had to have been more sophisticated."

"It couldn't have been all that sophisticated in the old days," Baldwin said, "because Leo was one of the writers. Yet—yet the show used to seem incredibly hip. But we were younger. Maybe our standards were lower."

Nacke coughed lightly. "It's like Roy said in the meeting. Ten years ago it was enough to put irreverence on the air. No one had ever seen anything like it on network television. But the stakes are higher now."

"Anyway," Vergaard ventured, "Leo wasn't the only writer on the show then. They had some really brilliant people writing for the show."

"No more brilliant than we are," Baldwin said. "The difference now is that we can't get our brilliance on the show. It's like Leo has a stranglehold on the content. You know, I was so excited when I got hired. After all those drunks in Dayton and Rochester. I thought I was going to be part of the Renaissance here, but it feels more like the Black Plague. Why does Ganz let him have so much control?"

"Maybe because he trusts Leo because he worked with him in the old days," Nacke said.

Baldwin pounded the arm of the couch. "But Leo is comically arrested at an adolescent stage of development!"

Nacke clucked. "Trust is thicker than talent." He was really playing elder statesman now.

"But that's no way to run a network comedy show! While the rest of us vegetate in our offices!"

"Except when we sit around here bitching," Causey said.

Baldwin was not through. "And the gall of Ganz to dress us down in that meeting! To lay the show's problems at our feet, as if Leo doesn't write most of what gets on the air himself!"

Nacke shrugged. "Hey, what're you gonna do?"

Causey, his little round body curled up in a corner of the couch, said, "Do you think some of us are going to get axed?"

"Ax me no questions, Chuck," Baldwin said, "and I'll tell you no lies."

"With jokes like that," Causey said, "no wonder your stuff's not getting on."

"Oh, fuck you," she told him.

"Sorry." Causey placed a pudgy hand on her shoulder.

Harvey had heard enough and began walking back toward Kasick's office. Karen Baldwin called out to him, "Hey, Harvey, welcome to the wacky world of network comedy."

"Don't mind me," Harvey said. "Just passing through."

"Exactly what we're doing," she replied.

Halfway down the corridor, he happened to glance into an open doorway and meet Curt Geller's eyes.

The "joke doctor" was sitting at his desk in front of a Kaypro word processor. "Hi," he said abstractedly, resetting his wire-rims on his nose.

"Didn't mean to disturb you."

"Whyn't you come in?"

Harvey checked his watch. He had ten minutes before he had to get Kasick in shape for dinner with Ganz. "All right."

"Have a seat." Geller had a soft-spoken but tense manner. Harvey took the other chair in the office. Geller picked at his short beard. "I heard what was going on out there." He tilted his head in the direction of the reception area. "I couldn't pick out all the words, but the music was familiar: the plaintive theme song of disgruntled employees."

"I've heard it before too," Harvey said.

"Let me take a guess. It reminds you of the locker room of a losing baseball team."

"It also reminds me of the locker room of a winning baseball team."

"It's the human condish," Geller said.

Harvey smiled. "This seems to be the losing team at the moment."

Geller shrugged.

"I saw your face at the meeting when Leo Rhoades proposed that thing about Kasick being exposed in the locker room."

Geller shrugged again. "A new standard for elegance in comedy."

"Is it true what they're saying out there? That his humor's dominating the show?"

"Oh, well, Ganz is going with what he knows," Geller said. "He and Leo go way back."

"I understand that, but it seems like Leo's humor's aimed at fifteen-year-olds." Harvey was quickly developing a taste for the office politics.

Geller didn't say anything, but reached for an index card taped to the wall over his desk and pulled it off. "Goethe," he said to Harvey, "age seventy-five, speaking to his legal executor, a man by the name of von Muller. Quote: 'Only a man with no conscience or sense of responsibility can be a humorist,' " he read. " 'Of course, we all have our humorous moments, but the point is whether humor remains a constant lifelong attitude of mind. How dare a man have a sense of humor when he considers his immense burden of responsibility toward himself and others?' " Geller laid the card down next to his Kaypro, readjusted his wire-rims, and smiled mildly at Harvey.

"So how do you explain your being a humorist?"

"Oh, like a lot of humorists, I guess I suffer from an inability to pay attention to reality. Also, I didn't read you the end of Goethe's quote." He retrieved the index card. " 'However,' Goethe said, 'I have no wish to pass censure on the humorists. After all, does one have to have a conscience? Who says so?' " He retaped the index card to the wall.

There was a knock on the door behind Harvey. He turned to see Chuck Causey.

"Excuse me," Causey said to Harvey from the door-way, and addressed Geller. "Doc, I need a diagnosis. I wrote two versions of a joke for 'Views on the News' and I don't know which one to submit to Leo." He was holding a single sheet of paper.

"Let me hear them," Geller said, tilting back in his swivel chair.

Causey cleared his throat. "Okay, here's the first version. The premise," he added quickly, "is from an actual story in the *Times*. Here goes: 'A new study circulated by the American Civil Liberties Union this week claims that since the beginning of the century twenty-five people have been wrongfully executed. The American Nazi Party promptly distributed a study of its own, claiming that since 1900, over seventeen million people should have been executed, but weren't.' "

Harvey laughed; Geller didn't.

"Here's the second version," Causey said. " 'A new study circulated by the American Civil Liberties Union this week claims that since the beginning of the century twenty-five people have been wrongfully executed. Yale public policy professor Michael Gelhard called the twenty-five wrongful executions, quote, a very acceptable number, unquote. The ACLU released another study claiming that Professor Gelhard was one of eighteen people in this century who had been wrongfully allowed to live.' "

Harvey laughed again; Geller merely stroked his beard and asked, "This Gelhard business is true?"

"Yes," Causey said.

"Go with the second one," Geller said.

"The second one? Why?"

"Why?" Geller said with mock impatience. "Why?? Because it's *funnier* than the other one. That's why."

"Okay, Doc," Causey said. "Not that Leo'll go for either one of them."

"Just one thing, Chuck," Geller said. "Put a 'promptly' in there. You know, 'The ACLU *promptly* released another study. . . .' Rhythm."

Causey looked at his sheet of paper for a moment. "Yeah," he said. "Thanks." He left, closing the door behind him.

Harvey had been studying something else on Geller's wall— one of those cheap mass-produced plaques inscribed with comical business wisdom. The one Harvey remembered best from the clubhouse of the Providence Jewels, his last team, read: "Winning Is Better Than Losing, But Losing With Pride Is Better Than Winning Without It." The one on Geller's wall read:

SIX PHASES OF A PROJECT

1. ENTHUSIASM
2. DISILLUSIONMENT
3. PANIC
4. SEARCH FOR THE GUILTY
5. PUNISHMENT OF THE INNOCENT
6. PRAISE & HONORS FOR THE NONPARTICIPANTS

"What phase is 'Last Laughs' at?" he asked Geller.

"We're at the tail end of disillusionment," Geller said, "and coming up fast on panic."

Fifteen minutes later Harvey Blissberg and Dave Kasick were sitting on either side of Roy Ganz in the back of the latter's limousine. The small-boned executive producer hunched between them on the gray velour banquette as the limo swam through Times Square. Harvey looked out the one-way opera window at a derelict sleeping in a large cardboard box that had once contained a Maytag washing machine.

"This business about one-way windows in limousines," Ganz suddenly said. "There's something wrong about celebrities being able to look out, but people not being able to look in. It's an inappropriate metaphor. It should be the other way around, shouldn't it? The celebrities shouldn't be able to see *out,* and people should be able to look *in* and see everything we're doing in here. Because that's what our life is like."

"I get your drift," Kasick said.

Harvey said nothing, and the limo moved quietly through the East Forties.

Ganz put his little black shoes up on the mahogany television console. "I think the Lincolns ride better than the Caddies," he said. "But, in any case, isn't this a nice way to defy death?"

"Absolutely," Kasick said. "Sure, because in a head-on collision, we're so damn far back from the front end of the car that we probably wouldn't even know we'd been hit."

5

By the time cast members Rob Whent and Nancy
Pildone, reading aloud, had reached page seven of
Karen Baldwin's sketch about a pair of homely, near-
sighted people falling in love with each other across
the counter of a luncheonette, hardly anyone in the
reception area of the writers' wing was paying attention.

It was Wednesday afternoon and virtually everyone
associated with the show—Ganz, Rhoades, the writers, director Ralph Morello, the stage managers, the
set designers, prop master, choreographer, two men
from Standards and Practices, and the music, wardrobe, and makeup people—had congregated to hear
the six regular cast members and two featured players
read through the best of the mass of material—as
determined by Ganz and Rhoades—that the writers
had been working on through the night. Each key
member of the production cast had photocopies of the
script package in order to follow along. Listening,
Harvey had to admire the Byzantine cerebral process
by which some of the writers had, overnight, con-
verted raw pieces of reality into finished comedy.

Baldwin's sketch, the last of twenty-two to be read,
was, Harvey thought, well-written, but several people
were now rustling pages to see just how much longer
this sweet, pathetic love affair could possibly continue.
The sketch had none of the mean-spiritedness or shock
humor of the scripts that had so far earned laughs.

Joey Hanes, sitting next to Harvey, leaned over and whispered, "This one doesn't have a chance. It's about people and the sort of thing that actually goes on between them. Fatal."

As Whent and Pildone droned on with diminishing affect, Karen Baldwin sucked in her upper lip and picked sullenly at one of the plates of cheese and fresh fruit provided for the occasion. Doubly handicapped by its tenderness and its position as the last script read, the sketch at its conclusion was greeted with a silence so burdensome that Baldwin could not raise her head.

"Well," Leo Rhoades coughed. "The good news is that this sketch is going to be performed inside a dead cow."

Several people laughed. Karen Baldwin looked dolefully at a slice of kiwi fruit in her hand.

"That will gradually be cut open during the performance," Rhoades added, "to reveal the action inside."

Even the Joke Doctor allowed himself a reluctant laugh. Harvey could not suppress a smile, either. Nor, finally, could Karen Baldwin who, gazing about her at the rubble that had once been her hopeful creation, smiled oddly and joined in.

"So," said Roy Ganz, who had been presiding over the read-through with the air of a tired parent whose children had insisted on presenting their version of *The Music Man* in the garage, "I guess that's it. Thank you all for coming. It's been a long read-through, but entirely worthwhile." He flashed an impish, calibrated grin to undercut his last remark. "A few of us will now retire to our chambers to decide which of these sterling scripts are meritorious enough to begin going into production. I strongly encourage all the writers to be back here in a couple of hours to discuss rewrites. Thank you."

At dinner the night before, Harvey had been impressed by the opacity of Ganz's personality. Harvey knew no more about him at the end of their meal than he had at the beginning, despite Ganz's volubility. But his monologues gave off a sour odor of premeditation. "In my experience," he had said, "I've found that most people say they find one thing funny, but they laugh at quite another." And: "Some of the best cast members I've had over the years were funny people who had no sense of humor. Take Warren Howard—he could make you laugh just by licking his lips, but he was incapable of understanding even a knock-knock joke." His only personal questions were designed to determine the extent of Kasick's drinking problem and the likelihood that he would have to deal with it before Sunday morning.

The read-through broke up with a scraping of chairs and a last-minute raiding of the candy dishes and plates of homemade chocolate chip cookies. Harvey found himself in Kasick's office watching Kasick pace back and forth between the window and the door. Before Kasick could find the words to express this agitation, Joey Hanes, the head writer, came into the office chewing on one end of his black mustache.

"I'm not telling you this to make you feel better," Hanes said to Kasick, "but because it's true. I've sat through a hundred read-throughs and there's no relationship between how scripts go over on Wednesday and how they go over on the air. Some of the weakest read-throughs turn into the funniest shows."

Kasick stopped pacing. "You're saying that because there weren't many laughs out there today—at least only a few that were audible to the human ear—that the show's gonna knock 'em dead on Saturday night?"

"What I'm saying is that read-throughs can be misleading."

"I think it's gonna bite the big one, Joey."

"Dave, you've got a cast of professionals behind you on this show. You're not going to be out there alone." Hanes didn't look quite as if he believed this. "You'll be fine. Hell, America doesn't expect you to *act*. You're going to get laughs just by showing up."

Kasick was pacing again. "I'm not sure how to take that one, pardner. But thanks for the pep talk."

When Hanes was gone, Kasick picked up his stack of photocopied scripts, glanced at the one on top, and fired it across the office against the wall. "I will not play an aging Hall of Famer with Alzheimer's!" he shouted.

He flung the next script against the wall. "I will not play the father of a teenage daughter whose prom date is extremely uncoordinated!"

The next script hit the ceiling and fluttered to the carpet. "I will not play a ballplayer being exposed by a female sportswriter!"

And the next one. "I will not play a man desperately trying to arrange a men-odge a troy in a triples bar!"

He heaved the remainder of the stack against the wall. "And, Harvey, I swear on my grandmother's grave that I will not play a man with syringes in his urine!"

Harvey waited until Kasick calmed down before saying, "Shake it off, Dave."

"Yeah," Kasick said after a moment, "I've got to stay within myself."

"That's right. Stay within yourself."

"Suck it up."

"Suck it up," Harvey repeated.

"Be the ball."

"Yeah," Harvey said. "Be that ball."

"It's only a game," Kasick said.

Harvey tapped his index finger against his temple. "And the game's in here. That's where it's won or lost. Hum babe."

"Harvey?"

"Yeah?"

"Harvey, it's already lost."

"Game's not until Saturday."

"Naw, I can't be the ball, Harvey. I can't stay within myself. The game's lost."

"We're only in about the third inning here."

"Can't go the full nine, Harvey."

"You're doing it, an inning at a time."

"Not a money player." He looked at the script pages on the floor. "I'm going to get my clock cleaned on Saturday night."

"Let me ask you a question," Harvey said. "What'd

you think you were getting into when you agreed to host the show?"

"Huh?"

"I mean, you've seen the show. Didn't you realize you'd be out there performing live in front of millions of people?"

Kasick looked dazed.

"Well, didn't that occur to you?"

Kasick pondered his huge callused hands for a moment, studying his palms and turning them over and studying the backs with their moss of hair.

"No," Kasick said. "I guess it didn't occur to me."

"Then why're you doing it?"

"Why? Because my agent said it would be good for me."

"But what did *you* think?"

"I didn't."

"You let your agent do your thinking for you?"

"Hell, who else is gonna do it, Harvey?"

Six years ago, when they were teammates in Boston, Kasick had taken Harvey aside one day and asked him how checking accounts worked because he had just learned that it was not one of the Red Sox organization's duties to pay his utility bills. In the world of professional sports, one could be the Most Valuable Player and not have the faintest idea how to write a personal check.

"I can't stay within myself!" Kasick shouted. "I'm not in myself at all! I'm outside myself! I'm nowhere near myself!" He collapsed heavily into a chair.

Harvey was grateful he was not a guest host. He had not been a great ballplayer like Kasick. He had been just a good ballplayer and therefore had all the advantages of a limited celebrity. He had not been asked to guest-host network shows; he had been asked to make commercials for local insurance companies.

"Guess what time it is, Harvey?" Kasick was studying his Rolex.

Harvey saw by his own watch that it was a little before six.

"It's the cocktail hour."

"Not for you," Harvey said. "No sauce."

"No sauce? I haven't had a drink since last night."

"Let's keep up the good work."

"For God's sake, Harvey, you're just supposed to keep an eye on me, not change the drinking habits of a lifetime. Let's run down and I'll buy you a pop. Look, it's humiliating, you looking after me like this. I need a drink just to restore my dignity."

Harvey's silence suggested a softening of resistance.

"Nothing's happening up here for an hour or two," Kasick said, taking his sheepskin overcoat off the peg behind the door. "That gives us a nice window of cocktailability."

On their way to the elevator, they ran into a group of writers huddled together in the reception area, laughing hysterically at a piece of paper Rick Vergaard held in his hand.

"Hey, Dave," Dickie Nacke said to Kasick, motioning him over, "you'll enjoy this."

"Oh, c'mon, don't show it to him," Karen Baldwin said. "He's nervous enough as it is. This," she added, tapping the sheet of paper, "is really the bottom of the barrel."

"What is it?" Kasick asked, peering over Vergaard's shoulder.

"Barry Sondell just submitted it by courier," Nacke said. "It's a totally unusable opening monologue for you. Sondell at his most perverse."

Curt Geller was looking at the page in Vergaard's hand, shaking his head. "Gee, if you ever needed proof that humor is motivated by anger, hostility, contempt, and self-loathing, well, this is the smoking gun you're looking for."

Baldwin looked at Geller. "You," she said with mock awe, "are *such* an amazing intellectual."

"Thank you," Geller said.

Kasick and Blissberg read over Geller's shoulder:

GUEST HOST MONOLOGUE/DAVE KASICK

BARRY SONDELL

KASICK

Hi, everybody. My name's Dave Kasick, and you

probably know that I am one of the American League's most popular players. I know you think that's why I've been asked to guest-host "Last Laughs" tonight. Well, actually, that's not the real reason. You see, baseball players are widely thought to be, well, less than really intelligent. You know, we don't read books and we're always saying the same things over and over to sports reporters. Let's face it—people think we're completely dumb. That we're just these physically skilled individuals with no brains in our head. Well, ladies and gentlemen, it's true. In fact, this past summer a prestigious medical research institute X-rayed the heads of each and every major leaguer and discovered that none of us has much of a brain. It's shocking, but true. What little brain I do have allows me to read box scores, third base coaches' signals, and cue cards. That's about it. I'd always suspected this about myself, but now there's medical proof. Like every other major league baseball player, I am an idiot. Hey, what can you do? However, there are a couple of advantages to this condition. First, we can, and do, take enormous amounts of illicit drugs without impairing the functioning of our brains. I mean, hey, we don't have brains whose functions could be impaired! Second, and probably most important, the fact that I do not have a brain makes me extremely well-suited to host a show as stupid as this one. I hope you enjoy it. (looks offstage) Now, if someone could come out and show me what to do next . . .

For the next three days Harvey followed Kasick into the complex, chaotic process of the show's production. In his office Leo Rhoades coached Kasick and the cast on dialogue. Kasick was fitted for wigs, prop glasses, spent two hours in the wardrobe room while a seamstress let out costumes to accommodate Kasick's Brobdingnagian torso. He struggled with cue cards during dry-blocking in the tenth-floor studio—itself a miniature city of sets, frantic humanity, and technology

—while on the twenty-fourth floor those writers whose sketches were in the show polished pages of their scripts, which were then ferried down to the studio by sleep-deprived production assistants.

"Getting a script approved's like trying to push a bill through fucking Congress!" Rick Vergaard blurted to Harvey on Thursday night as he emerged from a conference with Rhoades and Ganz. "It's incredible—there's no end to the lobbying, the buttonholing, cajoling, compromising, amending, courting, the filibustering—" He threw up his hands.

"I'm sorry," Harvey said.

"Corporate creativity! I've rewritten this eight times," he shouted. "Two hours ago they loved the spider therapy! Now they want me to get rid of it! I don't get it!"

Harvey lost track of time, had to consult his Casio wristwatch on Friday to make sure it wasn't still Thursday. People napped when and where they could. Kasick tripped over a slumbering Rick Vergaard on the way to his office after camera blocking on Friday. ("Too much eye cheat, Dave," Ralph Morello, the director, had boomed repeatedly over the studio loudspeaker from the control room. "Don't fight the cue cards—they're your friends." "If they're my friends," Kasick replied, "let's see them buy me a drink after this goddamn rehearsal's over.")

"How do you do it?" Harvey asked Karen Baldwin, who was staggering, red-eyed, down the hallway. "How do you guys do it on no sleep?"

"Sleep?" she mumbled, propping herself up against the wall. "Sleep? What's sleep? Harvey, sleep is just something you do to make yourself feel better while you're awake." She yawned magnificently and proceeded blindly down the corridor, reaching out every step or two for the wall. The only creature well rested was Dickie Nacke's dog, the springer spaniel who spent most of her time napping on the floor of Nacke's barren office.

Bits that weren't working in the studio were continually sent upstairs to be repaired by Marty Beaver and Curt Geller. At one-thirty on Saturday morning, Harvey heard, through the open door of Leo Rhoades's office, a heated argument between Rhoades, Ganz, Beaver, and Geller about the propriety of a joke about South African apartheid. In a hallway the choreographer was trying to teach a simple dance step to three cast members for a spoof of a public-access cable variety show.

On the twenty-fourth floor delivery men kept showing up with stapled bags of food. They glanced around expectantly, like tourists, hoping perhaps to glimpse some real evidence that this was indeed—or at least had been—a seat of great comic power. The only observable relic, and it was hidden around the corner by the popcorn machine, was the tuft of hair—pressed under glass and framed—that cast member Tony Rocchio had pulled out of his own head several years before in a characteristic rage.

The number of unfinished containers of sesame noodles and chicken wings continued to grow. On Saturday afternoon Karen Baldwin and Chuck Causey, who didn't have any sketches on the show and were therefore excluded from the delirious activity around them, sat glumly in the writers' wing reception area, watching, on closed circuit television, the run-through taking place fourteen floors below them.

"My stand-up career really took off," she was telling Causey, "when I finally understood the comic value of consonants. I didn't have enough hard consonants in my material. You know, words like 'buck,' 'trick,' 'charcoal briquet,' 'crate,' 'stack.' I was amazed how much mileage I could get out of 'clitoris.' "

Joey Hanes walked by in his socks and said, "Chuck, Karen, give me the name of a funny piece of furniture. I'm stuck. All I've got is 'piano stool.' "

"Credenza," Baldwin said.

"Ottoman," Causey said.

"Gout stool," Baldwin said.

"Rococo Revival laminated settee," Causey said.

"Thanks," Hanes said, hurrying on.

"Mind if I join?" Harvey asked the two of them. He sat on the sofa and watched Dave Kasick's performance of a man trying to arrange a *ménage à trois* at a triples bar. Kasick, wearing five or six gold chains around his neck, was plowing uncertainly through his lines.

"So, Harvey, what do you think of the show so far?" Karen asked. After four days in the show's hothouse atmosphere, Harvey had come to feel like an honorary member of the writing staff. The cast members, occupied by rehearsals, had been less accessible, and seemed protected by a thicker shell of self-absorption.

"Oh, you know, I'm no judge. Dave's acting style has a certain—" Harvey searched for the right phrase.

"—a certain sweet but stiff quality," the pudgy Causey broke in. Among the writers, he was known as Tweedledumpling, his thinner partner, Rick Vergaard, as Tweedledee. "Sort of like the theatrical equivalent of a frozen dessert."

"Chuck, how'd you know exactly what I was going to say?"

"You know great minds," Causey said.

Harvey turned to Karen. "Nothing on the show, huh?"

"No, that's not true. There're a couple of 'the's on the show this week that I wrote. And three or four conjunctions. Hell, I don't even know why they bother to give me one of these." She picked up her bound copy of that night's complete show script. Her name was impressed on the lower right corner of the leatherette cover in gold leaf.

On the closed-circuit channel Kasick was trying to describe to two people at the "triples bar," using extravagant hand gestures, all the polymorphous sexual acts he had in mind if they would just come back to his apartment.

A woman strode into the reception area and stood before the three of them in a bright red sweater and jeans. "Excuse me," she said, "has anyone seen Dickie around?" She was thirtyish, with a moppy blond perm, an economical nose, and a pouty mouth. She held a lit cigarette at her side between two straightened fingers.

"I think he's out walking his dog," Karen said. "He should be back soon. You want to sit down and watch run-through with us?"

"That's all right, I'll just wait in his office. That's Dave Kasick, huh?" she said, bending toward the TV. "He's cute."

"Who's that?" Harvey asked when she left.

"Dickie's wife, Sally," Karen said. "She's none too happy Dickie took this job."

"The hours?"

"More the geography. She was perfectly happy in L.A. I think she feels lost in New York."

"Oh, I know the feeling," Harvey said.

When everyone broke at six for dinner, Kasick came up to the twenty-fourth floor, still wearing the six gold chains from the triples-bar sketch.

"Well, Mr. Baby-sitter," he said to Harvey, "five and a half hours to live. You watch the run-through?"

"You were great," Harvey said.

"Don't bullshit me."

"Really. I was impressed."

"Don't give me that." Kasick actually looked fairly calm. Did he owe his placidity to the ingestion of some foreign substance that had escaped Harvey's vigilance?

"Yeah, it was very good," Harvey said. "Polished. Mainly Very Polished."

"You think so?" Kasick's eyes widened with tentative delight. "Mainly Very Polished?"

"That's what I said."

"Good enough for me," Kasick said. He clenched his right fist inspirationally and headed off to change into his terry-cloth robe.

"Mainly very polished?" Chuck Causey said.

"Just a joke between us," Harvey told him. "You know—M.V.P., Mainly Very Polished."

Causey turned around to make sure Kasick was out of earshot. "How would you feel about, say, Monumentally Vacuous Performance?"

"You could give the guy a break."

"A break? Harvey, this show's D.O.A."

Harvey accompanied Curt Geller downstairs for the staff dinner on the tenth floor. Geller first had to stop at the script room where production assistants were busy typing and collating the latest dialogue changes.

"This'll just take a minute," Geller told Harvey.

"Kasick was having trouble pronouncing 'salacious' in
the triples-bar sketch, so I changed the line and I want
to make sure they got the change, see how it reads."

While Geller looked over the freshly photocopied
insert, Harvey looked over a production assistant's
shoulder as she retyped a corrected page of a script for
a parody commercial about a kitchen appliance that
did everything from dice vegetables to resurface
driveways.

"Let's go," Geller said, wiping the lenses of his
wire-rims on his shirtfront. "I'm hungry." He looked
like he could use a couple years' sleep.

"Me too," Harvey said. As he turned, he saw a
handwritten sign on the bulletin board. It read: "Who
Do I Have to Fuck to Get Off This Show?" Harvey
broke into laughter. "That's great," he said. "You see
this?"

Geller glanced impassively at the sign. "Whom," he
said.

"What?"

"It's whom," Geller said.

6

The dress rehearsal, which began at nine P.M. before a packed studio audience, was very bad.

It was hard to say, given the vast complexity of a "Last Laughs" live production, what or who was responsible, although flubbed lines, overlong sketches, wooden acting, poor direction, missed lighting cues, and unfavorable celestial alignments were all mentioned. The informal consensus in the windowless Tan Room near the studio, where the writers traditionally gathered to witness both dress and the broadcast on a twenty-nine-inch RCA television, was that dress rehearsal was so bad that Dave Kasick's limitations as a comic performer went relatively unnoticed. Harvey counted three jokes about the weight problems of older film stars and two at the expense of homosexual posture. The inspired irreverence of the old days shone through only faintly, reflections from another light source.

Joey Hanes, Karen Baldwin, Marty Beaver, Chuck Causey, Curt Geller, Dickie Nacke, Rick Vergaard, Paula Coles, and several others Harvey didn't know suffered through dress in noble silence, except for the occasional comment, such as: "Let's see what else is on?" (Karen); "I'm too young to die" (Rick); "Does anyone know an effective way to kill an entire cast without raising the suspicions of the authorities?" (Joey);

57

and "I've seen worse shows over the years . . . maybe they'll come to me . . . maybe not" (Paula).

The dress rehearsal was over at 10:40. When the beleaguered cast members had made their way up to the Tan Room in their matching terry-cloth robes, Roy Ganz emerged through a door at one end of the room, followed by Leo Rhoades, who was wearing a New York Yankee cap and chewing gum with a vengeance. Ganz's palm was pressed Napoleonically against his heart.

"Well, we're long by about half an hour," Ganz said, reaching leisurely for a stalk of celery on the buffet table. "I would like to be able to cut everything but the opening sequence and the credits, but, unfortunately, I am contractually obligated to provide at least forty-one minutes of material. This forces me to make some difficult decisions in the next few minutes"— Ganz observed the celery in his upheld hand—"mostly involving some fine distinctions between the merely abominable and the truly execrable."

"Don't just look at us, Roy," Baldwin said. "Whyn't— whyn't you look at Leo—look at Leo too when you say stuff like that?"

Rhoades stiffened next to Ganz, who flicked Karen's remark away with a hand gesture. "Dave," he said.

Kasick froze in the middle of transporting a slice of honeydew melon from a tray of fresh fruit to his waiting mouth. "Sir?"

"You did a good job out there, Dave," Ganz said. "You didn't get much support behind you, but you did a good job. I thought the triples-bar sketch worked as well as anyone could hope. Joey?"

"Yes," Hanes said from one of the couches.

"I'd like to see you first, if I may."

Hanes rose, holding his bound show script.

"Marty, I need the benefit of your wisdom as well. In this dark hour."

Marty Beaver straightened his navy blazer, placed the latest in a succession of mangled orange toothpicks in an ashtray, and followed Hanes and Ganz into the latter's adjacent office.

In the fifty minutes between the end of dress and the start of "Last Laughs" 's fourth live broadcast of the season, most of the writers and their friends remained in the Tan Room. For once, no one angled for the funny crack or the self-effacing witticism. The mood was stoically professional. Occasionally one of the writers would assure another that a certain line in the script, which had been amusing all week, had failed during dress because of the delivery, not the writing. The studio audience, which everyone agreed was skewed toward the young and uninformed, was blamed for the failure of a couple of topical gags. The broadcast audience, papered with Ganz's friends, would be hotter. The writers were admirably frank about their own scripts—a frankness extending in Tweedledee's—Rick Vergaard's—case to his announcement that his monologue for Tom Angel about single fatherhood was not one of his better efforts and didn't belong in the show. "I think it ought to go," he said.

He got his wish when Hanes and Beaver came out of Ganz's little office and explained that Angel's monologue and five other sketches had been deep-sixed. While the saturnine Beaver moved to the buffet table and began gnawing carrot sticks instead of toothpicks, Hanes summoned Geller and Vergaard into Ganz's office. "Roy and Leo want you to clean up a couple more lines in the triples-bar sketch," he said. "Standards and Practices still has problems with it."

"Cheer up, gang," Hanes announced when Geller and Vergaard had disappeared into Ganz's room. "Some of the weakest dress rehearsals have turned into some of the strongest shows over the years."

Dave Kasick and the core cast members—Tom Angel, Eddie Colasono, Ron Fellows, Nancy Pildone, Candee Wersch, Rob Whent—as well as the two featured players, Brenda J. Johnson and Jimmy Lanahan, were all called to makeup at 11:05. Kasick, who had been quietly swigging V-8 juice, lifted his eyebrows at Harvey and went to his doom. The cast's exit had an immediate effect on the atmosphere in the Tan Room. The air of earnestness that had developed in the wake

of Ganz's post-dress appearance lifted to allow the
discharge of some damned-up bile.

"A bunch of thespian cripples," Causey said, slump-
ing on one of the couches.

Karen: "Dramatic dim bulbs."

"I've never s en so much flop sweat," Marty said,
deigning to speak.

Karen again: "Go a wonder how Whent ever made
it in the movies. He's got the comic timing of a
sturgeon."

"I resent that," Tweedledumpling said. "A very
funny sturgeon gave me my first big break in this
business."

The quips abated as the Tan Room began filling up
with new faces—friends of the cast members and writers, a few of Ganz's friends. At 11:25 a plump woman
in her late thirties came in. For an instant Harvey
thought he recognized her as Claire Strawbridge, a
member of the show's original cast ten years ago. But
this woman's small nose and perfect chin had little in
common with what Harvey remembered of Strawbridge's
elaborate facial features, assets that had greatly er
hanced her impressions of Golda Meir and even Lyndo
Baines Johnson in a sketch called "Night of the Living
Dead Presidents." This woman, dressed in a violet
muumuu, slipped quietly into the now packed Tan
Room and stood against the wall under a broad-
brimmed hat, where she watched the end of the local
New York newscast on the RCA mounted on the wall.

A voice came over the studio intercom: "Five minutes to air. Five minutes to air. Mr. Kasick, please
come to wardrobe. Mr. Whent, Ralph would like to
see you."

Harvey, sitting in a chair at the long conference
table in the middle of the room, turned to Karen
Baldwin and said, "For a minute I thought that was
Claire Strawbridge."

"It is," Karen said.

"Doesn't quite look like her. I mean, her features,
her nose and chin."

"Plastic surgery."

"Oh," Harvey said. "What's she been doing the

last, what, seven, eight years? I haven't seen her in much."

Karen kept an eye on the TV. The sportscaster was winding up. "She's been in and out a lot," she said. "In and out of a marriage, in and out of drug rehab, did a commercial or two."

"She was once on the cover of *Newsweek*."

Karen inspected his face with a comical expression of disbelief. "Well, aren't we being naïve."

"Yeah, yeah, I know."

"Look at you, Harvey. From the cover of *Sports Illustrated* to Dave Kasick's nurse."

"I was never on the cover of *Sports Illustrated*."

"Well, surely you were on the cover of something."

Harvey reached for a handful of the trail mix sitting in a plastic bowl on the table. *"The Sporting News,"* he said. "May eleventh, nineteen eighty." Curt Geller came back from Ganz's office and sat across from Harvey. The local news was over, and a commercial for stone-washed denim clothing was on.

"So," Harvey said to Geller, "how'd it go with the triples-bar sketch?"

Geller touched the stem of his wire-rims. "Any resemblance between the original triples-bar sketch and what you are about to witness on national television is purely coincidental."

The theme music for "Last Laughs" erupted on the television set. The Tan Room clock said 11:30. Harvey felt a surge of excitement, forgetting for a moment that he had already seen the show in its bloated, abysmal dress rehearsal state. He said a silent prayer for Kasick.

"Turn it up," someone yelled behind Harvey.

"No, turn it down," Tweedledee said. "Turn it way down."

The post-show party was held on the building's top floor, in an airy penthouse whose southern wall was one long floor-to-ceiling window. A dense fog had moved in during the evening. Harvey, standing alone by the windows with a plate of boiled shrimp, could see only a faint scattering of lights suspended in the gray view. The fog tightened the claustrophobia that had wound itself around him over the past four days. The few hours he had not spent in the offices or studio he had spent asleep on his bed in the hotel room he shared with Kasick. And now, although he had discharged his duties, he had still followed Kasick upstairs to all this numbingly loud music, dim smoky light, and jacked-up energy.

An English rock star, whose first album Harvey had danced to a dozen years ago at the University of Massachusetts, was mincing about, doing a little tender-footed jig all by himself, balancing a plate of hors d'oeuvres on his left hand. Not far away, in a pool of admirers, a young starlet with a recent hit movie smoked a nonfilter cigarette. The role, Harvey recalled, had not required much from her in the way of actual speech. Dave Kasick had the inside position with her.

On the dance floor Dickie Nacke, too early a member of the Baby Boom to know moves of recent vintage, puttered around with his wife, Sally, looking like a man stamping out a fire in slow motion. Ash-blond Candee Wersch was bouncing around with fellow cast member Rob Whent. A large-nippled breast popped out of her little cotton top. She ignored it for ten or fifteen seconds before, without interrupting her frenetic shuffle, casually reaching over with her left hand to cup and stuff it back into her shirt. In his sight line, beyond Candee Wersch, Harvey glimpsed Roy Ganz, who had also been watching. Their eyes met across the dance floor, joined by a moment of male servitude. Then Ganz folded himself back into a group of friends and admirers.

The show had seemed less bad than dress rehearsal, owing in part to the sometimes forced laughter in the Tan Room from friends and guests. Also, perhaps, the writers, desensitized to the show's shortcomings in dress, could devote themselves to the minute study of subtle improvements in the delivery of one line or another. Kasick had once again acquitted himself well. Compared to the cast members' frequent efforts to wring some laughter out of their dialogue, Kasick's natural stiffness had been refreshing. The studio audience warmed to his every fluff. Even the look of genuine distaste that crossed his face when his urine sample was shown to contain barbiturate capsules and syringes—actually a look of distaste for the sketch itself—was a hit.

A beaming Kasick had found his way to the windows, where he took Harvey's face between his hands and kissed him on the forehead. "That's for looking after me," he bellowed over the dance music. "And this is Jeannie."

Harvey shook the starlet's small white hand. "Glad to meet you."

"What?" She tilted her head, squinting. The squint made her face suddenly common. She was young, her blush-on was too thickly applied, her "What?" had a harsh Midwestern twang. Celebrity, Harvey thought—sometimes it seemed like a time-share condo that almost anybody could spend the weekend in.

"I said it's nice to meet you," Harvey yelled.

"Oh," she yelled back. "Yeah. Do I know you?"

"Now you do."

"Well, this is great, huh?" Kasick spread his arms joyfully.

"What a night," Harvey said. Maybe Mickey and he could get up to see the Vermont foliage after all. He had never felt so far from nature.

"Straight orange juice," Kasick said, holding his drink in front of Harvey's nose. "Sip?"

He held up his hand. "What you drink, when you drink, how much you drink, Kasick—that's your business now. Your parents came home. I'm going."

"What?" Kasick yelled, trying to surmount a solo drum riff.

"I'm going back to the hotel."

"I'm a star, Harvey."

"Good for you. But you were a star before tonight."

"Ten million people, Harvey. Losing the Series doesn't hurt so much right now."

"Dave," he shouted, "if I don't see you before I leave in the morning"—he glanced quickly at Jeannie—"it's been real."

"Real," Kasick said and hugged him.

In the elevator Harvey felt a touch of anxiety. For a second he considered going back up to the party. Mickey would insist on more high-level show business gossip than he had exposed himself to. When would he ever be in a room with so many culture heroes again? His misanthropy, Mickey complained, was always robbing her of significant trivia. Also, he had not said good-bye to Geller, Baldwin, Nacke, Tweedle-dumpling and Tweedledee, or any of the handful of people he had come to like. During a commercial break while they were watching the show, Geller and Baldwin had presented Harvey with a bottle of nonalcoholic wine in recognition of his labor.

As he walked through the empty lobby, he thought one last time about going back up to ask Karen to dance or something. He paused just inside the revolving door, then continued on. It was nothing more than the fear of missing out on something he was fairly confident didn't exist.

Out on Forty-seventh Street, a school of waiting limousines crowded the curb in front of the network building. Most of their drivers leaned against polished fenders, smoking with secondhand prestige. Harvey walked east to the hotel, showered, and slept. The hotel phone rang him out of a deep sleep.

"Harvey?" the voice said.

"Yeah." Dawn seeped through the curtains.

"This is Leo. Leo Rhoades."

He half expected Leo to break into his mechanical laugh. The man was his own standing ovation. "Hi, Leo," Harvey said. "What's up?"

"Sorry to wake you."

"You looking for Kasick?" Harvey heard himself say. He had been dreaming that he was looking for Kasick again, that he was forced to devote the rest of his life to finding Kasick. Now, as Harvey ascended to the next level of wakefulness, he thought with a jolt, something's happened to Dave. He looked over at Kasick's bed. But Kasick was in it, alone, undisturbed by the phone call.

"I'm not looking for anybody. We found somebody."

"Good, Leo. Who'd you find?"

"We found Roy."

"Roy Ganz."

"Yeah, we found Roy Ganz in the alley here."

"Oh, yeah?" Harvey stifled another yawn. "What was Ganz doing in the alley?"

"Completing a fall."

7

Harvey walked west the six blocks to the network building on West Forty-seventh, one foot still in his dreams, the call from Leo Rhoades almost a dream, the landscape a collection of images from deep sleep: the damp silence, a fat man on Sixth Avenue carrying potted ferns from a panel truck to the sidewalk, the pyramids of dark green polyurethane garbage bags, a tidy row of small dumpsters. Garbage in, garbage out. He stepped over a broken bagel in the diamond district. The fog of a few hours earlier had lifted but not cleared. The few skyscrapers on Forty-seventh blurred after the twentieth floor. It was still night, although behind him pinkish light had crept up over the East River.

As he approached Broadway, with its big painted hamburgers and thirty-foot-high chorus girls, the city stirred. Hookers in short slickers, twirling their collapsible umbrellas by the handle loops; a pigeon-toed tourist couple in matching windbreakers; three homeless men in front of Florsheim discussing shoe styles —"Go for the tassel loafers, man," "Naw, them fall apart," "Them good shoes," "Y'all need shoes take you right through the winter." Cadmium-yellow taxis hissed on the wet street, up and down Broadway.

In the next block, two-thirds of the way down, was the network building, pimpled with air conditioners, an older forty-story building with Art Deco styling. It

had been built of white brick, soiled now to the color
of used adhesive tape. Its upper floodlit reaches burned
eerily through the fog. In the alley that ran along the
east side of the building, several police cars and an
ambulance had converged. Two dozen people formed
a semicircle on the pavement.

Harvey talked his way past a cop and ducked under
the yellow tape sealing off the alley. Candee Wersch,
wrapped against the cold in a man's sports jacket,
passed him coming out of the alley, a startled deer.
When he reached the crowd, he recognized a few faces
from the show: Joey Hanes, Paula Coles, Ron Fellows, Brenda J. Johnson, Karen Baldwin.

"Oh, Harvey," Karen said. She had been crying.
"Looks like the party's over."

Leo approached them, wheezing, his hair damp, eyes
smaller than ever, dots in his huge head. "Somebody
pushed him," he said. "Roy wouldn't jump. Want to
see him?"

"Not particularly."

Leo ran an index finger across his nostrils. "He
looked like a broken puppet."

"Does anybody know anything?" Harvey asked.

"I went upstairs with two of the cops before," Karen
said. "He could have come out of his office window.
Twenty-four floors. But it was only open a few inches."

"Were both of you still at the party?" Harvey looked
at his Casio: 5.49 They said yes. "Did Ganz stay
long?"

"I lost track of him," Leo said.

"I don't think I saw him at all," Karen said.

"He was there, I saw him," Harvey said. "But I left
before one-thirty."

"Somebody pushed him out a window," Leo said.

It seemed to Harvey they were all just talking—
sleepless, disconnected talk. Harvey couldn't see what
the cops were doing behind Leo. Through someone's
legs, he saw a bit of body bag.

"He was like a father to me," Leo said.

Harvey almost expected a punchline, but Leo fell
silent. A squad car turned up the alley, forcing the

three of them to the side. Two more plainclothesmen got out and headed for Ganz's body.

"I'm sorry," Harvey said.

"I'm going to get some shut-eye," Karen said. "Good night."

"Get some rest," Harvey said.

"Night," Leo said. When Karen was gone, Leo turned to Harvey. "Mike Altiser wants to talk to you."

"Who's that?"

"Vice-president of business affairs. Mike's sort of one of the show's godfathers in New York. Mike's the first person I called. You were the second. Just talk to him."

Twenty minutes later Harvey sat in Mike Altiser's thirtieth-floor office. Altiser, a man in his forties with a Princeton haircut, very orange tortoiseshell glasses, and unusually small ears like Turkish dried apricots, calmly opened a paper bag and took out two containers of coffee. He removed the lids, handed one of the containers to Harvey, and then folded his hands in front of him on his desk. Outside his window it was light.

"I believe this is the first time I've been in my office without a tie and a clean shave." He had thrown on a well-worn yellow chamois shirt and a pair of jeans. "Where to begin, where to begin," he said. He had the firm, pleasant manner of a man who could be counted on, even if awakened in the middle of the night, to patiently resolve some corporate difficulty.

"I'm very tired," Harvey said. "Let's begin with why you wanted to talk to me."

"Roy was a very old friend of mine. I don't believe he'd kill himself. He was recently divorced, but not despondent. Careful with that coffee."

Harvey had scalded his tongue and paused a few seconds before speaking. "I suspect the cops will determine whether he killed himself or not."

"Yes." Altiser sipped his coffee thoughtfully and began loading up a small Danish pipe. "I've always been close to the show. I'm young enough to understand it and old enough to police it."

"Police it?"

"You know, keep the, uh, self-inflicted damage to a minimum."

"Okay," Harvey said. He was much too tired to ask follow-up questions.

"We've got to throw a net around this thing and contain it."

Harvey took a more prudent slurp of coffee. "What do you mean 'we'?"

"We want to hire you." Altiser sucked the match flame into his pipe with a series of short, desperate inhalations. "You've been around the show this week. You know the cast of characters." He tamped the tobacco down with a chrome pipe nail.

"I don't understand. You think someone on the show's involved in this?"

"No, no, I don't know. Look, privacy's very important to us here." He put down the pipe and pressed the heels of his hands against his eye sockets for a long time. "I agree with Leo that you should be here, to, uh, find out, uh, what you can, uh, find out"—he clasped his hands together—"and to, uh, keep it"—he unclasped his hands and made the motions of someone packing a mound of dirt together on his desktop—"well, contained."

Harvey blew on his coffee.

"Obviously, there'll be full cooperation with the police. But, of course, we're, uh, dealing with a group of individuals on the show whose personal lives, whose, uh, habits, if held up to the, uh, microscope, may well raise . . . peripheral suspicions. Which is to say that in the context of, uh, what may well be a murder investigation, a certain degree of exposure . . . incidental exposure of, uh, details— Look, Harvey, 'Last Laughs' is not, uh, a Xerox Corporation or a, uh . . . these are *creative* people, many of whom lead lives that are unconventional . . . this show has, as you know, a, uh, history of public perception, if you will. . . . Are you falling asleep on me, Mr. Blissberg?"

"I'm listening," Harvey said without bothering to open his eyes. "Are you saying you want to hire me just to babysit the truth so nothing bad happens to it, like getting out, or are you saying that you want me to help investigate the possible murder of Roy Ganz and be discreet about it?"

"Well, uh, I think you've said it very well there. If Roy was pushed out a window, I want you to talk to people on the show and ascertain, uh—"

Harvey opened his eyes. "Put the thesaurus away. I take it you want me to find out if anyone on the show's involved."

"There're individuals on the show with habits of, uh, an eccentric nature."

"Like what?"

Altiser put his pipe down and pressed the heels of his hands against his eyes again. "Well, you got your drugs, of course, but it's, uh, nothing compared to what you had here a few years ago. You got your drinking problems, you got your, uh, hell, you got your boys who like boys and your girls who like girls, hell, I don't know."

Harvey was dazed with fatigue. "You got your guys who like to chew on orange toothpicks."

"Oh, yeah, Marty Beaver and his goddamn Stim-u-dents."

"Is that what they're called?"

"You know what I'm talking about, don't you?"

"You're talking about drugs, booze, homosexuality, and a guy who's always got food in his teeth."

"That's it."

"We're not talking about anything else that you know of?"

"What do you mean?"

"I just thought maybe some image of a specific something or other might have leaped into your mind in some connection with Ganz's death."

"No," Altiser said, and paused. "You can name your price."

"It's not the price."

Altiser leaned forward, pipe protruding. "What is it then?"

"I'm not sure, to tell you the truth. I can't think too clearly on three hours' sleep."

"Would you consent to spend, say, uh, two or three days just looking into it?"

"Two or three days? If Ganz didn't jump on his own, I have to tell you, two or three days isn't much. I mean, this isn't like one of those things where you scratch that little patch with the edge of a coin and you get your answer."

Harvey and Mike Altiser looked at each other in silence for thirty seconds, not tired enough to actually fall asleep, too tired to negotiate.

"You know," Altiser finally said, "Roy used to say, 'I've been in show business since I was seven, Mike, and I expect to be in it when I'm seventy. There'll always be something I can offer the industry.' "

"Are you sure it wasn't Sammy Davis, Jr., who said that?"

Altiser ignored it. "I don't believe for a minute that he jumped, and to tell you the truth, it scares the hell out of me. From child star to geriatric star, I think that's how he saw it. He had the touch."

"Yes," Harvey said.

"This is going to be all over the papers, you know. The heat's going to be on."

Harvey nodded. "Let's see what the preliminary police report says, and then I'll see what I can do." Beyond Altiser's office window the dawn was burning off the fog. The sound of clanking dumpsters and down-shifting trucks floated up from Forty-seventh Street. "In the meantime, can you get me the bios of the cast and writers?"

Altiser made a note, then opened one of his desk drawers and extracted a single sheet of network letterhead stationery. He slid the paper across to Harvey and said, "Would you, uh, mind?"

Harvey examined the sheet, blank on both sides except for the network symbol, a simplified eagle, and Altiser's name and title. "I hope this isn't my contract."

"No, no. For my ten-year-old." He jerked his head to the right, in the direction of a family portrait on the sideboard: Altiser, the pretty wife, the young son and daughter. "He's a baseball nut."

"What's his name?"

"Noah. Kid already hits the ball real well."

Harvey plucked one of Altiser's desk pens from its holder and wrote: "Dear Noah, Keep your eye on the ball and your mind on the homework. Good Luck, Harvey Blissberg."

"He'll really appreciate this," Altiser said.

"My pleasure."

8

Three homicide detectives from the Midtown Precinct North, two men and a woman, sat side by side on one of the couches in Roy Ganz's former office. They all smoked cigarettes, as if this were part of their job. Arrayed around the office were the show's cast members, writers, production people, support staff, well over forty in all, many of them sitting on the floor. There was no show this coming Saturday—every fourth week in the schedule was an off-week—and many of the people in the room had had to forfeit or postpone vacations at the request of the police. On Sunday morning, following his talk with Altiser and a three-hour nap, Harvey had broken the news to Mickey by phone from the hotel and promised to get back to Boston as soon as possible.

Since early Monday morning the three detectives had been questioning "Last Laughs" personnel individually in the twenty-fourth-floor offices. It had been thirty-six hours since Ganz's body was discovered by one of the building's night security guards, but the intensity of the press coverage had pushed the event backward prematurely into historical perspective. It was as if Ganz had been dead for months. With the exception of one New York tabloid, whose splashy front page sneered GANZ'S LAST PRATFALL, the coverage had been dignified, befitting a youth culture hero who had turned his generation's sense of humor into serious business.

"Let me try to capsulize," one of the male detectives, a fiftyish man with thick black hair and a grayish complexion, told the assembled staff. He cradled a small notebook in his hand. "We've talked briefly to just about everyone, give or take a few regular employees, and I'm going to tell you what we know. We know a lot of you saw Mr. Ganz at various times at the party pursuant to the show itself. The latest any of you remembers seeing him at the party was around three-thirty Sunday morning. Various ones of you saw him talking at the party with a variety of other people, some connected with the show, some of them guests. None of you says you left with Mr. Ganz. None of you saw him leave the party. We understand there were well over two hundred people at the party, many of them going in and out a lot. None of you remembers anything unusual at the party involving Mr. Ganz—no arguments, no altercations, no mysterious conversations. Mr. Ganz was discovered in the alley, dead, at roughly four-thirty Sunday morning by Mr. Fekaris, a security guard. Some of you have mentioned various areas of disagreement between Mr. Ganz and various other employees. But I can't say that any of it seems the basis for throwing Mr. Ganz out of a twenty-fourth-story window."

The detective put out his cigarette and rose slowly from the couch. "We know that Mr. Ganz was going through a divorce. He may have had reason to be depressed." He walked slowly toward one of the three windows, carefully stepping between Rick Vergaard and fifteen-year-old cast member Eddie Colasono, who were sitting on the floor. "Naturally, we have considered the possibility of suicide." The detective stopped at the middle window and looked out, his back to the crowded office. "Well"—he pivoted to face the room —"we found a distinct set of Ganz's fingerprints on the wall on either side of this window. Now Mr. Ganz could've been leaning against the wall on either side of the window as he looked out and contemplated jumping, but in such an eventuality he undoubtedly—and I think you'll agree—would've been *facing* the window. However, the prints showed his thumbs down." The detective demonstrated by slapping his hands against the wall behind him without taking his eyes off his audience.

"Did I say we found a distinct set of Mr. Ganz's prints on the wall here? Well, it's rare to find a usable print, but we did. We found a few sets and some smudges, all in the same area." The detective rapidly moved his hands around the wall, capping his demonstration by pressing them forcefully against the wall and dragging them downward an inch or so. He managed to summon the agonizing image of a man trying to prevent his assailant from pitching him out a window. It was perhaps the best piece of theater any of them had seen recently.

The detective turned again and opened the window as far as it would go, admitting the crisp early November air. Harvey swept his eyes around the office and saw more than a few visible gulps. Kasick p led nervously on his nose. Even Marty Beaver had stopped chewing his Stim-u-dent.

"A few of you," the detective said while gently closing the window, "said you came down here to the twenty-fourth floor at one time or another during the party, or to get your belongings on your way out, but none of you remembers seeing him down here in the early morning hours, or remembers seeing him in the elevator coming down from the party, or recalls anything, it seems, that could make our job a little easier. Furthermore, I'm aware that there were many people at the party who don't work here, who were friends and acquaintances, and maybe even just hanger-ons, and that they were free to come and go from the party, as well as free to travel between the fortieth floor and this one. There were no signs of struggle here other than Mr. Ganz's fingerprints on the wall. Nothing written in Mr. Ganz's calendar showing that he had planned to meet anyone in his office after the show or after the party. No"—he searched for the phrase—"beautifully incriminating piece of evidence left behind by Mr. Ganz's assailant."

He paused here, in the vain hope that someone else in the room would speak. "Well," he said, "once again my name is Detective John Generra, and those are Detectives Miriam—"

He stopped in the middle of his introductions because the door to Ganz's office had suddenly opened and a very strange sight had entered, turning every head in the room.

It was someone completely concealed inside a gigantic bright-red foam-rubber costume in the general shape, if Harvey was not mistaken, judging from the intermittent arrangement of cloth scales sewn into the foam rubber, of a fish.

The figure took two steps into the office. Then, from somewhere inside the fish's head, a rather high male voice screeched, "Well, as you can obviously see, I sure as hell didn't do it!"

No one laughed.

"Could someone please—" Detective John Generra began.

Head writer Joey Hanes, who was sitting nearby, looked dismally at the detective and said, "Red herring. Get it? He's a red herring. It's from a mystery satire we did on the first show."

The red herring stood near the door. Its occupant's labored breathing was audible inside the foam head with its round plastic eyes.

"Oh, Christ," Karen Baldwin muttered.

"Good timing, Sondell," Leo Rhoades yelled across the room. "Really good timing."

"As I was saying," Detective Generra said, gesturing toward one of the couches, "my colleagues are Detectives Miriam Ortiz and Wayne Pittell. If any of you—including, of course, the fish—remembers anything that sheds some light on Mr. Ganz's death, we'll be very happy to hear about it."

9

Harvey stopped at a Korean market in the West Village on Monday night and addressed the sprawling, fastidiously arranged salad bar. His final selection leaned heavily toward Chinese barbecue ribs and tiny meatballs. Watch what you eat, his mother had reminded him only recently on the phone. "If you'd watched what you ate, you'd still be playing baseball." She had a way of reducing fate to a question of diet. He had been, he was sure, the only major leaguer whose mail regularly included clips from the *Boston Globe* Food Section on the subject of riboflavin. He ate his meal on a Christopher Street stoop and washed it down with a quart of fresh-squeezed orange juice.

Harvey turned down Barrow Street, looking for the address of Curt Geller's sublet. After the meeting with the detectives had ended, and Barry Sondell had unzipped his red-herring suit (his entrance line, Harvey learned, had been written by Sondell for his sketch "Mystery Theater for the Slow-Witted"), and Kasick had been allowed to leave New York finally for his home in Pennsylvania, but had been told by Detective Generra to stay in touch . . . after all that, Harvey had followed Geller into the latter's office and said, "Curt, the network has hired me to investigate this thing."

Geller had gone to his desk and written something on a pad, ripped off the sheet, and stuffed it in the breast pocket of Harvey's shirt. "My address. Whyn't you come over tonight at about nine and we'll see if we can crack this nut."

Detective John Generra had intercepted Harvey outside Geller's office and pulled him into an alcove near the reception area. His complexion really *was* sort of gray.

"I'm told you're going to have your own line in the water," he said.

"That's right," Harvey said.

"You know we're not going to help you." Generra said it with almost corny antagonism.

"Fine, but have I done something wrong? Did I bug you in a previous life or something?"

"Just steer clear, all right, Professor?"

Harvey started. "Well, frankly, Detective, I'm flattered you remember my old nickname."

"I'm a big baseball fan, and a big baseball fan even remembers the nicknames of not-so-great players."

He didn't go for the bait. Dickie Nacke passed by with his springer on a leash, and Harvey signaled a greeting.

"But you will stay out of our way, won't you?"

"Oh, I'm very quiet," Harvey said. "Very well behaved."

Curt Geller came to the door of his West Village sublet with a towel around his waist. Water glistened in his little concave diamond of chest hair. Without his glasses, he looked less academic, more vulnerable. "Come in, make yourself comfortable. I just got out of the shower." He showed Harvey to the front room of the dark, snaky apartment. "I'll be with you in a minute."

Harvey suspected he was in the living room, although it did not appear that much living went on in it. It possessed an unintentional asceticism. An institutional couch—green vinyl cushions on a chrome frame—and a round oak table were the only furnishings of any consequence, with the exception of books. There were books on the table, on the couch, on the floor. Harvey picked up a few: *The Denial of Death; Prisoners of Childhood; The Culture of Narcissism; Social Amnesia; Zen Mind, Beginner's Mind; Stress Without Dis-*

tess; The Myth of Neurosis; Making It on Your Own; The Divorce Book; Star Signs for Lovers. There were three books with the word "loss" in the title.

Geller came in, wearing pleated khaki pants and a loose black crew-neck sweater.

Harvey put down the book in his hand—*The Bible: For Students of Literature and Art.* "Well, Curt," he said, "looks sort of like you're going through a rough time."

Geller plopped down on the couch. "Oh, no, not at all. I've just split up with my wife, moved to a strange city, I live in someone else's place, and I don't like my job. This is one of the best times of my life. I don't think it gets any better than this."

Harvey was off-balance. "Well—well, I never cared much for this city. It's so—it's so—"

"It's so *there*," Geller helped out. "It's is-ness is is-ier."

"Yeah."

"And its business is busier." Geller fidgeted with the seam of a vinyl cushion. "I came, I saw, I went bonkers."

"Uh-huh."

"I'm going mental in my rental. Ganz's death is just another nail in the psychological coffin." He picked up a book and said, "Did you ever read *The Denial of Death*?"

"No."

"The single most depressing book ever written. Depressing because it's true. If you can read this book all the way through without killing yourself, then you're probably going to be all right."

Wit and despair had combined in Geller to produce an ambiguous mania. Harvey said, "And did you read it all the way through?"

"Twice."

"Maybe that means you're immortal. What does it say?"

Geller threw *The Denial of Death* onto the floor at his feet and looked scornfully at it. "Well," he said, "one of the things it's about is the irreconcilable urges in man to be separate and unique on the one hand,

and on the other to—to identify with the whole, to blend in, to escape one's unavoidable aloneness. In other words, it's about the urge to diverge, to"—he ran his hand through his wet hair—"to narcissistically splurge, vying with the urge to merge, and how, well, how we keep trying to purge one or the other urge. Anyway, after reading a chapter of *The Denial of Death,* I have to take a little S. J. Perelman as a nightcap or I'll never get to sleep."

Harvey quietly belched up some meatballs and slapped himself on the chest.

"It gets so bad sometimes I have to read a Zen lecture at three in the morning to try to get back into Big Mind. That, or some Martin Buber."

Harvey crossed his legs. "Curt, what's a guy who reads"—he swept his eyes around the living room— "books like these doing at 'Last Laughs'?"

"Oh," Geller said. "Well, I—let's see—I ended up on the show because I'd just split with my wife and I was tired of the West Coast. I wanted to try something new. A mutual friend of Ganz's and mine recommended me to him, and he offered me a job. I'd always had a kind of reluctant admiration for Ganz, and I thought I could contribute."

"You don't seem too happy there."

Geller leaned forward, elbows on his knees. "Harvey, I know you're here to find out who killed Ganz, so I'm going to tell you about myself and the show so you don't have to keep asking me questions. I've got nothing to hide, which I'm going to prove to you"—he glanced at his watch—"in about fifteen minutes."

"What happens in fifteen minutes?"

"In fifteen minutes I'll tell you something you'd have a hard time finding out on your own. I'll save you a little shoe leather."

"What's wrong with telling me now?"

"I've got to wait for my visual aid to arrive. But first things first. You said I didn't seem too happy on the show. Quite correct. Let's just say I don't see eye-to-eye with the prevailing comic mentality of the show. I thought I would. I misunderstood Ganz. I thought he wanted to bring the show up to a higher level. I was wrong."

"What's the prevailing mentality of the show?" As if Harvey didn't already know.

Geller stroked his beard. "These guys—I'm talking about Ganz and Rhoades—well, it's like they come from a different emotional gene pool. Now I'm not trying to get up on some high horse about this—I mean, it's not a high horse I'm on, is it?"

"More like a very tall pony."

"Anyway, these guys have . . . to them, the whole world is designed to end in a tasteless sketch. Now, I suppose I'm no one to talk, since I've worked a little in Hollywood, but the truth is that what little reputation I have is based on a, on a light touch. I, well, I once got paid a handsome amount of money for polishing a script, where all I did was take out a dozen words and add a joke that didn't require a single syllable, and they loved it. But these guys, these guys measure jokes according to how much damage they do and, particularly in Leo's case, by how loud they can laugh at their own jokes."

"So I've noticed."

"Yeah. Look, Harvey, I don't want to read you my résumé, but I don't really belong on this show. I used to teach college, I wrote humor on the side, I backed into scriptwriting. I never went to live in Hollywood, I stayed in San Francisco. I like to work alone. I probably've read ten books for every good joke I've written, you know, like those sixteenth-century French chefs who used to boil a ham for six days to get a tablespoon of essence. I—" He stopped and smiled. "A little bit too much false immodesty, huh?"

"I'm listening," Harvey said. He was pretty sure Geller had had a couple of belts.

"All right. So I got to the show, thinking I'd be able to help, but I failed to size up the situation."

"Size it up?"

"They drive the fast track with no rearview mirrors. I didn't get the game, Harvey. In the sizing-up category I struck out. Whiffed."

"What do you mean, whiffed?"

"Okay. The first week I was there, I handed in my first sketch to Rhoades. It was a thing about yuppies, about a Yuppie Detox and Rehab Center, you know, where yuppies who no longer wanted to be yuppies could check in to be weaned away from their conspicuously consuming behavior. So Rhoades comes into my office a few hours later and asks me to hold out my hand. I'm thinking, he wants to shake it to tell me how much he likes the piece. I mean, I thought it was a funny bit, so I hold out my hand and he says, 'No, turn it the other way.' So without thinking, I turn my hand, palm down, and he slaps it."

"Wait a second—Rhoades slaps the back of your hand?"

"Yeah."

"What'd you do?"

"Well, I should've ﹍ ﹍ ked him up against the wall."

"Okay, but what did you actually do?"

"I just looked at him, sort of stunned, and then he said, 'We don't do sketches like this on the show.' "

"Sketches like what?"

"He said, 'We don't do sketches that aren't funny. Sketches that are just fill-in-the-blanks satire.' "

"What's that?"

"I think he meant, you know, take a drug rehab and detox center and take out 'drug' and put 'yuppie' in the blank. I thought it was a little strange, coming from someone who himself had written any number of such sketches, like a thing he did a few years back called 'What's My Crime?,' a take-off of 'What's My Line?' So when he slapped my hand, I said, 'What's the matter, not enough vomit in the sketch for you?' And, needless to say, it was all downhill from there between Leo and me."

"What about you and Ganz?"

"Ah. You know Marty Beaver?"

"The older guy."

"Yeah, well, I was under the impression that when Ganz hired me, it was to act as a, you know, joke doctor. My principal job was to improve the work of the other writers. I was to get a credit on the show as script consultant. Well, I show up two months ago

only to discover that Ganz has also hired Marty
Beaver—*rehired* Beaver—who was Ganz's script consultant during Ganz's first tour of duty as executive
producer. I find out he's brought him back."

"So now you're competing for your own job with
Beaver?"

"Exactly."

"You're pissed off."

"No, I'm delighted beyond your wildest imaginings.
You know what it's like trying to compete with a guy
who's known Ganz for years, worked for him? I've got
about the same status as the office popcorn machine."

"Beaver couldn't've been too happy about your being
there, either."

"I know he's not happy about it, but he never
speaks to me on the subject. I mean, he literally won't
even respond to a hello."

"You've had no contact with him at all on the
show?"

"Only in script conference when Ganz is present,
and then he doesn't talk to me. He refers to me, when
addressing Ganz, as 'Mr. Geller.' I take it back, I've
had some contact with him. He came up to me one
day and handed me a four-pack of Stim-u-dents."

Harvey laughed. "He gave you those orange toothpicks?"

"I suppose it was a peace offering, or maybe just a
veiled comment on my dental hygiene." Geller rose
from the vinyl couch and started pacing. "You know, I
went to Ganz about the third week I was there, and I
said, 'This won't do, you know, having me and Beaver
doing the same job.' And Ganz gave it the royal, 'Well,
it'll just *have* to do, won't it?' Basically, he left me no
choice except to quit, if I wanted to keep my dignity."

"Why didn't you quit?"

Geller stopped in the middle of the floor. "It's the
human condition." He sighed. "Harvey, didn't you ever
sit through a really bad movie to the end? Transfixed
by how bad it was. Because you know something this
bad just has to get better?"

"I've sat through a few bad movies. I'm assuming
you didn't work on any of them."

"Let's hope not. Ganz and Rhoades've had me for breakfast, Harvey. And I've been just dumb enough to show up at noon, and so they've had me for lunch too. You know Emerson's line in 'Self-Reliance,' 'Insist on yourself'?"

"Not offhand, no. But I *am* familiar with 'To thine own self be true.' "

"Well, that's what I'm not doing, and it keeps me up at night."

"That should give you plenty of time to read Emerson."

"I'm a fringe character there. They think I'm aloof. And surly. I'm a surly on the fringe. On top. Of it all." Geller chuckled. "I'm a who-and-whomer."

"A what?"

"You know, the difference between 'who' and 'whom'—that's like something that matters to me. I got into a fight with Tom Angel once about his misuse of the word 'fortuitous.' I couldn't help myself. I feel like a librarian there. Once in a while a writer'll come in and ask my opinion about something, but everyone knows I have no power. I mean, I get along with most of the people there, but Ganz and Rhoades basically wrote me off a while ago."

"So why don't they fire you?"

"I don't think they fire people there, unless you do something really outrageous."

"Like toss Ganz out a window."

"I think that might be a fire-able offense," Geller deadpanned. He sat down on the couch again.

"Curt?" Harvey said.

"Yeah?"

"*Whom* do you think killed Roy Ganz?"

"If you'll excuse me, it's 'who.' "

"You're excused, but the question stands."

"How the hell do I know who killed him?"

"I said, who do you *think* killed him? Correction: among the people on staff, who might've been capable?"

"Cold-blooded murder, I don't know, that doesn't exactly—"

"Forget cold-blooded. Assume there was an argument. And Ganz lost. Now who has a real problem with Ganz?"

Geller stood up again and walked to the narrow windows overlooking the street. "Who doesn't? Where do you want me to start?"

"Leo Rhoades."

"Okay. Rhoades. I've heard that Ganz stole a screenplay idea from Rhoades when they were both out in L.A. a couple of years ago. Something about Libya. A comedy, I think, involving guns, Islamic fundamentalists, the CIA, and circus performers. It won't surprise you, perhaps, to learn that it was never made. Had it been, I'm sure Rhoades would've been upset."

"Even as it is, isn't it a little strange that Rhoades works for Ganz? I mean, if what you say is true."

"Hey. Hostility is these people's form of love."

"Who told you about Ganz's alleged theft of Rhoades's idea?"

"I heard it first in L.A. Word gets around. Then Dickie Nacke was talking about it in the writers' wing a couple of weeks ago."

"What about him?"

"You mean, why would Dickie chuck Ganz out the window?"

Harvey nodded.

"I don't know about Nacke. It looks to me like he struck up a nice rapport with Ganz from the beginning. Maybe because he's roughly Ganz's age. Of course, Nacke hasn't had much luck getting his stuff on the show, but that doesn't distinguish him."

"Joey Hanes," Harvey said. "He's chief writer, right?"

"Head writer." Geller returned to the couch and sat down. "Joey Hanes is a nice guy. Hanes worked under Ganz in the way-back, first few years of the show. Quit, came back, even ended up writing a Ganz TV special in L.A. a few years ago. Hated it. Hates Ganz. Loves Ganz. Heavy ambivalence. Couldn't resist when Ganz offered him the head writer's job this year, a job he had last year when Stuben was executive producer of the show. Hanes couldn't resist even though Joey told me his shrink told him not to come back and work for Ganz. Joey couldn't help himself. It's kind of sad. Ganz is kind of an abusive father to Joey, never misses an opportunity to ridicule Hanes's passivity in front of others. Ganz calls him 'Rough and Ready' Hanes. 'Cause Joey's soft and usually late. Speaking of abuse, you know Jimmy Lanahan?"

"He's one of the cast members."

"Ah," Geller said, holding up a finger. "No, Lanahan's a featured player. Second string. Important distinction. Here's that story. I know because one night, the week after the first show, Lanahan wandered into my office. Deeply in the bag. Throwing things around. He'd been bumped at the last minute from a small role in the first show. He was pissed enough at being just a featured player to begin with. To be bumped from a cameo was salt in his wounds."

"Why'd he get bumped?"

"He was in the bag half an hour before air on the first show. Ganz took one look at him between dress and air and gave the part to Nacke. Nacke wasn't half bad, either. But here's the thing: Lanahan sits down on the couch in my office and tells me that Ganz"— Geller held up the quote sign—"discovered Lanahan five or six years ago in a New Jersey comedy club. Told him he was great, that he'd make Jimmy a star, all that bullshit that really goes on in this business. Ganz apparently even paid him a retainer for a couple of years to bind him, keep him away from other opportunities."

"And Ganz never did anything for him, right?"

"Worse, he basically kept Lanahan off the market for two or three years. Of course, Lanahan did it to himself, no? So Lanahan throws some of his best years at Ganz's feet, and Ganz steps all over them. Then, this year, Ganz finally throws him a bone—featured player on a show that's already been brought to its knees by comic arthritis. Big deal. No meat on that bone. No wonder Lanahan was throwing shit around my office."

"One thing you can say about Lanahan, he's big enough to have thrown Ganz out the window," Harvey said.

"And he was probably in the bag enough. He was tossing them back at the party. When I left, he was dancing in his underwear."

"There's another featured player, isn't there?"

"Brenda Johnson."

"The black woman."

Geller sat down and clapped his hand against his forehead. "There was a writers' meeting a couple of weeks ago where Brenda complained that she wasn't getting any good parts on the show. She said she felt like she was going to get nothing but bit parts as domestics, receptionists, and unwed mothers. I remember she said, 'I've spent enough time in the ghetto in my life. Why doesn't someone write me a fucking color-blind role?' She was really steamed. I've gotta hand it to her. Took some guts to say that to a room full of white men."

"Well, did anyone respond to Brenda?"

"Ganz said she was absolutely right, and on the very next show the only part she had was playing a nurse with two lines."

"The list keeps growing, doesn't it?" Harvey said.

"Hey, you asked who had a problem with Ganz. And don't forget Beaver. By an irony that's all too familiar in the industry, as they call it, Marty Beaver and I have the same agent, and he told me a week or so ago that Beaver was threatening to leave the show."

"Why? It sounds like his power's intact."

"My—our—agent says that at some point this fall, Ganz had discussed letting Beaver go."

"Discussed this with who?"

"With whom. With Beaver himself."

"I don't get it."

"I don't either. Maybe Ganz felt guilty, after all, about hiring me and not getting rid of Beaver. Maybe there was something else."

Harvey bummed a Lucky Strike from Geller and lit it. After his first drag he said, "I think I need to rest for a minute."

"Then there's Karen Baldwin," Geller said.

"What the hell is this, an Agatha Christie novel?"

"Have you ever seen Karen do stand-up?"

"No."

"She's terrific," Geller said. "She's a great comedian. She wanted to be in the cast. There's no way in hell she shouldn't've been hired as a cast member slash writer. Particularly when you look at the cast Ganz ended up with."

"Well, what happened?"

"Well, she never even got to audition. Ganz called her in after seeing her tapes—excerpts of her appearances and some other stuff—and Ganz told her it sucked."

"Why?"

"I guess because he thought it sucked. And this is the man legendary for his nose for comic talent. He told her it sucked, and then he offered her a job as a writer. And she took it. This is part of Ganz's genius, Harvey—he spits in people's faces and they think his saliva's good for their complexion."

"I get it," Harvey said, blowing smoke. "This is that Agatha Christie novel in which it turns out that all twelve suspects killed the murder victim."

"There's only one person I can think of offhand who can spit in Ganz's face and get away with it."

"Leo Rhoades?"

"Barry Sondell."

"Sondell?"

"Yeah, Sondell. Of course, keep in mind I'm not a true insider here. This is the first time I've worked with any of these people. I'm just giving you my thoughts. But here's Sondell, who was responsible years ago for some of the show's best moments, if abusive and self-abusive humor is your idea of a good time. But he hasn't written anything worthwhile for years, he just holes up in his Manhattan penthouse with his collection of antique weapons, and what does Ganz do? He hires Sondell for a huge amount of money, and then Sondell never comes to the office, never turns in anything usable, and to boot he gives interviews to the press about how pathetic the show is. Talk about biting the hand that pays you several thousand bucks a week."

"So why does Ganz put up with it?"

"Well, now, Harvey, would it really surprise you that a man who often treats others with such casual disregard would, at some level, I mean at *some* level, have an equally perverse need to be the object of precisely that treatment?"

Harvey put out his Lucky in the ashtray sitting on the floor between him and Geller.

"Don't you think it possible that a man like Ganz might, in some other, better concealed area of his life, subject himself to another?"

"You're losing me, Geller."

"I'm just saying that someone like Ganz just might need, unconsciously at any rate, to reap what he sows, to, uh, invite small disasters to even the moral score in his own mind. You know, the urge to merge back into the humanity from which he has so colorfully distinguished himself."

"Being thrown out a window's not exactly inviting a small disaster."

Geller's buzzer rang. He got up and started walking toward the kitchen. "Well," he said over his shoulder, "small disasters have a way of turning into bigger ones, don't they?"

Harvey heard him buzz in his visitor.

"My date's arrived," Geller said, going to the front door. "Remember I told you fifteen minutes ago that I was going to prove to you I had nothing to hide?"

"I remember."

Geller opened the front door and admitted an extremely good-looking woman in a yellow scarf and black Perry Ellis coat. Her straight dark hair was fashionably cut shorter on one side than the other. She hugged Geller tightly for a moment and turned toward Harvey, who stood.

"Harvey Blissberg," Geller said. "Mimi Weiss."

"How do you do," Mimi said, extending her hand. She had deep brown eyes and a pair of small moles below her left eye. She looked distraught, but managed a tepid smile.

Harvey said, "Nice to meet you."

"The same," she said.

"Can I get you something?" Geller asked her.

"No, I'm fine."

The three of them stood in silence by the front door for several seconds, with an awkwardness that Harvey did not feel was warranted.

"I was going to show you I had nothing to hide," Geller finally said to Harvey.

"Oh, it can wait." Harvey reached for his parka on the back of a chair by the door.

"It doesn't have to wait."

"Don't worry about it, Curt. Why don't I give you a call tomorrow and we can talk some more."

"Mimi's what I don't want to hide."

"Come again," Harvey said.

Geller ran his arm gently around Mimi's waist. "Mimi," he said, "used to be married to Roy Ganz."

10

At first Mimi Weiss struck Harvey as someone whose personality had been patched together from pieces of upper-middle-class American culture. Over the course of the first twenty minutes, the facts emerged: raised in Great Neck, educated at Bennington, a stint as a "Last Laughs" production assistant in the early days before becoming a buyer for Bloomingdale's, reacquainted with Roy Ganz on one of his trips East four years ago, a furious love affair ending in marriage. . . . She referred to Woody Allen as "Woody," to Steven Spielberg as "Steve." . . . She was wearing more gold jewelry than looked good on her. But gradually, as she talked, she relaxed, seemed to detach from the trappings of that world. Fnally they were talking about Ganz.

"When we got together four years ago, he was at a low point," she said through intermittent tears. "When we got married, he was no longer *the* Roy Ganz, which was what I liked. When he was away from the center of attention, he was a person. Roy didn't know that, but I did. Our marriage got bad when he started to inflate up. Then I felt like I was living with a press clipping. I kept telling him, 'I'm your biggest fan, you don't need the others.' "

"Why'd he start to inflate?" Harvey asked.

"Oh, I guess he started hanging out with a new Hollywood crowd out there, he got a deal for a TV special, maybe people started paying him a certain kind of respect he thought he'd lost, I don't know. His disappointments began to fade."

"You weren't living out there with him?"

"No, I spent time out there with him, but basically I lived here, in the apartment."

"Don't get her wrong, they lived together here," Geller said, for some reason eager to rush to the defense of their marriage.

"Roy just spent a lot of time out there, doing business," Weiss said. "But it was lonely, that's why I pushed him to come back to the show last spring when they started looking for a new executive producer. I mean, I knew it would be risky for him to come back to his old stomping grounds, to compete with his old success here, but I thought—I thought it would be good for us. I had to be here for my job. And I thought New York'd be a healthier environment for him. Of course, that was the end. If he hadn't come back to do the show, we'd probably still be married. Unhappily married, but married. I take responsibility for that."

"Why was it the end? Because—what? Because he resented your pressuring him to return to the show?"

"Yeah, that was part of it," she said. "I guess he thought I was trying to control him. All I was trying to do was have a real marriage."

"What was unreal about it, as it was?"

"Oh, I don't know, we were apart so much. It was like we were on parallel tracks, waving to each other from the train windows. It wasn't my idea of intimacy, but he didn't seem to mind."

"He didn't like you to make demands, huh?" Jesus, Harvey thought: Fourteen months ago I was still playing major league ball; now I'm playing shrink to Bennington graduates.

"You got to understand one thing about Ganz," Geller interceded. "All those years he was a child-actor, his life was controlled and manipulated by his agent, his parents, the network. You know, his parents basically sold him into a life of very lucrative slavery. Well, maybe that's a little strong."

Harvey looked at Geller, who was sitting next to Mimi. They both faced him with their hands in their laps, not quite touching. Harvey felt like their chaperone. "Curt, you know his parents?"

"Oh, no. I'm just saying this thing about child-actors. It's part of the bargain for them. They lose their childhoods. Between the ages of whatever it was—seven and ten, let's say—Roy Ganz was a blond-haired, blue-eyed commodity." Geller glanced quickly at Mimi. "Of course, I never really watched the show all that much. I was too young."

"Me too," Harvey said. He wished Geller would shut up.

"I watched 'Leave It to Beaver' when that came on."

"Yeah," Harvey said. "What was the name of Ganz's show?"

" 'My Baby Brother,' " Weiss said.

"They rerunning it these days?"

"Naw," Geller said. "But I think they had it on cable here a couple of years ago."

"Mimi, did Roy talk much about the show? I mean 'My Baby Brother.' How'd he feel about being a child star?"

"He didn't talk about it at all, really. He was too busy being an adult star." She stopped to reconsider the tone of her last comment. "Don't misunderstand me—I loved Roy, I really did. Even after I told him I wanted a divorce. I loved the little boy in him, I loved the good parts of him."

"But," Harvey said, "the little boy, at least the little boy who was a child star, was the part of him he liked least in himself?"

Mimi Weiss looked at Harvey for a moment. "Well, you're right. But the little boy I loved in him was not the 'My Baby Brother' little boy. I liked something else. I guess it was the nice, spontaneous little boy I could see in him, but he couldn't, because he'd never been allowed to experience it. He was always trying too hard not to be *that* little boy."

"You know," Geller said, "when he was a kid star,

they used to call him 'The Miniature Man.' I think it was *Time* or *Newsweek* that tagged him with that."

"Mimi," Harvey said, "where were you the night of the party, the night he was killed?"

Her face froze. "We—Curt and I—were at my place. When Roy and I separated, I took another apartment."

"We didn't go to the party," Geller said.

"Listen," she said, "I've already been through this with the police. I don't like the sound of your question. Curt told me to talk to you because you wouldn't—you wouldn't be so—"

"So blunt?" Harvey said.

"Yeah."

"It just helps to know your whereabouts between the hours of, say, midnight and five on Sunday morning."

"I was at the apartment. Curt came over after the show, so he got to my place around, I'd say, one A.M. We didn't leave until Leo called me about, I guess, a little after five."

"You have a doorman at your building, right?"

Mimi Weiss jumped to her feet and clattered across the living room in her black leather boots, kicking a couple of Geller's books out of the way. "Stop it! I had nothing to do with Roy's death, and you know it!" Geller chased her across the room and held her tightly by the bare wall. "Enough!" she said, pressed against Geller's shoulder.

"I'm sorry," Harvey said.

She broke away from Geller's embrace and disappeared into the bathroom.

"Hey, go easy, Harvey, for God's sake," Geller said.

"You're right."

"It's traumatic enough for her, okay?"

"Right."

"All right?"

"Yeah," Harvey said and stood up to stretch his legs. "Curt," he said, pressing his thumbs into the small of his back and arching backward, "did Ganz know about you and Mimi?"

"No."

"How long have you two been together?"

"Just about three weeks."

"How'd you meet her?"

"I met her waiting for the elevator leaving the show one day. I think she'd been up there seeing Roy on divorce business. We started talking, she was making conversation about the show, you know, and I said I was pretty miserable there, and so she started telling me about what it was like years ago when she was a production assistant, and I told her I couldn't figure out why Ganz would come back to the show, and then she said, just as we were leaving the network building, 'He came back because I asked him to.' And so she started telling me that she was Ganz's wife and hoped soon to be his ex-wife, and we ended up having coffee, and I'll tell you, so you don't have to ask, that it was seventy-two hours later that Mimi and I went to bed together, two lonely people on the rebound."

"How's the divorce? Messy?"

"No. There's a bunch of property to divide, but the feelings aren't—weren't—too split."

"Ganz wasn't contesting it?"

"No. I don't think he was too happy about it, but he didn't raise a stink. He kind of had porcelain-coated feelings. The shell was real hard."

When Weiss came back and sat down, Harvey leaned forward in his chair, elbows on knees, and said, "I know you've already answered this for the detectives, but I'd like to know if you have any ideas about who would've wanted to push Roy out the window."

Geller turned to her. "I've already told Harvey about some of the people on the show who had beefs with Roy. You know, Leo, Marty, Joey, Lanahan, even Karen—you know, what Roy said about her audition tape. Not that I think any of those people would ever do anything like this."

"Well, in a moment of rage," Harvey said. "Mimi, can you add anybody to the list?" He could see that it was getting to her, that behind all the words she was now simply trying, unsuccessfully, to reckon with the fact that the man she had loved was dead. She looked blankly at Harvey, playing with the trio of thin gold bracelets on her right wrist.

He made one more attempt. "Mimi, did Roy owe anyone a lot of money, or did he have any mortal enemies you know of? Was he thinking of firing anyone—except Marty Beaver, that is?"

She shook her head tightly at each question.

"All right," Harvey said. "It's late." He stood up.

"Roy made a lot of small enemies," she said quietly. "It came with the territory."

Geller got up to see Harvey to the door. "I'm sorry," Harvey said to Mimi, who remained on the vinyl couch. "I'm sorry about Roy."

She said, "Thank you," without looking up.

At the door Harvey asked Geller if he was going to be around for the week.

"Police orders." He seemed exhausted too. Over the course of the evening, his mania had wound down like a toy with weak batteries.

"Curt, answer one more thing for me: did Ganz have any vices I should know about?"

"Like what?"

"You know, anything I should know about."

Geller poked his glasses back up his nose. "Does treating people badly count as a vice?"

In the taxi on the way back to his midtown hotel, Harvey asked the Iranian driver if he could look at his newspaper. Roy Ganz's death still dominated the first three pages of the tabloid. The police were "looking at many possible suspects." " 'No,' Detective John Generra said, 'drugs did not appear to be involved in any way.' " Blah-blah-blah. Unless Generra and his colleagues were holding something back, this whole thing was a mess. It could've been almost anybody, Harvey thought. It could've been the rock star with the mincing dance step. It could've been some hanger-on stoked on crack who had taken offense at some sketch on the show. It could've been some right-wing fundamentalist who took offense at every sketch on the show. It could've been one of the hundreds of writers and actors who had not been hired by Ganz. But

Harvey had to go for now with what he knew; he was curious about Jimmy Lanahan. He had a long-term and short-term grievance, and he had a substance-abuse problem. Harvey felt he was about to fall through the thin, slick surface of the show.

As the cab rocketed up Sixth Avenue, his thoughts turned to baseball. He had just missed his first season since he was a nine-year-old Little Leaguer. The Providence Jewels, the last team he played for, had managed to tie Cleveland for sixth place. They could have used him. His rookie replacement in centerfield, M.O. Givens, had shown something at the plate, batting .261, with a bushel of RBIs, but the kid had been a little light on the leather in the field, misplayed a few late-season line drives—he had followed the kid's year more closely than he liked to admit—and raised some questions about his future. Maybe Harvey could squeeze back into the lineup, but he'd have to do it soon, next season, before Givens had time to refine his fielding or before Marshall Levy, the team's owner and general manager, traded for someone better. Before the gristly creaking in both of Harvey's knees got any louder.

Harvey had the taxi drop him off at Forty-seventh and Madison. He needed a couple of blocks of fresh air, such as it was. The night was cool, but not exactly crisp. Perhaps it was the best Manhattan could do in the way of autumn. He found an old Winston in his parka and smoked it as he walked east toward the Boswell House.

A block from the hotel, a derelict motioned to him from the shadows of an office building entranceway. "He'p a guy out?" he said wheezily.

"Next time," Harvey said without stopping.

The derelict came out of the shadows and followed Harvey for fifteen or twenty yards. "Hey, man," he rasped. "He'p a guy out."

Harvey walked on, thinking about catching Ganz's eye at the post-show party two nights ago when Candee Wersch's breast popped out of her dress on the dance floor. What was that expression on Ganz's face? Had it been just mild disdain for her exhibitionism, mixed

with simple curiosity? Or was there something disap-
provingly possessive about his gaze? Harvey had spent
a good part of the evening concerned with Mimi Weiss's
affair with Curt Geller and whether Ganz's possible
discovery of it ought to be factored into his fate; but
who—whom?—the hell had Ganz been seeing? Had
Harvey been observing a little drama two nights ago,
in which Candee Wersch had been taunting Ganz,
demonstrating the limits of her availability? I may be
sleeping with you, but I sure as hell don't belong to
you, even if you are the executive producer. If Geller
was right, and Ganz had been susceptible to domina-
tion by a few—by Barry Sondell, by Mimi—what's to
say that Candee Wersch hadn't been exerting a frus-
trating influence on him?

"He'p a guy out, now," the voice behind him said.
"Habn't eaten today."

In a pedestrian passage under a network of construction scaffolding, Harvey pivoted to face the wiry
derelict, who was wearing a soiled hooded sweatshirt
and a moth-eaten cardigan over it. In the shadows,
Harvey thought he could've been anywhere between
thirty and fifty. He made out a fresh abrasion on one
side of the bum's face, and a nose blooming with
nodes. The man held out a begrimed hand and wheezed,
"He'p me out, he'p me out." He pushed himself close
to Harvey. "God bless you, and he'p me out."

Harvey felt around in his change for a quarter and
pulled it out. "Here," he said, dropping it in the
bum's hand.

The bum looked at it in his hand and mumbled,
"You can do better'n this, Harvey. He'p me out."

"What'd you say?"

The bum wiped a fingerless glove across his nose. "I
ask you to he'p me out."

"What'd you say before that?"

"I ask you for mo' money." He flipped the quarter
back at Harvey, who made a backhand grab. "My
machine don't take quarters."

"No, no, you said my name."

"I did?"

"Yes."

"No, man, you gotta he'p me out."

Harvey shoved him against the plywood wall separating the pedestrian walk from the construction site. "Who the hell are you?"

"Easy, man," the bum said, this time in a faintly familiar, high voice.

"If the next move you make isn't to tell me who you are, I'll rip your nose off your face."

Raising a hand to his nose, the bum said, "You don't have to do that. See, it comes right off." He yanked off his cauliflower nose and winced. "Damn, I always put on too much spirit gum."

"Oh, Christ—" Harvey said. "Barry—"

"Sondell."

"You asshole." Harvey dropped his Winston on the pavement, where it hit a puddle with a *pssst*.

"Thank you," Sondell said, peeling the abrasion off his cheek. He held out the flimsy piece of latex to Harvey. "Want this? Guaranteed to scab over in a day or two." He laughed shrilly.

Harvey slapped him across the left side of his face.

"Hey, wait a second!" Sondell said. "How come you get to call me an asshole with impunity, and when I offer you my sore, you get to slap me?"

"That's just the way it goes."

"Nobody likes being called an asshole."

"Then why the fuck'd you thank me?"

Sondell was wiping some of the dirt off his face. He wore a thin silver-and-turquoise ring on his right middle finger. "Just being polite."

"Polite, like showing up in Ganz's office a few hours ago in a fish costume?"

"You didn't like that?" He pulled back the hood of his sweatshirt.

"Look, Sondell, here's the deal." He poked him in the chest. "You can dress up any way you want in the office, okay, but when it comes to me, you show up in the face God gave you, or I'll give you a permanent disguise."

"You're one tough hombre." He rolled his *r*.

Harvey slapped him on the right side of his face.

"Hey, man, he'p me out." The phony tracheotomy voice.

"What do you want, Sondell? I'm bored."

"I want to help you out." His own voice. Harvey wasn't so sure he didn't prefer the other to the high, sniveling thing that naturally came out of his mouth.

"Know how you can help me out, Sondell? You can help me out by dressing up next time as a suppository and shoving yourself up your own ass."

Sondell's dry mouth broke into a sticky smile. "That's pretty good. Almost reminds me of a Sondell line."

"Maybe I can get a job on the show, make a couple hundred grand, ~nd never even have to show up at the office."

"Hey, I do my best work in the friendly confines of my own room. A man of my creative magnitude needs to be left alone."

Harvey looked at his watch. It was ten after midnight. "I'll give you five more seconds, Sondell."

"Beaver," Sondell said. "Marty Beaver."

Harvey waited for a couple to pass by under the scaffolding. "What about him?"

"I thought your job was to figure out this Ganz business."

"What about Beaver?"

"I told you. Beaver."

"What're you saying? Beaver threw him out the window?"

Sondell shrugged.

Harvey was annoyed now at wanting something from Sondell. "Stop shrugging, will you? What about Beaver?"

He shrugged again.

" 'Cause Ganz wanted to fire Beaver?"

Shrug.

"After all these years?"

Shrug.

"Bringing Geller in to replace him? Anyway, Geller's the one with more to be angry about, if you ask me." Harvey was testing him.

"Beaver," Sondell said.

"You're gonna have to say more'n that, Sondell."

"Think of this as a Socratic dialogue."

"Beaver's an old man. He'd never have the strength to throw him out."

"Golden Gloves champ back in the forties. He still works out. He'd throw you out a window with one finger."

"Did Ganz really have plans to dump Beaver?"

"That's part of it."

"What's the other part?"

"Can't tell you any more," Sondell said, putting up his hood again. "It'd give it away. I've already told you more'n I've told the cops. Night, Harvey." He started walking away, in the opposite direction of Harvey's hotel.

"What about you, Barry?" Harvey called after him.

Sondell turned and raised a precious finger to his lips. "Shhhh," he hissed.

Harvey walked a few paces toward him. "I've heard a few things about you."

"Oh, I'm sure you have. I don't have any secrets."

"I'm watching you," Harvey said. Christ, he thought, I sound like the bigger asshole.

"Watch all you want. I had nothing against Roy. Roy was very, very good to me. Too bad about the show, though."

"How's that, Sondell?"

"Used to be so good, when I was writing most of it. Imagine," he said, "a man of my creative magnitude being forced to work for a shit show at these wages. Remember what Chaplin once said, Harvey—that comedy arises from the attempt to maintain one's dignity in the face of bizarre events."

"What's that got to do with anything?"

"It's hard to say, hard to say. Well, Harvey, I guess I'll see you around, where the rubber meets the road." Once again Sondell began walking away into the shadows.

"The rubber meets the road?" Harvey called out. "What's that mean?"

Sondell stopped and turned again. "I don't know. I just like the way it sounds. Sometimes I just say things, Harvey."

"Hey, Sondell, let me tell you something—your problems run faster than you do." Now, where did *that* come from? Harvey thought.

"Gosh, that's a beautiful piece of philosophy," Sondell called to him. "Harvey, I know that if I spent more time listening to you, I could be a better person."

11

With a fistful of phone messages collected at the front desk, Harvey returned to the hotel room that, for six nights, he had shared with Dave Kasick. Now there was a chocolate mint on only one of the beds. Harvey ate the candy, crumpled its wrapper, opened one of the windows, and walked to the op site side of the room. He faced the window, wound up, and threw the ball of foil out the window into Manhattan.

A little up and in, Harvey thought, but not a bad pitch at all. He knew half a dozen American League umpires who would have called it a strike.

He sat on Kasick's former bed and pawed through the phone messages for a second time. "Entertainment Tonight," the syndicated evening television digest of entertainment news, wanted to interview him about the Ganz investigation. Joey Hanes wanted to talk to him. Mike Altiser of Business Affairs wanted to talk to him. One of the researchers for the *New York Post*'s gossip column had called—twice—to talk to him. *Rolling Stone* wanted to talk to him. *The New York Times* wished to have a word with him.

He had also just missed a call from Kasick in western Pennsylvania.

Kasick answered on the second ring. "And how's your large and exquisite person, Harvey?"

"Fine."

"You miss me?"

"Yes," Harvey said.

"Harvey, I want you as my first guest on my new show."

"Oh, yeah? What show's that, Dave?"

"I think I'm going to be able to swing a talk show on public access cable in Pittsburgh."

"This is why you called?"

"No, I called—I called because I had to tell you something."

"What?"

"I should've told the cops, but I didn't, so I'm telling you."

"Well?"

"It's something someone on the show said to me last week. Thursday or Friday, I don't remember."

"Yes?"

"You know Jimmy Lanahan?"

"Yeah."

"Lanahan told me ᴸe was gonna kill the fucker."

"Lanahan said that to you?"

"He was drinking, you know."

"What were the circumstances?"

"Oh, we were down in the studio dry-blocking," Kasick said. He threw out the "dry-blocking" with the casual assurance of a newly minted star. "Jimmy-boy was having trouble with his line in the sketch, the one about the triples bar. Ganz yelled at him, he said something like, 'Lanahan, if you put less garbage in your mouth, less garbage'd come out of it.' I think that even the folks in the control booth could smell the gin on his breath. Anyway, Ganz told Jimmy to take five to sober up—'I don't care how you do it, just do it' is how Ganz put it. Lanahan stomped off, stood next to me fuming, and said, 'I'm gonna kill the fucker.' "

"Did he say anything after that?"

"Not that I heard. He was sort of saying, 'I'm gonna kill the fucker,' to himself. Then he walked off."

"What do you think? You think Lanahan's the type?"

"Hell if I know, Harvey. I'm just telling you."

"Did anybody else say anything else to you about Ganz?"

"Na, that's it. I was too busy learning my lines. Incidentally, Harvey, you think I ought to renegotiate for next year?"

"Huh? Oh—I don't know. How many years you got left on your current?"

"Two. But."

"But what?"

"But how'd I know I was going to be this good?"

"How much you making now?"

"Comes to seven hundred thou and change next year."

Harvey had never made half that. "You want a million?"

"I want what the other guys make."

"What other guys?"

Kasick quickly ticked off half a dozen premier players, one of them a two-time American League Most Valuable Player. They all made more than a million.

"Look, I don't know, Dave. Sure, see if the Red Sox'll bend. Worse comes to worst, you can always go to arbitration. Don't worry about it. Anyway, after taxes it's the difference between a Porsche and a Chevy station wagon."

"Yeah, but don't you think I should make at least what Camins and Frain make?"

"I don't think you should anything. Sometimes a poor slob like you just has to settle for seven hundred thou and change. Hey, go to Russia if you want to make the same as everybody else."

"Russia?" Kasick said. "When they'd start playing baseball over there?"

Harvey went through his phone messages and separated out the ones from the media. He squared them off in a little pile and ripped them into eighths. He went to the open window and thought about tossing the pieces out. He would have liked to see the pink flutter of paper against the navy blue night.

Harvey had not expected to see any of the show's personnel around the office during the off-week, even if they had been requested by the police to remain in the city, and he least of all expected to run into

Lanahan, whom Harvey, in his thoughts, had just been indicting on the way in.

When he got to the "Last Laughs" offices at noon on Tuesday, the large actor was snoring liquidly in a worn armchair in the cast's wing, his head thrown back, mouth dryly ajar, long legs splayed before him, ending in purple high-top Converse All-Stars. His features, even in repose, had all the delicacy of a semi-trailer cab seen head on. Facial fate, if not limitations of talent or his unfortunate attachment to Ganz, had consigned Lanahan in advance to character roles.

As Harvey watched him, Lanahan stirred and blinked his eyes open. After a long stale yawn he said, "Hey, Harvey, whatcha doin'?"

"Wondering what *you're* doing."

"Catchin' some shut-eye."

"Why're you sleeping here?"

Lanahan looked about him for a moment, as though to confirm where "here" was, smacked his big lips, and said, " 'Cause my apartment's too depressing."

Harvey glanced at his Casio.

"I had a late night," Lanahan said. "What time is it?"

"A little after noon," Harvey said. "What kind of late night did you have?"

Lanahan stretched, elbows out. "Oh, I sat up here late with Brenda, drinking," he said very matter-of-factly.

"Brenda Johnson?"

"Yeah, you know, us obscure cast members have to stick together. Brenda and I have our own little mutual admiration society. You know, we sat around talking about Ganz's, you know, death."

"What'd you decide about Ganz's death?"

Lanahan tucked his T-shirt into his jeans. "You got a cigarette?"

Harvey said no. "You have any more specific thoughts?"

"You mean, like who did it?"

"Thoughts in that general area. I'm just trying to get a feel."

"Whyn't you go feel somewhere else, Harvey?"

Harvey held up a conciliatory hand. "Easy, Jimmy, I'm just asking."

Lanahan sat up in his chair. "Harvey, I've played a lot of cops, detectives, and busybodies, and I gotta tell you your performance doesn't move me. I got a feeling you suspect me or something, based on my relationship with Ganz. Am I right?"

"Not really."

"Am I right?" Lanahan shouted at h

Harvey leaned back, out of the path o' 'anahan's abominable breath. "I know a little bit ab ~ your background with Ganz, and Dave Kasick told me 'bout the flare-up with Ganz during dry-blocking last week—"

"What flare-up?"

"That you said, referring to Ganz, 'I'm gonna kill the fucker!' "

"That's not true," Lanahan said in a more civil voice.

"You weren't referring to Ganz?"

"No, I was referring to Ganz when I said what I said, but I didn't say, 'I'm gonna kill the fucker.' "

"But you said something?"

"Yeah," Lanahan said. "If I remember correctly, what I said to Kasick was, 'I'm gonna kill the *mother*fucker.' "

"Have it your way."

"Come off it, will ya, Harvey?" Lanahan yelled. "I won't read these lines."

"Huh?"

"This script sucks, Harvey. Don't make me say, 'Hey, man, just because in a moment of anger I said I was gonna kill the motherfucker, that doesn't mean I went ahead and did it,' okay? Get yourself a new writer. This is bad melodrama."

"Ganz made you a few promises he couldn't keep. Tied up your career and didn't do much with it."

A wave of despair crossed Lanahan's face, "Yeah, Roy—" he began, "he did a number on me . . . yeah, it pisses me off. I coulda been a contenda, Chollie. But I don't go around fuckin' throwin' people outta windows!"

"You know, no one's saying Ganz was murdered in

cold blood. Things happen, a dispute, you know, turns
into a shoving match. Things happen."

Lanahan fixed his eyes on Harvey's. "Somebody,"
Lanahan said coldly, "had to open the window."
He paused. "It was about forty degrees out, Harvey.
Ganz's window wouldn'ta been open. Listen to me,
Harvey. Somebody . . . had . . . to . . . open . . .
the . . . window. Ganz didn't exactly fall by accident
out a window in the middle of a scuffle. Do you
understand?"

Lanahan was right; someone had to open it.

"You figure it out," Lanahan said. "Anyway, I was
nowhere near Ganz's office after the show. I was at
the party until four or so—"

"Dancing in your underwear, I understand."

"Oh, yeah?" Lanahan almost smiled. "Well, I don't
rightly recollect. I kinda party hearty."

"Where'd you go when you left the party? Or don't
you recall that either?"

"That's my business."

"That's not much of an alibi."

"Oh, fuck alibis. I don't have to defend myself to
you."

Harvey headed for the writers' wing. Turning the
corner from the corridor into the reception area, he
was surprised to find a congregation of writers on the
couches—Joey Hanes, Karen Baldwin, Rick Vergaard,
Chuck Causey, Dickie Nacke, and Marty Beaver. People didn't seem to be able to get enough of the office
atmosphere.

"So," Nacke was saying, "he can't find the houses
on his route anymore. He's losing it. So he tells his
wife, 'Linda, they've moved them. They've moved the
houses. And the dogs—they're not afraid. They don't
bark anymore.' "

Hanes, who was wearing a Chicago Bears jersey,
noticed Harvey and said to him, "Dickie's got an idea
for a spoof called 'Death of a Mailman.' It looks like
Andy Seif, who's in *Death of a Salesman* on Broadway,
is going to host a week from this Saturday."

"And Willy complains that people are forgetting to
stamp their letters," Nacke went on. "And his wife,

you know, tells the kids, she pleads with them, 'He's a human being, and a terrible thing is happening to him. Postage must be paid.' "

Marty Beaver, standing in his blue blazer, said, " 'It's not enough for the mail to be sorted. It must' "—he paused—" 'be *well*-sorted.' "

Vergaard and Causey looked blankly at Beaver, but Karen Baldwin stopped sucking on her pendulous lower lip to say, "So Willy tries to kill himself by putting his head in a postage meter, right?"

A rustle of laughter, which Beaver allowed to subside before saying, "But Leo won't go for it."

"Why not?" Baldwin said.

Beaver raised his right arm and passed his hand over his head. "What's the average age of our viewers? Eighteen? You think these people have ever been to a play? You think they've ever even heard of Willy Loman or Arthur Miller?" He smirked. "Look at Tweedledumpling and Tweedledee here"—he tossed his jaw at Causey and Vergaard—"you guys a little lost?"

"Some of it sounds familiar," Vergaard said.

"Let's ask Harvey," Causey said. He turned his head to Blissberg. "Do you get it?"

"If you want my opinion," Harvey said, "I think you ought to be using your week off to work on a sketch called 'Death of an Executive Producer.' "

"I like it," Nacke said, turning to the others. "But who can we get to play the murderer?"

"Hmmm," said Baldwin.

"Lanahan," Hanes said.

Nacke darkened. "Too obvious."

"That's why no one'll suspect him," Hanes argued.

"What about Pildone?" Baldwin said. "Nancy's got that character she does. You know, that shrew."

"And what's her motive?" Causey asked.

"I didn't know we were typecasting," Baldwin said. "But if we are, why not Candee then? Ganz always treated her like doody. I think he thought that anyone as pretty as Candee Wersch couldn't be taken seriously as an actress. Personally, *I* think that anyone as pretty as Candee ought to get life in prison."

Marty Beaver reached over and tapped Nacke on the knee. "What about you, Dickie? You were terrific filling in for Lanahan a few weeks ago."

Nacke examined his I.D. bracelet. "I don't act. I was just doing Roy a favor."

"You certainly act like you can act," Beaver said.

"I'm too old to make a fool of myself on TV." Nacke cracked a knuckle.

"But wait," Vergaard interjected. "Who'll play Ganz? Now that's a tough role to fill. Do we know anyone with an ego big enough to handle the job?"

There was a pause, then Baldwin, Hanes, and Nacke simultaneously said: "Sondell."

"Perfect," Beaver said quietly, and everyone laughed.

Harvey went down the hall to the office formerly occupied by Kasick, sat at the desk, and looked around at the spare furnishings—the tan couch, the metal file cabinets and bookshelves, the white walls pocked with little foxholes in the plaster where push pins had once held up posters. Like most of the "Last Laughs" offices he had been in, this one reeked of temporary tenants hired over the years, passing through to practice their wit for a single show or a season, or two or three. Funny for money.

He rummaged through the desk drawers to find the inhouse phone directory and dialed Mike Altiser's extension.

"Business affairs," a woman chimed. "Mr. Altiser's office."

She put Harvey through to Mike Altiser, who said, "How are you, Harvey?" and without waiting for a response added, "Can I get right back to you? I've got Detective Generra in here and we'll be through in a few minutes. Where are you?"

"Extension seventeen-thirteen," Harvey said.

"Oh, good, you're in the building. Whyn't you come up to the thirtieth floor in fifteen minutes?"

From the inside pocket of his suede sports jacket, Harvey took the confidential list of home addresses and phone numbers for "Last Laughs" personnel that Altiser had given him on Sunday morning. He dialed Candee Wersch's sublet on the Upper West Side. While he listened to her phone ring, he glanced over his copy of the *New York Times* article on the show: ". . . plucked 24-year-old Candee Wersch from relative obscurity, in her case a small improvisational comedy troupe in Detroit."

A woman picked up the phone on the sixth or seventh ring. "Hello?"

"Is this Candee Wersch?"

"Yeah. Who's this?"

"This is Harvey Blissberg."

"Who?"

The closest contact he'd had with Wersch during the past week was observing her dance at the party after the show. "Harvey Blissberg. I'm the guy who was looking after Dave Kasick last week."

"Oh, the baseball player."

"The ex–baseball player. Now I'm a professional baby-sitter for guest hosts. Actually, I don't know if you know, but I've been hired by the network to help investigate Roy Ganz's death."

"Hey, that's a pretty big promotion, baby-sitter to detective."

"Candee, I don't know if you've talked to the police—"

"Not since yesterday. They asked me a bunch of questions. I don't think I helped them much. I'm pretty freaked by this whole thing."

"Did they ask you if you had been dating Roy Ganz?" Maybe he should have taken a more leisurely windup before throwing the fastball. Not only was Harvey unsure what he would make of the revelation if Ganz secretly had been dating Candee, but he knew the whole notion was a wild inference.

"No," she said.

"No, they didn't ask you?"

"And no, I wasn't dating Roy. Why'd you ask—you think it would've been a good match?"

"I—gee, I wouldn't want to say."

"I'll tell you the truth," she said. "I did try to interest him a while back—this was a couple of weeks before we went on the air. I always thought he was kind of excellent."

"What happened?"

"Nothing. It just didn't take. You know, I asked him if he was dating or anything, you know, with the divorce and everything—I can be a little forward. He told me he wasn't leading a monk's life, and then he smiled in this way that . . . well, it was a real diplomatic no, is what it was. So ma‿‿e he was seeing somebody. Or somebodies."

"How'd he treat you generally, Candee?"

"Oh, okay, I guess. I mean, I don't get as much to do on the show as I'd like, but I'm just glad to be part of it. The whole place seems so clubby, and I accept the fact that I'm not really part of it, you know. Not yet, anyway. I mean, I have my ambitions, and this is just the beginning for me, if you ask me."

"Who's in the clu‿?"

"Oh, you know, G‿‿ ‿nd Leo Rhoades and Marty and Joey, they've all worked together before, and then Rob Whent, 'cause he's been in movies and everything, he seems to have more status." Candee Wersch gasped for air and continued. "You know, I wasn't interested in Roy to get in the club or anything. I just liked him and wanted to get to know him, right?"

Harvey said, "Right."

"Anyway, let's face it—he was kind of ancient. I'm only twenty-four. Anyway, there turned out to be somebody else on the show I started to like a lot, who's more my age, so I kind of forgot about Roy, romantically I mean. I mean, I really admired him as a genius, I don't know who could've wanted to push him out a window. My mother called me yesterday and wanted me to quit the show and come home. She was already worried about drugs on the show and everything."

"Candee, you said there's someone else on the show you like a lot. Who's that?"

"Do I have to tell you?"

"It would help."

"I mean, not too many people know we're seeing each other, you know what they say about the—about, what is it, something about company ink."

"Dipping your pen in it."

"Yeah."

"Well, you can tell me and not worry about it getting around."

"You sure?"

"Yes."

"Okay," she said. "I guess. I've been seeing Jimmy Lanahan."

"Jimmy Lanahan?"

"Yeah. For about three weeks now. But not too many people know about it."

Harvey looked down at the scratch pad on which he had been doodling during his conversation with Wersch. He had written down: LANAHAN, RHOADES, BEAVER, SONDELL, HANES, BALDWIN, and finally WERSCH. He crossed out WERSCH. "Do you have any idea who might've been in Ganz's office with him when he went out that window?"

"No, I don't," she said.

Harvey believed her. "Tell me," he said, "how long did you stay at the party Saturday night?"

Wersch thought for a moment. "Until about three-thirty or so."

"Then where'd you go?"

She hesitated. "I was, well, to tell you the truth, I was in the wardrobe room, you know, off the studio on the tenth floor, until maybe close to five. We didn't know about Roy until we left the building, when he was, you know, already dead."

"We? Who were you with?"

"Jimmy."

"What the hell were you and Lanahan doing in the wardrobe room?" Harvey fleetingly pictured Barry Sondell in his red herring outfit.

"Do I have to answer?"

"I'm asking."

"We were having oral sex."

"I see," Harvey said, uncapping his Rolling Writer. He drew a single line through LANAHAN.

—— 12 ——

The reception area was empty when Harvey passed through on his way to take the elevator up to Mike Altiser's office on the thirtieth floor. Through a sliver of open door, he glimpsed Marty Beaver in shirtsleeves reading a newspaper at his desk. Beaver's rust-colored pompadour was just visible over the paper. Where the sun hit it coming through the window, his curly hair looked like a copper scouring pad. Harvey rapped lightly on the door.

"Come in," Beaver said without lowering the paper.

Harvey stepped into the office. Towering stacks of old newspapers formed a skyline against one wall. "It's Harvey," he said.

"So it is." Beaver accompanied the words with a brief rustle of *Newsday*.

"You don't throw much out, do you?"

"Old news is good news." He laid the paper down softly on his busy desktop, where it tented over a chrome desk pen standing in its holder. "What can I do for you?" A Stim-u-dent was crammed between a lateral incisor and a canine. Beaver looked at him with an air of infinite patience, an old pro biding his time until something better—or at least funnier—came along.

"I wonder if this is a good time to have a word or two about Ganz's death."

The muscles in Beaver's massive forearms tensed. Ex–Golden Glover.

"No time's a good time for that," Beaver said.

"So that makes this as good a time as any."

Beaver's response was to lift the newspaper back into reading position. For the first time, Harvey noticed the headline: GANZ PROBE WIDENS. He shifted his weight from one loafer to another. Beaver remained hidden behind his paper, silent except for some faint sucking sound that had to do, Harvey imagined, with his Stim-u-dent.

"Marty," Harvey began, "I know about the situation with you and Curt Geller." He paused. "You know, it seems he was hired to do your job." No response. "I've heard you were very unhappy about it. Understandably." Still no response. Harvey cleared his throat. "I also understand you've been thinking of leaving the show the last week or two."

Beaver softly turned a page.

"I also understand," Harvey said, but with difficulty because his mouth had gone dry, "that Roy Ganz had been contemplating letting you go."

Beaver said nothing from behind his paper.

"That makes a certain kind of sense, I guess, or he wouldn't have hired Geller in the first place. What I don't get is why he would hire Geller with you still in place here. I mean, I figure that since you and Ganz had known each other for a long time, well, it doesn't make sense he'd put you in such a bad position." Harvey jiggled the change in his pants pocket.

Beaver lowered the paper again and narrowed his eyes at Harvey. He pulled the Stim-u-dent from between his teeth and put it in a dish that already contained several dozen used Stim-u-dents.

"When I wrote for 'The Jack Beaton Show' back in the fifties," Beaver said, "I think you're probably a little young to remember it, but we created this character who reminds me a lot of you."

Harvey stopped jiggling his coins and felt around in his pocket for his lighter.

"You know, Jack ran a neighborhood variety store with his wife, and he was always bumbling, always getting himself into one fix or another. And one season we created this character, a distant relative, a nephew around thirty or so, a kind of ne'er-do-well, who kept showing up at the store to pester Jack about one damned thing or another. He always wanted something. He either wanted to borrow money or borrow tools, and get Jack involved in some harebrained business scheme. He was always hanging around, shuffling his feet. And the funny thing is that the actor who played him looked a little like you, Harvey."

"How interesting," Harvey said.

"But you know, it just never worked. The nephew was boring. We gave him some laugh lines, but the problem was he was *boring*. The character just didn't work."

"About Ganz," Harvey said.

Beaver lifted the paper again and disappeared behind the headline. "So after a few episodes," he said, turning a page, "we just killed him off. And, Harvey, when you leave, please close the door behind you."

Detective John Generra stopped Harvey outside Mike Kaiser's office on the thirtieth floor. He was wearing a wash'n'wear suit and black ankle boots that zipped up the side.

"Hey, rookie," Generra said.

"Detective," Harvey said.

Generra stroked his gray face. Harvey wondered how skin could achieve such an absence of color. It was as if the concept of middle-age had chosen Generra to exemplify itself.

"How's your probe going?" Harvey asked.

"My probe's fine."

"I heard it's widening."

Generra smiled, his pale lips stretching over his big teeth. "There's nothing like a widening probe. Though I can't say any pasta's sticking to the wall. And how's your probe?"

"I think my probe's narrowing instead of widening."

"Oh, I see. A narrowing probe. Been eliminating suspects, have you?"

"Yeah."

"Anything I should know about?"

Harvey glanced at his Casio. "I'm supposed to see Altiser."

"Hey." Generra smiled. "Are we working together or not?"

"I thought I was supposed to stay out of your way."

"I'll let you know if you're in my way."

"I'll be happy to tell you what I know, but I gotta know what's coming the other way. You trading players or cash?"

"Players."

Harvey pulled him around the corner, away from Altiser's secretary. "All right, you know this guy Lanahan, one of the actors?"

"The big guy with the chip on his shoulder that's got the career that Ganz was dicking with?"

"That's the Lanahan I'm talking about."

"Yeah, we've been looking at him. Lanahan has a rap sheet. A short one."

"What's on it?" Harvey said.

"Assault and battery four years ago in a comedy club. He beat up the club owner for trying to short-change him. The owner dropped the charges."

"I think you can eliminate him."

"How's that?"

"When Ganz went out the window, he was with another member of the cast."

Generra's gray eyes brightened. "Which gender?"

"The opposite one."

"And Lanahan told you this? Because if you got it from Lanahan, I'll tell you, rookie—"

"I got it from the opposite sex."

"Well, don't we have a way with us."

"People just like to talk to me," Harvey said.

"Well, are you going to tell me who you got this out of or not?"

"No."

"You believe her?"

"Yes."

"You don't think she'd be protecting Lanahan, do you?"

"Protecting him? That'd mean she was in on it."

"I guess you're right."

"Now," Harvey said, "for your end of the deal, tell me about Beaver. I think Ganz wanted to get rid of him. I think Beaver had reasons to wish Ganz ill, but I admit I can't quite see a guy his age giving Ganz the heave-ho."

"Forget Beaver."

"Forget him?" It grieved Harvey to lose him as a suspect.

"Yeah, Beaver and his wife were out after the show with Altiser and his wife. They're all friends. They were out until three or so. And the guard downstairs here didn't see Beaver come back to the building that night. No, it was someone who was probably at the party, but, in any case, someone who was in the building and didn't leave until after four-thirty. We even?"

"One more thing," Harvey said. "Was there anything in Ganz's blood?"

"He had an antidepressant in his system. A moderate dose of imipramine."

"That's it?"

"That's it."

"That's one of the drugs they use to help people get off cocaine," Harvey said.

"I know. But—" Generra shrugged.

Harvey shrugged back. The story was not going to be told in Ganz's bloodstream.

When Harvey sat down across from Mike Altiser, the network vice-president was pulling down on the lobe of one of his small ears. A pipe was clamped in one corner of his pinched mouth; the other corner emitted ceremonious puffs of smoke. "How's it going?" he said.

"I just saw Generra. We've eliminated Jimmy Lanahan and Marty Beaver."

"I'll vouch for Marty's wherabouts."

"Generra told me."

"What about Lanahan?"

"He was with another cast member all night," Harvey said.

"I see." Altiser clicked his pipe stem against his teeth.

"It checks out. For what it's worth, Curt Geller's

got an alibi too. Just out of curiosity, Mike, was Ganz trying to get rid of Beaver?"

"Well, yes, Beaver's agent and I had been talking about a way out of here for Beaver."

"Beaver was unhappy because Ganz also hired Geller to do basically the same job?"

"Well, it was really Leo who hired Geller."

"Didn't Leo and Ganz know what each other was doing? I mean, they ended up with two people in the same job."

"That's right," Altiser said, relighting his pipe.

"How the hell'd that happen?"

Altiser waved a hand at his pipe smoke. "You'd be surprised what happens on this show, Harvey. A few years ago Ganz hired an old friend of his as assistant production designer, brought her all the way out here from California, even though there was no money in the budget for the position."

"What happened?"

"Oh, we let Roy keep her. Found the money somewhere. It was hard saying no to Roy."

"That's very interesting," Harvey said. For a moment he felt his enthusiasm for the case drain away, and his mind wandered. There were too many players in it playing by too many rules he didn't understand. He was beginning to develop a slump mentality about the whole thing; he felt his spirits turning a familiar corner onto that street where a guy could go 0-for-29 before pushing one through the infield.

"What's very interesting?" Altiser asked.

"Interesting? Oh, interesting—I don't know, Mike." Harvey looked out the window framing Altiser's head. The gargantuan torso of a woman in a bathing suit rose above a neighboring rooftop on Broadway. "What about Barry Sondell?"

Altiser tapped out some pipe ash against a cork knob attached to a large glass ashtray. "Well, you know Sondell *was* on his way out."

"I didn't know that."

"I spent a few hours last week looking over his contract and talking to Sondell's agent to see how we could buy him out. Roy wanted Sondell gone."

Harvey shifted. "I thought the two of them went way back."

"Oh, they do, but Sondell's sort of slipped over the edge. He always did think of himself as God's gift to comedy—"

"I'd say he's more like a party favor."

"Okay, I'm inclined to agree, but it turns out that the time he's been spending *not* fulfilling his obligations to 'Last Laughs,' he's been spending writing sketches under a pseudonym for a competing comedy show."

"Oh, that's charming," Harvey said. "Couldn't you just fire the guy?"

"Not that easy. Contracts. Just like they can't simply fire a major league ballplayer, right?"

"I don't know, it's kind of difficult to play for two teams at the same time, which is what Sondell's been doing."

Altiser held up his hands, as if to stop the analogy from proceeding any further. "In any case, Sondell was not seen at the party after the show. No one saw him."

"Doesn't mean he wasn't there."

"No?"

"Mike, here's a guy who shows up in a fish outfit yesterday afternoon when Generra's talking to the staff, then last night he accosts me on Forty-seventh Street disguised as a derelict. I wouldn't be surprised if he came to the party dressed as a cocktail knish."

"I'll grant," Altiser said, "that Sondell could've been there, but I simply can't see a guy like him—"

"You know, Mike, that's the problem—we got suspects up the yin-yang, but nobody can see any of them chucking Ganz out the window. This is wreaking havoc with my wu-wei."

Altiser leaned back in his tufted black vinyl chair. "You want to forget the whole thing?"

"No."

"You know, when I was at Yale," Altiser said, "I played hockey. Center. I used to score a lot of garbage goals. The other guys on my line were better athletes, stronger shooters. I'd just hang back and wait for loose pucks and rebounds. I always found that a little forechecking and a lot of hanging around in the slot made all the difference. I let my linemates wind up for the big slapshots. Sooner or later I'd find the puck on my stick, the goalie out of position, and twenty-four square feet of net looking at me. You know what I'm saying."

"Yes," Harvey said. "Now tell me—Generra's probe is widening. Where's it widening?"

"Well, L.A., for one thing. The cops're looking at some drug dealers there who seem to know, or have known, Roy at some point."

"Yawn," Harvey said.

"Yawn?"

"Yeah, if it were drugs, why would anyone knock Ganz off, except that he didn't pay up, and Roy's not short of cash. Besides, I thought Ganz only did Diet Coke these days. That's what he told me, and for some reason, I believe him on that. Where else is it widening?"

"Well, they're interviewing as many people at the party as they can get hold of, hoping for some lead, some description of someone. You know how it works, Harvey—looking for some crack in the veneer, some seam in the fabric—"

"Some figure in the carpet?" Harvey said. "Some chink in the armor, perhaps?" Altiser looked at him queerly. "Sorry, Mike. Just trying to get rid of some tension." Harvey rose. "Do you have those publicity biographies for the writers and cast members?"

Altiser got to his feet too. "Publicity was supposed to send them down to you. I'll goose them again."

"It's been a pleasure, Mike."

"Likewise. My boy loved the autograph."

"I'm glad."

"Maybe someday you can teach him how to hit the curve."

"Mike," Harvey said, "if I could teach him how to hit the curve, that would mean I knew how to hit one myself, and if I knew how to hit the curve, my career batting average would've been higher than two-sixty-eight. But I'll be glad to teach him how *not* to hit the curve. It's really pretty simple, all you do is pull your head out of the box at the first sign of a curve, then step in the bucket and wave your bat wildly at the ball."

Harvey spent the rest of the afternoon of Tuesday, November 4, obtaining two pieces of information that were not, in retrospect, worth the time and trouble, except that in obtaining them Harvey was able to cement a feeling of professionalism and competence that had been coming loose. First, by calling the Writers Guild of America's health fund and pushing enough to violate his own sense of decorum, Harvey was able to procure the name of Joey Hanes's Upper East Side psychiatrist, who told him on the phone, "If what you're asking me is whether, in my professional opinion, Mr. Hanes would be capable of pushing this gentleman out of a window, the answer is no."

Second, he went to Mimi Weiss's apartment building on Park Avenue near Eighty-eighth Street and from the day doorman got the name and home phone number of the night doorman, who confirmed that Mimi Weiss had come home at around eleven on Saturday night; that a man in wirerimmed glasses visited her some time after one in the morning; and that both of them left the building around five in the morning.

Harvey decided to walk back to his hotel down Park Avenue, between parallel waves of pre-war apartment buildings undulating down toward the Pan Am building. In the smoky, granular light he could just detect that it was beginning to snow. The fur coats were out—matrons in pairs. A few had had so many facelifts that their skin had the quality of Cling Wrap pulled tightly across the top of a bowl. Under one of the apartment building awnings, a young, uniformed doorman shot his cuffs, examined the chunky rings on each pinky, grazed the brim of his cap at a passing heiress, and patrolled the sidewalk with the jauntiness of a lounge singer.

At Sixty-fifth Street Harvey detoured over to Third Avenue and had a dinner of marinated flank steak in a restaurant so chic he wouldn't have been surprised if the maitre d' had come on the PA system and announced that, regrettably, all those who were not extremely good-looking and well-dressed would have to leave the premises. Around him the tables were clogged with convivial men and women; they all appeared to be twenty-eight years old.

Over coffee Harvey looked at the short stack of official bios Altiser had sent down to him. There was nothing new on the writers, except for Marty Beaver. Harvey fanned through the telegraphic histories of the cast members: Tom Angel, Eddie Colasono, Ron Fellows, Nancy Pildone, Candee Wersch, Rob Whent, Brenda J. Johnson, Jimmy Lanahan. They told him little. Rob Whent's hobby was windsurfing. Nancy Pildone came from a family of eight children and used to organize her siblings for an annual Christmas show around the tree. Fifteen-year-old Eddie Colasono was not forsaking his education for his career; he was tutored daily by a former Brooklyn high school teacher. Candee Wersch's original ambition in life was to be a Navy pilot. Ron Fellows had a graduate degree in anthropology from Pomona College.

Harvey imagined his own life reduced to a handful of sentences: "Harvey, whose father owned an Italian restaurant in suburban Boston, can't stand stewed tripe. . . . His pet peeve is newspaper reporters' invasion of his privacy. . . . Harvey's older brother Norm still torments him by making late-night, long-distance calls to quiz him on baseball trivia. . . . His secret passion is devising new dishes in his spare time and forcing Mickey Slavin to eat them. . . ."

It was almost eight when Harvey returned to his hotel room. He had stopped at a bookstore on Madison and bought a collection of John Singer Sargent watercolor reproductions. He lay on the bed, studying Sargent's wet-in-wet technique in a 1907 Venetian boatscape called "Guidecca." He watched part of a New York Knick–Dallas Maverick game on television.

When the burst of impatient knocking on his door shook him out of his vegetative state, his first thought involved a fantasy about Candee Wersch having come to engage him in acrobatic sex before making a post-coital confession to the murder of Ray Ganz. He then quickly revised the fantasy to include just the acrobatic sex. Then he opened the door.

She stood there—garment bag slung over her shoulder, hip cocked—and regarded Harvey's midsection with narrowed eyes. He looked down at his unbuttoned pants, where a slight swelling of flesh drooped over his waistband. He looked up at her again and smiled innocently.

"Whose paunch this is I think I know," Mickey said. "Its owner is in real trouble, though."

"You're a redhead," Harvey said. "I asked the concierge to send up a blonde."

She tossed her hair. "The last blonde just went out to an ophthalmologist on the seventh floor. I'm all they left." Her tongue snaked out of her mouth and ssed her upper lip. "I think I'll be worth your whil

H rvey shook his head. "You don't know what I'm like in bed."

"I'm flexible."

"I like to wear spikes."

"I love it," she said.

"And a batting helmet."

13

Jammed together on a single bed in the dark cocoon of the hotel room, they came to their senses slowly. Mickey rolled over on top of him and pressed a series of milky kisses on his face and neck.

"Jesus, Bliss," she said. "That was quite a night."

"I always played well on the road."

She dangled a breast over his nose. "Is that so?"

"Hotel rooms"—he yawned—"are my métier. In fact once—I believe it was in Baltimore—"

"Skip it," she said, rolling onto her side, meeting up with unmistakable evidence of an erection. "For Chrissakes, Bliss," she said.

"Batter up!" Harvey announced.

"Batter down."

Harvey cupped his hands over his mouth. "Now batting for the Providence Jewels—wait, the opposing team is coming out of the dugout to protest, yes, they're claiming that Blissberg's Louisville Slugger exceeds American League regulations—"

"C'mon—this is a fungo bat."

"A *fungo* bat? How would *you* know the difference?"

"Actually," Mickey said, "it was in Baltimore—"

"All right," he said, clapping his hand over her mouth. Accustomed now to what little morning light forced itself through the heavy curtains, he could see the outline of her body above him, make out the dark disk of one nipple, a flash of tooth. He felt twice removed from the reality of Ganz's murder—by the room's soft featureless dark and by Mickey's presence. He sighed. He could easily disappear into the folds of the morning.

After Mickey had left the hotel to have lunch with the ABC News executive who had almost hired her for a network job the year before, Harvey, with the greatest reluctance, called Barry Sondell at home.

"It's time to talk again, Barry," Harvey said.

"I'm busy right now," he said in his high, thin voice. "I'm creating."

"For a competing comedy show?"

There was a beat of silence on Sondell's end. "When do you want to meet?"

"Now."

"Now? All right. Meet me at the Met in an hour."

"The Met?" Harvey said. He thought it a little odd, after their last encounter, that they should come to terms so quickly.

"The Metropolitan Museum of Art, tourist. Fifth Avenue at Eighty-second Street. Meet me in the Arms and Armor Room, at the Battle of Grandson."

"The what?"

"Just ask one of the museum guards. The Battle of Grandson."

"All right. And, Barry?"

"What?"

"Wear your own face."

For a late breakfast Harvey had something called a Super Bran Fiber Muffin at a coffee shop on Madison. It looked like it had wood chips in it. It looked like something you might buy at Scandinavian Design. The newspapers—he had picked through the *Times,* the *Post,* and the *Daily News* at the hotel newsstand—were absorbed with Ganz's death and the details of the private memorial service taking place today somewhere up the Hudson at Ganz's summer place. According to the various papers, Ganz's death marked the end of an era, called further into question the drug-related humor associated with his name, and proved that comedy can kill.

He strolled up Madison in the harsh sunlight. Last night's snow flurry hadn't stuck. He paused before an ethereal store window display—cotton clouds suspended by nylon thread over white wicker furniture and miniature white dresses. It took him a minute to recognize the object of his interest as a children's clothing store. He walked on, drawn in by one elegant window display after another in stores that sold nothing but yarn or all-cotton shirts or cheese or Tartan plaids or Italian paper goods.

As he was admiring some fussy, realist watercolors in a gallery window on Madison in the Seventies, a reflection joined his and said, "Harvey?"

Harvey turned to see Dickie Nacke next to him in a tailored navy blue overcoat. "Dickie," he said.

"I thought it was you. Appreciating a little art?"

Harvey turned back to the farmscape in the window. He admired the technique, but not the temperament that could spend so many hours on the details of an idle tractor. "What are you up to, Dickie?"

"I'm on my way to pick up the laundry on Seventy-fourth." He gestured vaguely up Madison with his left hand, the I.D. bracelet with the fat "R.N." glinting on his wrist. "How's the investigation going?"

"Actually, I'm on my way to see Sondell right now."

"Ah, Sondell," he said, flexing his eyebrows. "What can you say about a guy whose idea of comedy is barbecued babies and tap-dancing coroners?"

"That's a funny thing coming from the man who wrote a sketch about a crazed puppy killer."

"C'mon," Nacke said, "there's a big difference."

"Well, I haven't read your puppy sketch, but I guess I can see where there's a moral distinction between barbecuing *babies* and killing dogs."

Nacke ran a gloved hand over the sparse fuzz on top of his head. "Okay, I concede that the puppy sketch was in somewhat bad taste, but I was just trying to get something on the show."

"Ah, that's what they all say, Dickie." Harvey smiled. "They start by just trying to get something on the show, and before they know it—"

"Right, before you know it, sick humor's become a

way of life. But I don't worry about it. My humor's very gentle."

"Well, no wonder you can't get anything on the show." Harvey chuckled. "But, gee, Dickie, was that any reason to kill the executive producer?"

Nacke blanched for an instant before catching Harvey's tone, then laughed too. "Maybe I can still learn how to be crude. I've been studying Leo Rhoades. Look, if you're going uptown, I'll walk with you a block."

"Dickie," Harvey said as they began walking, "what's your real impression of Ganz?"

It was half a block before he answered. "Well, speaking of art. I knew him a little in Hollywood, where someone told me a story that I always think of when I think about Roy Ganz. As the story goes, he had moved into a new apartment with a lot of wall space. He had an art critic or art consultant friend or something, and he gave her a budget of something like twenty-five thousand dollars to buy him some art. And he told her, 'This is what I want the art to say: I want it to say that the person who owns it is a serious person who's not just interested in making an impression, but who *knows* something about art.' " Nacke scoffed. "And then he added, 'And get me a handful of paintings, predominantly in blue, to go with the living room set.' "

They were already at Seventy-sixth Street. Harvey stopped and said, "Your laundry."

Nacke looked confused.

"You said you were picking up your laundry on Seventy-fourth. This is Seventy-sixth. I just didn't want you to forget."

"Yes, my laundry," Nacke said. "On Seventy-fourth. I seem to have gone too far."

A Metropolitan Museum of Art guard pointed Harvey past Medieval Art, and European Sculpture and Decorative Arts, into the high-ceilinged Arms and Armor Room. He was met by a horse-mounted mannequin; both animal and dummy were attired in sixteenth-century German jousting armor, and the latter was leveling his lance just above Harvey's head. A glass case to the right contained several suits of tooled, engraved, and gilded armor. They were even more horrifying for the amount and delicacy of their craftsmanship, for the way in which the purposes of art and war were so well served in the same object. Even the hinged silver arm that connected the helmet of one of the suits to its backplate, a functional piece of hardware secured at either end by a large wing nut, had beautiful lines.

Along the wall stood a row of tall halberds in a rack. Harvey shuddered at the mere thought of the damage that their pike-and-battle-ax heads could inflict. He lingered for a moment in front of Matthias Corvinus's crossbow, its thick whalebone stock engraved with Biblical passages, before hailing another guard and asking directions to the Battle of Grandson.

The guard, a thin man with deflated posture, as if permanently cowering before the weapons it was his duty to protect, directed him to the staircase alcove at the end of the main hall. There, in a free-standing glass case, was a diorama of the Battle of Grandson, fought in Switzerland on March 2, 1476. On a snow-covered field several hundred medieval lead soldiers were poised for battle. Barry Sondell was nowhere to be seen, so Harvey read the notes about the Battle of Grandson mounted on a nearby wall. It seems that Charles the Bold, the Duke of Burgundy, had invaded Switzerland with 20,000 of the best-equipped and most modern professional soldiers of the day, including an elite corps of heavy-armored knights, plus artillery, infantry, and several thousand celebrated English longbowmen. They were confronted at Grandson by 18,000 Swiss civilian soldiers, 2500 of which fought off the Duke's forces by forming a dense square called a "hedgehog" until the main Swiss army could get through the pass to hit the Burgundian infantry in the flanks and handily win the battle, one of the most decisive battles won by citizen-soldiers over feudal forces.

"That old hedgehog defense'll do it every time," Harvey heard Sondell say over his shoulder.

Sondell was dressed entirely in shades of brown. His

pleated dark brown pants were held up on his negligible waist by a narrow belt. His sunken eyes, paper-cut of a mouth, pale tapered face, and pelt of close-cropped hair gave him the unhealthy, feral appearance of something in the Museum of Natural History on the other side of Central Park.

"Hello, Barry," Harvey said. "You want to tell me why we're meeting at this fascinating replica of the Battle of Grandson? Does it have some symbolic meaning?"

Sondell bent over and pressed one eye against the top glass of the diorama. "I don't see any symbolic meaning in there. Do you see any symbolic meaning in there?" He raised his head and tilted it toward Harvey. "This is one of my favorite places in New York. I like weapons of destruction."

"Your sense of humor, for instance?"

A series of squeaks came out of Sondell's mouth. "Harvey, you have a delightful sense of humor. Delightful."

Harvey bit his tongue.

"Follow me," Sondell said. "I want to show you something."

He led Harvey back into the main hall, where they paused to let a boy drag his mother across their path toward the rack of halberds. Sondell took Harvey into a room off the main hall and stopped before a case containing a long, curved sword.

"This is a class weapon, a Venetian falchion," Sondell said without referring to the card in the corner of the case. "The blade's inscribed with a Latin invocation for the user to be led out of tribulations. This is the weapon I really wanted to use on Ganz."

Harvey's head swiveled sharply. "Oh, is it now?"

"But I had to use my own hands instead."

Harvey lowered his eyes to Sondell's slight body.

"I would've enjoyed using a weapon," Sondell went on, eyes on the falchion. "I have my own personal collection, you know. A contemporary crossbow, a good replica of a state halberd, a prop mace, but it could do a lot of damage even though it's just a prop from a sketch I wrote called 'Jousting for Dollars.' I have a couple of real bayonets. One goes back to the American Civil War."

"No guns?" Harvey said.

"Guns? Not intimate enough. Anyone can use a gun."

"Tell me, did Ganz put up much of a fight? I mean, beyond the fingerprints on the wall by the window."

Sondell raised his eyes to Harvey's. "No. That was the funny thing," he said solemnly. "After that initial resistance, he just sort of went."

Harvey snapped his fingers in front of Sondell's nose. "Just like that?"

"Just like that. Harvey, I was going to go to the cops, but I felt I owed it to you first."

"I don't know what to say."

"I knew I'd end up doing something like this someday."

"Why'd you do it, Barry? 'Cause Ganz was trying to get rid of you?"

"That, and the fact that Ganz had been going around telling people I was washed up. That I was a sick person. A couple of my closest friends had come up to me and asked me if I knew what Ganz was saying about me. That's when I started writing for 'The Comic Dimension,' to get back at him. Then that got out, and he started to find a way to get rid of me. Hey, I helped make Roy Ganz. I wrote the sketches that made Claire Strawbridge and Tony Rocchio famous during the first two years of the show. I put Ganz on the map."

He walked a few feet, his little heels clicking, and stopped in front of a case containing several iron medieval helmets. "So I confronted him after the party last Saturday, and he confessed he was trying to get rid of me and that he had told two of my best friends that I was sick and needed professional help. He said he'd been spreading a rumor that I'm on a diet of raw duck liver. He said it right to my face. He told me that things had been good between us years ago, but they weren't anymore. That the magic was gone. He said he was planning to take over American comedy, to the extent that he would control what jokes could and couldn't be told at private parties all over the country. And he said there was no room for me in this plan. Then I told him I was going to throw him out the window. But first I made him eat some raw duck liver."

"And that's just what you did," Harvey said.

"What the man did, what the man did," Sondell said in a sorrowful whisper.

"I don't know why you're confessing, Barry. You might've gotten away with it."

"I don't know. It's a hell of a thing to live with. I've been thinking of killing myself."

"You have?" Harvey was looking at a black German helmet with, the description noted, 161 breathing holes.

"I'll probably get life."

"Yours wasn't worth living anyway."

"So what're you going to do with me? You want to go call Detective Generra?"

"No, Barry, I don't think that'll be necessary."

"You just want to take me down to the station?"

"Naw."

"What are you—a wimp? C'mon, take me in."

"Can you imagine fighting a medieval battle wearing one of these on your head?" Harvey said.

"You don't understand," Sondell pleaded. "I *killed* him. I killed Ganz. I made him eat raw liver and then I pushed him out the window. So what're you going to do about it?"

"I'm going to make things as tough for you as I can."

"You want my team of lawyers and me to hold a press conference? I'll confess it on television. Ganz was a piece of pompous poop. I'll say I was glad I killed him."

"That's too easy, Barry. You'd like that, a press conference. No, I think you ought to really pay the price."

"So take me in, you wimp!"

Harvey turned and seized Sondell by the front of his shirt and jerked him up on his toes. "I'm going to do much worse than that, Barry. I'm going to ignore you." He released Sondell and walked away.

"But I killed him!"

"Take care, Barry."

Sondell scurried after him. "What're you doing!"

"You don't interest me, Barry."

"Wait a second!"

"Bye now."

The guard was shuffling toward Sondell, saying, "Please, sir, this is a museum, I'm going to have to ask you to be quiet—"

Harvey was already out of the Arms and Armor Room, passing the dim sixteenth-century tapestries, wondering who—if Curt Geller and Joey Hanes weren't crazy enough to do it, Barry Sondell was too crazy, and Beaver and Lanahan had had better things to do that evening—had killed Roy Ganz, and why.

14

When Harvey returned to the hotel in midafternoon, his room's immaculate condition only garnished his gloominess. After-dinner mints on the pillow at three in the afternoon were not his idea of hospitality. How could he lay any claim to this provisional home if every day all the evidence of his occupancy—the damp towels, the uncapped Vicks VapoRub, the scattering of magazines—was removed, replaced, or rearranged? He considered calling the front desk to ask that henceforth the chambermaid leave the room in the same shape in which she found it, or, if possible, even worse shape.

The media continued to knock. *The New York Times* had called again. *Time*. Two local newscasts had left messages. *The Hollywood Reporter* had called. *The Village Voice* had called. Harvey wished he had some hard information to withhold.

The last phone message was from Curt Geller. Harvey punched in the Joke Doctor's number.

"Harvey," Geller said, "I think we've got something here that might interest you."

"What is it?" He'd take anything at this point.

"Well, Mimi was at Roy's co-op this morning, the place they used to have together. She was going through their things to figure out what she wanted to keep for herself, and she came across something that didn't belong to either her or Roy."

"Yeah?"

"I'll put Mimi on. I'm not even sure what it is."

"Hi, Harvey," Mimi said.

"Hi, Mimi."

"I found some women's makeup behind the toilet in the second bathroom. It's a jar of something called Dermablend Cover Creme."

"Not your brand?"

"No, not my brand. In fact, I never heard of this brand, and I don't know whose it is, but I thought you might want to know about it."

"Did you take it with you?"

"Yes, but I thought it would be all—"

"That's fine. Do you have any idea whose it is?"

"Not really."

"Could it be the cleaning woman's or something?"

"I doubt it. This looks like it's for fair skin."

"Who else?"

"Look, if Roy was dating someone, I wouldn't know. He's extremely discreet about that stuff. He and *I* were dating a couple of months before anyone knew, before it got in the papers. Roy'd never pick me up in his limo, that'd be too obvious, so I always had to meet him in those out-of-the-way spots."

"Oh, yeah? Like where?"

"I'd have to think about it."

"I'll hang on the line while you do."

After a moment Mimi Weiss said, "Well, Gsell's was one place, a dark little nondescript bar where nobody bothers anybody. It's on the Upper East Side, Lexington in the low Nineties."

"Who knows him there?"

"The only person who ever seemed to know him was the manager. I don't know his name."

Harvey was writing on hotel stationery. "And the other place?"

"An Italian place called Saletra's in the West Village."

"Thanks, Mimi. Do you have the makeup there?"

"In my hand."

"Can you give it to Curt and tell him to bring it with him to the office this evening?"

"Was he planning to go in this evening?"

"No, but tell him I'll see him at around eight in his office. It won't take long."

Harvey looked up the phone number of the "Last Laughs" Makeup Supervisor, Celeste Temkin, on the staff list Mike Altiser had given him. He got her answering machine and left his name and hotel room number. He had better success reaching the managers of Gsell's and Saletra's.

"To tell you the truth," the manager of Gsell's said, "I hadn't seen Roy around here for a long time. Last time he was with that dark-haired girl he married. But I'm talking years ago."

The manager of Saletra's in the Village told him, "Saw Roy here just last week. What a pity, poor guy."

"Was he with anyone?"

"He was with a woman."

"Did you recognize her?" Harvey asked.

"No."

"Can you describe her?"

"Very cute. Roy had a tendency in the direction of cute."

"Can you tell me more? Tall?"

"Medium height."

"Age?"

"Thirties?"

"Makeup?"

"I don't know. Probably. I don't know. The lights are pretty low in this place. That's one reason Roy liked it."

"How was she dressed?"

"She was dressed—dressed—I don't know how she was dressed."

"Do you know who waited on their table?" Harvey asked. "Maybe he'll remember more."

"Hold on." He was back on the line in fifteen seconds. "Hold on again. Here's Mark."

"Hello?" a different voice said.

"My name's Harvey Blissberg," and then he told Mark what his business was, and then, "You waited on them?"

"Yeah."

"Can you describe Roy Ganz's date to me?"

"She was very nice-looking and blond."

"Can you pin it down for me?"

"I liked her lips, I remember that. And she had bright red lipstick on. Beyond that—gee, let's see, she had that cheerleader look to her."

"What's that cheerleader look?"

"You know—"

"I don't."

"C'mon, you know, she had one of those faces, kind of corn-fed, small nose, what can I tell you?"

"You're not doing too badly," Harvey said.

"Beyond that, I can't say. New York's full of them, these facial masterpieces. Actresses, models. Gets monotonous."

Harvey gave Mark his hotel phone number and said, "Call me if you remember anything more."

"Dermablend," Celeste Temkin was saying in Curt Geller's office that night on the twenty-fourth floor of the network building on Forty-seventh Street. As Harvey and Curt looked on, the small woman in the oversized sweatshirt rotated the jar with her prehensile fingers. Her mascara was touchingly awry.

"You're familiar with it?" Harvey asked Temkin.

"Sure," she said.

"Well, is it a common makeup?"

"No. Originally, it was developed by doctors or scientists for medical use. People use it to mask hyperpigmentation." She handed the jar back to Harvey. "They use this stuff in burn units."

"Hyperpigmentation?" Harvey said. "Like what?"

"Oh, scar tissue or birthmarks or, basically, any gross irregularity."

"Does anyone on the show use this stuff?" Harvey held up the white plastic jar with the gold D on it.

"No." She glanced to the side for a moment, thinking. "No, no one uses it here."

"Including the men?"

"Including the men."

"No one with any scars or birthmarks or irregularities?"

"I can't think of any."

"What about guest hosts or bit players?" Next to

him, Geller had just lit a Lucky Strike, and Harvey reached over and with two outstretched fingers signaled for one of Geller's cigarettes.

"Can't think of any, no. Nancy Pildone has a little acne scarring on her chin, but we just use regular makeup foundation to cover it. You think that someone who uses Dermablend had something to do with Roy's death?"

"It's possible," Harvey said. Geller lit the Lucky for him with his lighter. "What else can you tell me about the person who uses this?"

"You see on the label where it says 'Chroma O'?" she said.

"Yeah?"

"That shade would be for the lightest skin."

"Does anyone in the cast have skin that light?"

"Well, Candee Wersch has pretty fair skin. Maybe not quite that fair, though."

"So, to the absolute best of your knowledge, no one in the cast uses this?"

"No."

"What about previous casts? How long have you been the Makeup Supervisor here?"

"This is my seventh year," Temkin said, "and I don't recall anyone on this show ever using this."

"Wait," Harvey said. "Couldn't someone use Dermablend on some other part of their body?"

"They could, I suppose, but it's unlikely. Clothes would cover it."

"But don't you occasionally have sketches on the show where the actors' bodies are partly exposed?"

"That's true."

"Well?"

"Well, I think I'd know even if one of the cast used Dermablend somewhere else on their bodies. And they don't."

"Okay," Harvey said. "What about Karen Baldwin?"

"Karen? Gee, I have no idea. I know she has very fair skin."

What *about* Karen Baldwin? She had bones to pick with Rhoades and Ganz, and a venomous streak. However, her professed animosity toward Ganz made it unlikely that she'd have had any occasion to leave makeup in Ganz's second bathroom. Harvey wanted to disqualify Baldwin on another count: she had been in the alley at the scene of Ganz's death, unlikely behavior for a culprit.

Half an hour later, on their way out, Harvey and Curt passed through the design department. A man was there, sketching at his drawing board.

"Hi, Miles," Geller said to him. "Whatcha doing here at this hour?"

"Oh, hi, Curt," he said, putting down his mechanical pencil. "I got bored at home, so I came in to work on a few problems with the show. Leo wants me to redesign the flats for Colasono's monologues."

Geller turned to Harvey. "Eddie Colasono, our resident fifteen-year-old comic genius, occasionally does these monologues about adolescence on the show. On acne, masturbation, first dates, that sort of stuff."

Harvey looked at what Miles had been sketching. It seemed to be an office with a sign on the wall that read "THE NATIONAL PUPPY-GRINDING COMPANY," and below that, in smaller type, *"We kill all kinds of puppies."*

"That doesn't look like a set for a monologue on adolescence," Harvey said.

"Oh, this," Miles said, picking up his pencil again. "No, this is something else. Leo wants to use this sketch next week, so I thought I'd get a head start on it, 'cause it might involve real puppies."

Geller picked up the copy of the sketch lying next to Miles's pad. "I thought Leo nixed this one a couple of weeks ago."

Miles ran a hand through his hair. "All I know is Leo told me to work on it."

"Isn't that Dickie Nacke's sketch?" Harvey said, trying to read over Geller's shoulder.

"But I heard Leo didn't go for it."

"Yeah, I overheard Nacke saying that Leo didn't think it was funny enough."

"So Leo changed his mind." Geller shrugged. "America must be entertained."

Miles shook his head. "Puppy grinding. Well, it's

still not as sick, if you ask me, as Sondell's sketch about the tap-dancing coroner. Propping all those corpses up in folding chairs while Tony Rocchio performed a buck-and-wing for them. Christ Almighty."

"Curt," Harvey said, "do you think you can make me a copy of Nacke's sketch?"

In the writers' wing Geller fed the pages into the mammoth copying machine. "Why you want to look at this?" he asked, the green light sweeping across their faces.

"Anything strange interests me at this point."

"What strikes you as strange about this sketch?"

"What's strange is that Leo didn't want it in the show, and now he does."

Geller inserted the last page into the machine. "Not the first time it's happened."

"Oh, has it happened before, this year?"

Geller stapled the two copies. "Well, actually, I can't remember when it happened before. Here you go." He passed one of the copies to Harvey. "So what do you make of it?"

"Doctor, what do you think of the idea that Leo didn't change his mind?"

15

PUPPY-GRINDER—Lanahan, Pildone, Whent,

Fellows, by D. Nacke

(OPEN ON: SIGN ON WALL: "NATIONAL PUPPY-GRINDING COMPANY")

(SFX: PUPPIES YELPING IN ANOTHER PART OF THE BUILDING, AND PERIODIC GRINDING MECHANICAL SOUND)

(DISSOLVE TO: LANAHAN IN BUSINESS SUIT, WORKING AT HIS DESK. HIS OFFICE IS LITTERED WITH PAPERS, PET CARRIERS, AND A PILE OF DOG LEASHES ON THE FLOOR.)

(Nancy knocks and enters)

LANAHAN:
Yes?

PILDONE:
Mr. Crockett, I just wanted to let you know that that shipment of German shepherd puppies is on its way.

LANAHAN:

Well, it's about time. I like to see those grinders going at full capacity.

PILDONE:

One other thing. There's another reporter here who wants to interview you.

LANAHAN:

Hey, what the heck is this! We were grinding chuck steak here for years. My father before me, and his father before him, and we never even got our name in the papers. But as soon as we convert into a puppy-grinding operation, we got reporters here all the time. I don't get it.

PILDONE:

(Shrugging)

Oh, I guess you never know what'll offend some people. What do you want me to tell him?

LANAHAN:

Send him in. I'll talk to him.

(Nancy leaves and Rob enters with reporter's notebook in hand)

WHENT:

(Shaking Lanahan's hand, after which he looks disgustedly at his own as if he's been contaminated)

Sam Fleisher, *Business Day.*

LANAHAN:

Sit down. What can I do for you?

WHENT:

(Sits, looking askance at the pet carriers and leashes)

Well, uh, Mr. Crockett, I'd like to do a story about your, uh, business.

LANAHAN:

Puppy-grinding.

WHENT:

(Wincing)

Uh, exactly. Puppy-grinding. It's a, uh, an unusual business, isn't it?

(He makes a pained face as the sound of yelping puppies momentarily increases)

LANAHAN:

(Proudly)

As far as I know, I'm the only one in it.

WHENT:

Well, uh, that's sort of what I mean.

LANAHAN:

(Growing impatient)

Look, what is this? I'm getting sick and tired of you reporters marching in here with your insinuations and innuendos. I'm a businessman. I saw an opportunity, and I grabbed it.

WHENT:

But, if you don't mind my saying so, *puppy-grinding?*

LANAHAN:

Let me explain something to you, young man. This great country needs a legitimate puppy-grinding company like mine. Before me, people had to resort to shady, fly-by-night puppy-grinders.

You never knew how they were going to treat the puppies.

WHENT:

(Furious)

But—but—but you GRIND UP PUPPIES!

LANAHAN:

And I do it *painlessly*. With the finest state-of-the art puppy-grinders.

(Whent starts to protest, but Lanahan holds up a hand)

Look, I've been through this a dozen times with the press. There's no law against puppy-grinding; in fact, I got this going with the help of a small-business loan from the government. My workers get excellent benefits. In case you have to be reminded, Mr. Fleisher, this *is* a free country.

(Nancy pokes her head in the door)

PILDONE:

Excuse me, Mr. Crockett, but the first batch of German shepherd puppies just arrived. You want to take a look at them?

LANAHAN:

Bring them in, Wendy. Thanks.

(Nancy leaves)

WHENT:

I gotta tell you, Mr. Crockett, I think what you're doing is unconscionable!

LANAHAN:

Oh, come off it, will you! Don't stand on stupid, liberal principles with me! I wouldn't be doing all this business if there weren't a lot of people out there with puppies who needed a good grinding. And that's exactly what we provide—a damn good grinding! My business has been going full-tilt since the very first day.

WHENT:

But it's sick! I'm disgusted!

(Nancy leads in three German shepherd puppies on a leash. Jimmy gets up from behind his desk, takes the dogs from her, and briefly examines them.)

LANAHAN:

Oh, these are very nice, very nice indeed.

(Cooing)

Here, puppy, here, puppy.

WHENT:

(Lunging for the puppies)

Give me those puppies!

LANAHAN:

(Wrenching them away from Whent)

Mr. Fleisher! Control yourself!

WHENT:

(Almost in tears)

But they're just little puppies, you maniac! I had a German shepherd when I was a boy. . . .

LANAHAN:

That's what all the reporters say.

WHENT:

His name was Chief, I remember he had this trick
he'd do, he'd . . . Hey! I won't let you get away
with this, you cretin!

(Lunges again)

LANAHAN:

Wendy!

*(Nancy goes over to try to restrain and soothe
Whent. This struggle is interrupted when Ron enters in a blood-spattered smock with bits of fur
stuck to it)*

C'mon, Mr. Fleisher. These puppies never feel a
thing!

FELLOWS:

(Ignoring the ruckus)

'Scuse me, Mr. Crockett. I was just wondering
whether the shepherd puppies had come. We finished with the Dalmatians and we're ready for—

(Noticing the puppies and going over to pet them)

Oh, *here* they are!

*(Whent wimpering, etc., face in hands, a helpless
mess)*

LANAHAN:

Bob, why don't you go ahead and start with these
three?

FELLOWS:

Check.

LANAHAN:

By the way, Bob, were you able to straighten out
that problem with the fifth grinder?

FELLOWS:

(Taking leashed puppies from Lanahan)

Oh, yes, sir, we cleared that up this morning.
Turned out that one of the poodles just got caught
in the blades. It's all taken care of.

(Whent dissolves into tears)

LANAHAN:
Excellent. Listen, why don't you and Wendy take
Mr. Fleisher with you? He's writing an article
about National Puppy-Grinding, and he's expressed
a desire to see the plant.

FELLOWS:
No problem.

PILDONE:

(Taking the blubbering Whent by the arm)

C'mon, Mr. Fleisher, I think you'll enjoy this.

*(Whent, Fellows, Pildone, and puppies disappear
through door)*

(SLOW DISSOLVE TO LANAHAN AT DESK)

(SFX: LOUD GRINDING MACHINE)

(SUPER: "TEN MINUTES LATER")

(Pildone and Fellows re-enter Lanahan's office)

LANAHAN:
How'd it go?

PILDONE:
Fine. Just fine.

FELLOWS:

(Handing Lanahan Fleisher's notebook)

I didn't know what to do with this.

LANAHAN:

I'll take it.

(Puts it in his desk drawer)

So how many does that make?

PILDONE:

Puppies?

LANAHAN:

No. Press.

PILDONE:

(Taking a piece of paper from her pocket and looking it over)

Let's see. That makes eight. Nine, if you want to count the fellow from that little suburban biweekly.

LANAHAN:

(Hands behind head, quite pleased)

God, how I love this country.

(Fade)

After she finished reading it, Mickey resumed spreading the coral-colored taramasalata on a chunk of bread. They were marooned at the back of a Greek place on Eighth Avenue. Between them and the front door was a sea of white tablecloths, unbroken except for the heads of two other diners bobbing in the distance.

"It has a certain nihilistic charm," she said.

Harvey took the script back and laid it next to his saganaki. "It's pretty sick."

"Oh, I don't know, it's got a certain something. I mean, it's more political than most of the crap that show's been doing lately. Who wrote it?"

Harvey sipped his glass of Hymettus. "The guy who wrote this, Dickie Nacke, is in his forties."

"Yeah, it sounds like it might've been written by someone who lived through the sixties." She clinked her wine glass against Harvey's and said, "Here's to hotel sex. But what's a guy in his forties doing with a name like Dickie? Shouldn't he be a Richard by now, or at least a Dick?"

"And he's got gray hair too."

"Gracious." Mickey gasped. "What're you doing with this script in the first place?"

"Dickie Nacke wrote it a couple of weeks ago, and a lot of the other writers thought it was funny, but for some reason, apparently Leo Rhoades didn't like it at all."

"Which one is Leo again?"

"He's the producer. He answers only to—answered only to Roy Ganz, the executive producer, and to the network censors. But here's the thing, Mick: suddenly Leo wants this sketch to go in the show. When I was up there tonight, one of the set designers was working on it, and he said Leo liked it."

"Now how do you know that Leo didn't like it in the first place?"

"Well, the only way I know that is because I heard Dickie Nacke telling some other writers that's why it wasn't used."

Mickey refilled their wineglasses. "Okay. What if this guy Dickie wasn't telling the truth?"

"If Nacke was lying about Leo not liking this sketch"—he tapped the script with a finger—"well, the question is, why would he lie? That's a pretty strange thing to lie about. But if he did, it must've been to conceal the real reason it wasn't used. And the real reason, I've been thinking, might be the objections of those with more power than Leo—either the censors or Roy Ganz."

"Hmmm," Mickey said, although it wasn't clear whether this was in reference to Harvey's deduction or her latest sampling of the taramasalata. "Well, let's take the censors."

"I asked Curt Geller about the censors. He can't imagine why they'd object to it. Their attitude is that you can't say 'fuck' and 'shit' on the air, but making fun of the halt and lame, hey, that's no problem. Puppy-grinding? Who cares?"

"That leaves Roy Ganz," Mickey said, dragging a piece of crust along the edge of the taramasalata plate.

"And this is why this sketch gets more and more interesting to me," Harvey continued. "Let's imagine that it was Ganz who didn't like the sketch and killed it, maybe even over Leo Rhoades's protest. Number one, why would Ganz feel so strongly about a sketch which, by the show's current standards, is more than passable? Second, why would Nacke attempt to conceal Ganz's role in killing it? See what I mean, Mick?"

"Of course I see what you mean. You mean if Nacke was the one who killed Ganz, and he knew he might kill him, he'd want to conceal all evidence of conflict between the two of them, even something as ostensibly insignificant as that sketch over there that you keep getting grease spots on. No, I get the red snapper," she said to the recently arrived waiter. "The lamb belongs to the gentleman I'm dining with."

"But, you know," Harvey said, "my mind resists this whole line of inquiry. There're a bunch of people on the show with less obscure reasons for wishing Ganz ill. Nacke isn't one of them, as far as I know."

"How far do you know?"

"The truth is, I know about as far as from here to the Sweet 'n Low over there." He gestured at the chrome rack halfway between them on the table.

"Well, maybe you ought to find out a little more about Dickie."

"But he's in his forties and he has *gray* hair."

"You got a couple gray ones there yourself, buddy."

"Be nice to me, Mick. You never know what I'm capable of when provoked."

"So find out what might've been provoking Dickie." She seemed to derive an unwholesome pleasure from saying his name.

"Wait a second." Harvey put down his utensils. "I just thought of something. Dickie Nacke has a springer spaniel, which he brings to the office. So what's a dog lover doing writing a sketch about puppy-grinding?"

"Well, I don't know if I'd make too much of that. I mean, he could just be making fun of the things that frighten him most. Isn't that what a lot of comedy's about? So Dickie Nacke loves dogs, and in order to exorcise his fears about what people do to animals, he writes this thing about puppy-grinding."

"What if Ganz is a dog lover," Harvey said, "and he nixed the sketch because he couldn't bear the cruelty of it? What if under all that fast-track ruthlessness, Ganz was just a complete softie about dogs? But, you know, we're talking about the man who raised the curtain on 'Last Laughs' a decade ago by threatening to cut off his finger if people didn't laugh."

"He might've been soft on dogs. Why not? That's all that may've happened, you know."

"Yeah, you might be right." He tore at his lamb for a moment. "But wait—that'd just explain why Ganz didn't like it. We're forgetting that Nacke said *Leo* didn't like the sketch. If it was nothing more than Ganz's objection on some quirky sentimental grounds, why the hell did Nacke lie?"

"I don't know."

"Oh, hell," Harvey said. "What if he didn't lie? What if Leo didn't like it, and then he just changed his mind, and there's nothing more to it than that?" He stopped. "Guard my lamb for a minute, will you, Mick?" he said, pushing back his chair. "I've got an itch I want to scratch."

He took his list out of his mountain parka pocket, found Leo Rhoades's home number, and walked past the empty tables to the pay phone at the front of the restaurant. He dialed Rhoades's number. Out on Eighth Avenue a vivid parade of midtown street culture drifted

by the restaurant window. One man caught his eye
through the glass and held up a Rolex knock-off.

"Leo?" Harvey said.

"Speaking."

"Harvey Blissberg."

"Well, how are you?"

"Hope I haven't disturbed you."

"Not at all. What can I do for you?"

"I wanted to ask you something, Leo. You know
that sketch of Nacke's about the puppy-grinding
company?"

"Yeah?" Leo said with a slight, suspicious, rising
intonation.

"I understand you want to use it in next week's
show."

"That's right. You're really getting around, aren't
you?"

"But I'd heard that you killed it when it first came
up a couple of weeks ago."

"That *I* killed it?"

"Well, that's what I heard, Leo."

"No, I always liked it. I think the line about the
poodle getting caught in the blades is terrific."

If Leo was telling the truth, Dickie was lying. "So
why didn't it make the show before?"

"Roy didn't like it."

"Ganz killed it?"

"Yeah."

"Why?"

"I think he said it was in bad taste. He just said no
to me. You know, a kind of off-with-its-head gesture."

"And you liked it?"

"That's what I said. I thought it went over great in
read-through that week."

"Now you want to use it?"

"Harvey, I always wanted to use it."

"I mean, now that Ganz is dead."

"Yeah, well, I know it seems a little ghoulish,"
Rhoades said. "Not exactly honoring his passing,
but"—he paused—"but we don't have a real glut of
great material right now, so I'd like to pop it on the
show next week. It's a nice part for Lanahan. He's

been awfully light on the show." Lanahan, whose career Ganz had held in hock.

"Leo, why do you think Nacke would say it was you who didn't think it was funny?"

"I have no idea. I really don't. Maybe he just got Roy and me confused. You know, maybe it's that Roy and I presented a united front on so many things, I think the writers sometimes just curse us as one when things don't go their way. You know writers. *I* know writers, 'cause I'm one. You know, authority's authority. Sometimes it's not that specific."

For an instant Harvey almost asked Leo if it was true that Ganz stole a screenplay idea from him. But he held his tongue and watched the hot candy-colored lights on Eighth Avenue.

"So how're you making out?"

"Making out?"

"With the investigation."

"Oh, I guess it's coming along."

"You know, it's so strange—so strange knowing this man for so long, and working with him so much, and he's dead, and there's nothing I can do about it, and I don't even know what the cops are doing, or what you're doing. I dread going back next week, knowing that office next to mine is empty. I don't know." Leo spoke with uncharacteristic softness; Harvey tried to catch the real sentiment in it.

"Well, listen, Leo, I'll let you go back to what you were doing. Sorry to bother you."

"That's all right, Harvey."

Harvey worked his way back to Mickey, who was meticulously working some snapper flesh off the bone with her knife and fork. Something in her squared-off shoulders and the childlike concentration in her lower lip made him feel newly attracted to her, the way he had felt once when he spotted her in the dugout before a Jewels-Indians game at Rankle Park in Providence a year and a half ago, writing in a notebook with a hand mike tucked in her left armpit.

16

Mickey left on Thursday morning, cursing, as Harvey held the cab door for her in front of the hotel, the documentary awaiting her in a Channel 7 editing room. Her departure left Harvey feeling newly displaced. The room he had shared with Dave Kasick and Mickey Slavin was all his again, his in the way a rental car inspired, after a few days, a vague sense of ownership. He paced the room, preoccupied, sliding open the closet to inspect the extra clothes Mickey had brought down for him, trying on the new raincoat he had bought on Madison Avenue. It was a voluminous, belted olive-green affair with a soft leather collar, poised somewhere between classic trenchcoat and frivolously dysfunctional high fashion. It was a garment of costly, somber subtlety. He strode back and forth in it, crossing his image several times in the full-length mirror bracketed to the outside of the bathroom door. If clothes made the man, Harvey thought, he'd very soon be someone other than himself. He took off the raincoat and sat at the desk, head in hands. Blissberg Held Hostage in Manhattan: Day 10.

He was floating numbly in some hazy investigative ether. He wondered if Detective John Generra was breathing the same air. He almost wanted to ring him up to compare notes, but the risk to him suddenly seemed too great. He couldn't afford to have the cops stumbling along the same obscure paths; the noise might scare everyone away. At the beginning, just a few days ago, everything had been possible, everyone had been suspect, every intuition interesting. Now alibis, intuition, and circumstance had eliminated some, leaving the names he kept overhearing in the cocktail party of his unconscious: Leo Rhoades, Dickie Nacke, and Barry Sondell, whose game of double- and triple-psych had backed Harvey once again into a corner. The narrowing of possibilities tightened his gut.

Rhoades, Nacke, and Sondell. He slid a sheet of stationery out of the desk drawer and wrote their names across the top. He looked at them. His only thought was, what if the three of them had collaborated on the script for Ganz's death? Ganz had possibly robbed Rhoades of a screenplay credit, arranged for the dismissal for Sondell, but done what to Nacke, except perhaps killed his puppy-grinding sketch? Harvey crumpled up the paper and banked it off the wall into the wastebasket imprinted with an English hunting scene.

He found Dickie Nacke's number on the staff list Altiser had given him, lifted the receiver, and paused. He had reached the stage where he didn't want to show any cards. On the other hand, he remembered what Wayne Gibbly of the Boston Celtics had told him nine months before when Harvey was trying to backdoor him for information about the disappearance of his teammate Tyrone Terrell. Don't upfake me, Gibbly had said; if you're driving at something, whyn't you go straight for the basket?

The woman who answered the phone told Harvey that Dickie would be back shortly.

"I'll call back," Harvey said. "Is this his wife?"

"It is. Who's this?"

"Harvey Blissberg."

"All right. I'll tell him you'll be calling back."

Harvey phoned Curt Geller and got Mimi Weiss.

"How are you?" Harvey said.

"Surviving," she said. "We had a little service for Roy up at the summer place yesterday and I'm a little shaky." She made a gobbling sound in her throat and broke into a sob. "Let me give you Curt," she mumbled.

"Hi, Harvey," Geller said.

"I've got you at a bad time."

"The anesthesia's wearing off."

"I'll call you back."

"No, that's all right. What's on your mind?"

"All right. I'll make it quick. Can I assume what we talk about stays between us?"

"Sure."

"Good. What can you tell me about Nacke?"

"Not much. All I know's he's a screenwriter and I'm pretty sure Ganz brought him in."

"Yeah?"

"I like him," Geller said with a flip conclusiveness. "And it's nice to have someone his age on the staff. His presence is reassuring that you can still be funny in your forties."

"What did Nacke do before?"

"All I know is screenplays."

"Did he work with Ganz in Hollywood?"

"I don't know."

"All right, Curt. Thanks."

"That's all I know."

"Go comfort Mimi, Curt. I'll talk to you later."

Next he got Leo Rhoades on the line.

"It's me again, Leo."

"Busy, aren't we?"

Go straight for the basket, Harvey said to himself. "Leo, I got another rumor I need you to scotch."

"Be my guest."

"I've heard there was some bad blood between you and Ganz."

"Some good, some bad."

"I heard he stole some screenplay credit from you. Just something I heard."

"Yeah, there's some truth to that," Rhoades said.

"There is?"

"Yeah."

"Well, can you tell me about it?"

"Is it pertinent?"

"I'm not implying suspicion, Leo."

"Let's hope not," he said. "Look, there wasn't much to it. Roy and I were sitting around in Hollywood a couple of years ago. Our respective careers were not exactly at their zenith, and we were just trying to talk down movie ideas, something to pitch. We were talking about political ideas, and I said something about Islamic fundamentalist terrorists. Roy said something like, 'What a bunch of clowns,' and I said, 'That's it, a movie about a bunch of terrorists masquerading as clowns.' I said, 'A traveling circus of terrorists—that's how they get in and out of countries easily.' You know, the metaphor seemed too good to be true. Then I guess I just forgot about it, and then about four or five months later Roy informs me that he's written a treatment about a group of Arab terrorists masquerading as a traveling circus. He tells me three studio execs are interested. So I say, 'Gee, why didn't you let me know you were going ahead with my idea?' And he had no recollection that it was mine. He thought it was his. He had no memory of our previous conversation."

"So what happened?"

"So I screamed at him, and he finally said, 'Look, Leo, I'm going to show my treatment to these three guys, and if I get any development money out of them, I'll let you know, and we'll talk about giving you idea credit. But honestly, Leo, I don't remember that we ever talked about this before.' He just went into his little-boy I-don't-know-what-you're-talking-about routine. As it turned out, nobody wanted to touch a movie about Arab terrorists in greasepaint."

"You must've been pretty pissed at him."

"No harm, no foul," Rhoades said. "It never came to anything."

"But the principle of the thing."

"Excuse me, Harvey, did I just hear the word 'principle'?"

"I believe I just used the word, yes," Harvey said.

"Hey, I thought I explained that these events took place in Hollywood. Principles?" Rhoades revved up his wheezy laugh.

"You didn't have any trouble going back to work for Ganz at 'Last Laughs'? After that?"

"After that? That was *nothing*. Harvey, if I can't

deal with Roy Ganz stealing an idea of mine, how'm I going to be able to deal with anything in this business? You can't deal with petty theft like that, how you going to survive the real larceny? Maybe in the game you played they don't do that, they got too many witnesses every time you get a hit or an RBI, but in show biz, Harvey baby, a lot of the time there aren't any observers. Why the hell do you think the Writers Guild's got arbitration up to its neck? You take what you can get away with, and what you can't get away with you try to take anyway. Roy was probably better than most. So did I have trouble taking this job when Ganz offered it to me? Fuck, no! You think this is a business for fucking Puritans? Look, Harvey, the thing about Roy is that I *knew* what he was capable of. I *knew* he could lie to my face. And I'd much rather work for someone where I knew what he was capable of than work for someone who could still pretend he was a sweetheart. You dig?"

"*Je* dig," Harvey said. He had to concede to Rhoades, reluctantly, a superior tolerance for human foibles. "One other thing, Leo. Did Dickie Nacke ever work with Ganz in Hollywood? They ever write screenplays together?"

"Not that I know of. I never knew Nacke before I met him this past September. He was Roy's man."

"You know his work?"

"No, just what he's done for the show this fall."

"Okay."

"Anything else I can help you with?" Rhoades barked.

"Not at the moment," Harvey said.

When he called Dickie Nacke's residence back, Nacke was in.

"I wanted to ask you something about the puppy-grinding sketch," Harvey said.

"Sure. Go ahead."

"I understand that Leo now wants to use it in the show."

"He does?" Nacke's surprise seemed authentic. "How do you know?"

"The art department's already working on the set design."

"No kidding. Well, I'm a little baffled."

"Why's that?" Harvey said.

"Leo must've changed his mind."

"What do you mean?"

"He didn't go for it the first time around."

"You think Leo's the reason it didn't get on the show?"

"I *know* that's the reason," Nacke said.

"I thought it was Ganz who axed your sketch."

"Where'd you get that?"

"Leo."

"Leo's lying," Nacke said. "But let's not make a federal case out of this. I'm glad he's decided to use the sketch. It'll be the first real piece I've had on the show."

"Wait, Dickie—so you're saying it was definitely Leo who rejected the puppy-grinding sketch? I just want to get it straight."

"That's what I'm saying. But what's it got to do with anything?"

"I don't know, Dickie. Now why would Leo tell me Ganz had rejected it?"

"Why would anyone care?"

"I care," Harvey said.

"Perhaps Leo forgot that he didn't like it at first. You know, I think he's the kind of person who doesn't like people to know he's capable of changing his mind. You know, he thinks it's a weakness."

"Yeah, I know the kind," Harvey said. "So why do you think Leo changed his mind about the puppy-grinding sketch?"

"How the hell do I know, Harvey? I don't live in his brain. C'mon."

"All right," Harvey said. "Sorry to cramp your morning."

"Aw, don't worry about it. We're all under strain."

"Yeah. By the way, Dickie, I was just curious—you write screenplays, right?"

"Yeah," Nacke said, adding quickly, "But, Harvey,

I can't help you get into the business, I have to warn you."

Harvey laughed as good-naturedly as he knew how. "Oh, no, I'm not *really* thinking of—anyway, like, is the Writers Guild the union you have to belong to?"

"Yeah," Dickie said and paused. "It's awfully hard to get anywhere in the business without belonging. But what—"

"You're a member, right?"

"Yeah, I'm a member, but, Harvey, everyone in the world's writing a screenplay, you know what I mean? I met a guy at a party and asked him what he did and he said, 'What I'm doing is I'm *not* writing a screenplay.' And I said to myself, now there's an interesting fellow."

Harvey laughed. "Yeah, I see what you mean."

When Harvey got off the phone, he looked up the phone number of the New York offices of the Writers Guild of America. The receptionist passed him on to a woman named Naomi.

"Naomi," Harvey said, "can you give me the movie and television credits for a writer I'm thinking of employing?"

"I can."

"I just want to check up on him before any money changes hands. You know what I mean, don't you?" He gave his voice the tonal equivalent of a wink.

"I think I do. What's the writer's name?"

"Dickie Nacke." Harvey spelled it for her.

"I'll have to call you back on this. I have to find his file."

"You'll be able to give me all his television and movie credits?"

"That's what I'm going to do, honey. Let me have your number and I'll get back to you. Give me ten minutes or so."

Naomi called back in fifteen minutes and said, "Okay. Dickie Nacke. N-A-C-K-E."

"That's right. What you got?"

"He's currently working for 'Last Laughs'?"

"That's the one. What else has he done?"

"Nothing."

"Nothing? No screenplay credits?"

"Nope," she said.

"What about projects he may have worked on, but that weren't, you know, produced?"

"That would be here, too, but there's nothing else on his record. See, when a member submits any literary work for television or motion pictures, he or she is supposed to send us what's called a Notice of Script Delivery or Commencement. If this person delivered any work for a project—it could be a treatment or an outline or a polish—even if it wasn't produced, then it would show up on a script delivery notice. But, see, Dickie Nacke's just down here for 'Last Laughs.' He only joined the Guild in September."

"This past September?"

"That's right."

"I see," Harvey said. "Listen, thanks, Naomi."

"There's one other Nacke here, but he's deceased. Died in 1982."

"Oh, yeah?" Harvey was barely listening. "What's his name?"

"Richard Nacke."

"*Richard?* A different one?"

"Yes, and it's funny—he's got only one credit too."

"What's that?" Harvey asked.

"He wrote for a TV show in the fifties called 'My Baby Brother,' " she said.

17

At the corner of Lexington and Fifty-fourth Street, as he simultaneously evaded a crazed bicycle messenger and intersected a particularly noxious current of bus exhaust, and then proceeded to eject a large strand of sticky saliva onto the front of his sweatshirt, Harvey began to seriously question his decision to jog to Central Park. No less disconcerting was his gut, this *thing* he now had to carry around, jellying with every stride.

In the park the air was better. Running past the empty children's zoo and cutting over toward the Sheep Meadow, he began to feel his lower abdominals tightening, his hamstrings stretching. He sprinted full out for fifty yards, and for a moment it brought back to him with uncanny, aching vividness the sensation of heading off a long drive to left center. This spurt of nostalgia almost embarrassed him because he recognized in it the same feeling he used to have as a kid, pretending he was Vic Davalillo or Adolfo Phillips or Willie Tasby or Gary Geiger or some other modestly endowed major league outfielder with whom Harvey had, prefiguring his own destiny, identified. Here he was, twenty years later, six of them in the majors, pantomiming what he had been. As he veered back toward the corner of Central Park South and Fifth Avenue, he laughed aloud, turning the heads of two elderly checker players on a bench.

Heaving and sweating under his three layers of clothing, he walked off a cramp on Fifth Avenue, heading downtown. He turned into the big B. Dalton book-store between Fifty-second and Fifty-third, asked directions to the television reference books, and took down a thick paperback called *The Complete Directory of Prime Time Network TV Shows, 1946–Present.* He fanned through the alphabetical listings to the M's.

MY BABY BROTHER

Situation Comedy, CBS
First Telecast: September 14, 1954
Last Telecast: April 9, 1957

CAST

Allan Bolling	Simon Durley
Midge Bolling	Catherine Marcus
Jimmie Bolling	Roy Ganz
Gerald Bolling	Steve Tolson (1954–56)
Margaret Rogers	Sarah O'Malley
Mr. Wax	Stewart Laness
Mrs. Finegold	Shirley Micklin (1956–57)

In a basically forgettable variation on the bratty-but-lovable little brother theme that would later be perfected in the more popular series "Leave It to Beaver," "My Baby Brother" featured Roy Ganz (seven years old when the series began) as Jimmie Bolling, the youngest son of Allan, a bumbling suburban gift shop owner, and his cheerful though fussy wife, Midge. Steve Tolson, who for the first two seasons played the straight-arrow older brother Gerald, provided the comic foil for the irrepress-ible and sometimes domineering Jimmie. A typi-cal episode would find the often eerily precocious Jimmie solving a family problem—such as the dis-pute with neighbor Mr. Wax over who should clean up a fence between their properties that had been defaced by Halloween trick-or-treaters—with a combination of childlike ingenuity and adult common sense.

With his finger, Harvey wiped off a drop of sweat that had fallen onto the page and returned the book to the shelf. On his way out he browsed at the magazine rack and found short articles in both *Time* and *Newsweek* about Ganz's death.

Time referred to his death as:

. . . the last tragic leg of Ganz's slow fall from grace in recent years. As so often happens in the wake of early success—Ganz was already the star of "My Baby Brother" at the age of eight—Ganz's legend seemed finally to have outrun his talent. During the four years since he left "Last Laughs" in 1982, Ganz was involved in largely unsuccessful movie and television projects, including a 1984 comedy special in which he worked with many of the mainstream Middle American comedians that "Last Laughs" had once scorned. This past summer he was lured back to restore his brainchild to its former heady glory, but the first four shows lacked "Last Laughs" 's earlier sparkle and courageous, if sometimes cruel, wit. Says Barry Sondell, one of the show's original writers, who had returned to Ganz's stable: " 'Last Laughs' now reminds me of a piece of dried fruit. Well, if not exactly a piece of dried fruit, it reminds me of some cheap variety of meat. Head cheese, perhaps, or maybe olive-and-pimiento loaf. You get the picture: the show's no longer using the finest cuts."

Like one of the absurdist sketches in which the show frequently specialized, the story of Ganz's fatal plunge out of his own office window early last Sunday morning appears—so far—to have no punchline, let alone an explanation. Spokesmen for the New York Police Detective Unit handling the investigation have not released the names of any suspects, raising doubts as to whether there are any yet. Suicide has been ruled out by the police. The network has retained the services of a private investigator, former major league baseball player Harvey Blissberg, who has not made himself available for comment.

In a long interview Ganz gave to *Esquire* magazine in 1978, the then 31-year-old producer said, "Comedy is dangerous. If it doesn't feel like something one ought not to be doing, then it *is* something one ought not to be doing." This week, with virtually nothing known about the circumstances surrounding Ganz's death, comedy has never seemed *more* dangerous.

Harvey drank two Yoo-Hoos standing at a Sabrett hotdog stand on the corner of Fifth and Fifty-first. It was already late afternoon, and workers were pulsing out of the buildings. The sweat had dried on his body, and he felt how chilly it was. The dropping sun was throwing itself coldly eastward down the cross streets, jolting the intersections on Fifth Avenue with stiff light. Before the pedestrian congestion could get worse, Harvey broke into a trot down Fifth along the curb, weaving in and out of the sidewalk vendors with their endless array of wool scarves, native jewelry perfectly arranged on small blankets, and electronic toys buzzing around the tops of cardboard boxes.

He turned right at Forty-seventh, crossed Broadway, and entered the ANC network building. He showed his temporary I.D. to the elevator security woman and rode alone to the twenty-fourth floor. As he walked through the show's offices, he nodded at a few women he didn't recognize who were typing at their desks.

The door to Ganz's old office was partially open, and Harvey let himself in. Trying to ignore that real or imagined chill, almost like a cold and audible hum, that clings to the rooms of the recently deceased, he went right to Ganz's impressive oak desk and started going through the drawers. He was looking for Dickie Nacke now. And he was looking for the connection between the Dickie Nacke he was looking for and the Richard Nacke who had written for "My Baby Brother" and died in 1982. Son and father? After pacing back and forth across the case, Harvey had finally stepped on a loose floorboard.

The first five drawers were empty, except for the odd paper clip, ball-point pen, or network memo pad. In the larger file drawer the dirty green file holders swung empty from the metal tracks. One more drawer to go.

"Can I help you?" a voice snapped Harvey's head in the direction of the door. He hadn't turned on the office lights, and now he squinted at the dusky figure, making out the large flat teeth in the middle of the gray face.

"Oh, hello, Generra," Harvey said, pulling out the last, empty drawer.

"Hello, Harvey." Generra sat on the edge of the desk, unzipped one of his ankle boots, took it off, and rubbed his foot. "Soaking up some atmosphere?"

"Something like that," Harvey said.

The detective replaced his boot. "What is it you're looking for?"

Harvey leaned back in the chair. "Your curiosity is flattering, Generra."

"Don't get a big head." Generra stared out the window.

Harvey snapped his fingers. "Hey, wake up, Generra. You looked depressed."

The detective sighed. "You have any idea how much I hate dusk in New York when it's cold? The older I get, the more fucking depressed it makes me. My doctor thinks I've got this thing called S-A-D. Seasonal Affective Disorder. I always get depressed when—the colder and darker it is, the shittier I feel. He wants to give me something for it. He thinks I should use these special fluorescent lights." Generra's gray complexion suggested that he had failed to make maximum use of the sun when it was out. "What the fuck do I care who knocked off some guy who's made millions making fun of cripples?"

"We've got to get you some sunlight, Generra. Ganz did some funny stuff in his day."

"You a TV critic too? In addition to being a ballplayer and a dick?"

*   *   *

Harvey left Generra looking out the window and walked down to the New York Public Library and in the *Readers' Guide to Periodical Literature* found the date of the 1978 *Esquire* containing the Roy Ganz interview and asked the librarian for the microfilm. The long introduction sketched in Ganz's life until the age of thirty. Born in New York City in 1947 to a mother who had been a summer stock actress in the 1930s and a father who ran a chain of dry-cleaning stores in the Bronx and Long Island. With his mother acting as his agent, Ganz was working as a child fashion model by the age of five and soon after was a regular on a local television kiddie show where he played, in his words, "the one who knew all the answers." In 1954 he auditioned for and won the part of Jimmie Bolling on "My Baby Brother," and moved with his mother to Hollywood. His father remained in New York for close to two years before joining his wife and only child in California.

When the network canceled "My Baby Brother" in 1957, Ganz, who was "determined to salvage some kind of normal childhood," stayed out of show business until attending UCLA, where he produced student variety shows. Upon graduation he joined ABC's programming department, where he helped to develop new shows. He left ABC in 1972, in his mid-twenties, and moved to New York, in part because his father was ailing. After an unsuccessful attempt at novel writing, he began to conceive of a comedy show "for his generation," and the rest is history.

In the interview itself, Ganz talked at some length about the slow gestation of the show, the virtues of live television, the conflicts with network executives and censors, and the trick, as he put it, "of being on the cutting edge of comedy without drawing too much of your own blood." Of his past as a prominent child-actor: "By the time I was ten, I knew I didn't want to be one of those child-actors who had made an astonishing amount of money but had no idea what things cost or how to do long division or kick a football. You know, the road from Hollywood to Santa Monica is paved with old child-actors. I mean, people walk all over them, when they're not walking all over themselves. I didn't want to be a character; I wanted to *have* one. I wanted to have a real life. I needed to know what real kids were like. I think that sense of really needing to be in touch with reality and have some real power over it came from my father. My mother would have been perfectly happy to have me live my entire life in a TV studio. I inherited my mother's exhibitionism and my father's presence—I guess you could call what I got from him a kind of imperiousness. Until the age of ten, the exhibitionism held the upper hand. After 'My Baby Brother' I wanted this to change. I feel I made a decision to be different. And my father was, let me say, not real encouraging about my continuing my child-acting career.

"Three years of 'My Baby Brother' was enough to teach me that—I understand this more, of course, in retrospect—that I someday wanted to be on the other side of the camera. Not necessarily as a director, but I did want to be in charge. It's funny, because Jimmie Bolling was all about being in charge. But that was just TV. I was a manipulated little bastard then, and manipulated little bastards either learn how to manipulate back or they may never realize they're not pulling their own strings. In fact, the person I was closest to on the set of 'My Baby Brother,' except my mother, of course, was Max Wiley, the director. He was my surrogate father in those years, and he kept me in line."

Toward the end of the interview, a comment by Ganz caught Harvey's eye. "My biggest enemy on the show? Myself. My temper, my impatience. So many things can go wrong. In television you're never really in charge, even as a producer, and you have to learn to tame your perfectionism at the same time you communicate that perfectionism to everyone else so that people do absolutely the best they can. Extend themselves. Because, if people don't extend themselves when you're doing comedy, you end up with just another sit-com."

Harvey walked back to the hotel and got in the shower. New York City water pressure had always been the best in the American League, and he stayed under the spray for ten minutes, on the theory that prolonged exposure of his scalp to hot water would clarify his thinking and return his thoughts to him nicely ironed and folded. In fact, he spent most of the ten minutes dwelling on the National Puppy-Grinding Company sketch. For the second time that day he laughed aloud recalling one of the lines intended for Lanahan: "Before me, people had to resort to shady, fly-by-night puppy-grinders. You never knew how they were going to treat the puppies."

After toweling off and stabbing his armpits repeatedly with a stick of Arrid Extra Dry Solid, he dabbed a little Vicks VapoRub in the corner of each nostril. He still felt chilled from three hours in a damp sweatsuit. He blow-dried his hair. He gargled at length. In the full-length mirror he retracted his stomach until it resembled its former contours. He acted in general as though preparing for a smoldering date—the image of Candee Wersch briefly danced across the dimly lit stage of his libido—but he knew he was simply procrastinating.

When Harvey was at last able to tear himself away from his grooming, he got dressed and dialed the Los Angeles telephone number for Dickie Nacke that he had copied down from Ganz's Rolodex. A recorded voice told him it had been disconnected.

Harvey went to his briefcase and took out the stack of press biographies that Mike Altiser had given to him. He looked at the group bio for the writers.

For the first time, he realized there was no mention of Dickie Nacke. Nacke had lied about being a highly paid screenwriter. He may have lied about who it was who had really rejected his puppy-grinding sketch. It was, Harvey thought, a measure of the transience of the world of "Last Laughs," maybe even a measure of the transience of television itself, that the show could have on its staff a grown man making, Harvey guessed, an easy six figures, and yet no one would have any clear idea who he was. Except, of course, Roy Ganz. Everyone seemed to agree that Dickie Nacke was Ganz's man, and Harvey, frankly, had a feeling that

Ganz had been Nacke's. In what way, Harvey had no idea. All he knew about Nacke was that he appeared to be a perfectly likable, graying, knuckle-cracking, dog-loving, puppy-hating, early middle-aged man.

18

Harvey decided to stay in New York over the weekend to sift through the modest material of his investigation so far, but he needed some distance. On the phone Friday, Mickey gave him the name of a small hotel on Madison in the Nineties favored by musicians and people of sensible means. With its faded white front, white fire escapes, and variety of white friezes over the windows, the nine-story Crown Hotel looked remarkably like a two-week-old wedding cake. Its informal lobby featured matted blue carpeting, a glass chandelier, a large floor-model humidifier, and a collection of Victorian lamps involving black lead figurines holding harps or performing some species of eurythmic dancing. Over the radiator three potted rubber plants with brown tips strove bravely to lighten the mood. The entire lobby looked as though it needed watering. When Harvey checked in at the small desk squeezed into the rear of the lobby by the marble staircase with its Doric touches, he was received with the wary nonchalance of a co-conspirator. He had to carry his own bag into the grunting elevator and ride up to his eighth-floor room with a downcast French horn player.

He was glad to be out of Midtown with its impinging concrete and glass. Here the scale was almost that of a village. Midtown smelled of money changing hands; on the Upper East Side it was the very faint odor of money quietly earning interest and throwing off dividends. Across the street, out of Harvey's room window, the shops lined up in quaint succession: a china and glass restorer, housewares, children's clothes, a Northern Italian restaurant, a purveyor of soap. It was midafternoon, and the streets were swarming with schoolgirls on their way to the brownstone stoops on Ninety-second and Ninety-third to smoke cigarettes.

On Saturday Harvey rang up Joey Hanes, the show's head writer. He asked Hanes about Dickie Nacke, but only after inquiring about Sondell and Karen Baldwin to disguise the real target of his interest.

"Yeah, well, as head writer, naturally I assumed I had the power to hire the writing staff I wanted," Hanes said, "but the facts were that Leo insisted on hiring Geller and the kids from St. Louis, and then Ganz politely informed him he wanted this Dickie Nacke on the staff. And then, of course, Marty Beaver rode back in on Ganz's coattails, and then Sondell— well, Sondell was just there, you know, suddenly soaking up a big chunk of the writing budget. I basically got to hire Karen, but there were a bunch of other writers I wanted too. There's one woman who does her own radio show in Atlanta who's terrifically funny and writes all her own stuff, and I really wanted to give her a shot, but the money was all gone before I knew it."

"Now let's see," Harvey said. "Where did Nacke come from?"

"Well, Ganz introduced me to him one day in September as a comedy writer from the Coast, and then Ganz came by my office later in the day and told me he was going to hire him because he had just what the show needed."

"And what was that?"

"Hell if I know, but let me guess. The, uh, ballast of maturity? A tamer sense of humor than Leo's? But he did do that sketch about grinding up puppies—now that was beating Leo at his own game."

"You know it's probably going in the show next week?"

"Puppy-grinding?"

"Yeah."

"C'mon."

"No, it is."

"Now you see what kind of power I have at the show," Hanes said. "No one ever tells me anything."

On Sunday night Harvey walked down to Eighty-sixth Street and saw two movies. He slept fitfully that night, finally turning on a rerun of "Gunsmoke" on cable television at four in the morning. When he fell asleep again, he dreamed in black and white. When he awoke at eight, sleep had made the connection that no amount of consciousness could.

At nine he was on the street flagging down a cab with the decisive gesture of a man who either had recently renewed his faith or else had mistaken a shadow on the wall of his reasoning for a piece of the real puzzle. When he climbed into the taxi, he asked the Arab driver to take him to the Museum of Broadcasting.

On the Museum of Broadcasting's third floor, in the card catalogue room with its coffee-and-cream-colored walls and portraits of Bob Hope, Ernie Kovacs, Walter Cronkite, and Sid Caesar, Harvey pulled out one of the *M* drawers and found listings for six kinescopes of "My Baby Brother" episodes. He picked one.

MY BABY BROTHER: (TV)

CBS September 14, 1955 Wednesday 8:30 PM NYT 30 Min. B&W

Credits: Prods—Jack Dworkin, Alan Stern. Creator—Babs Golick. Dir—Max Wiley. Cast—Simon Durley (Allan Bolling), Catherine Marcus (Midge Bolling), Roy Ganz (Jimmie Bolling), Steve Tolson (Gerald Bolling), Sarah O'Malley (Margaret Rogers), Stewart Laness (Mr. Wax), Shirley Micklin (Mrs. Finegold).

Summary: For a fifth-grade school project, Gerald needs to dig up an Indian artifact in their community. As a prank, younger brother Jimmie buries one of their father's old hatchet heads in the backyard and has the family dog "unearth" it the next day. An excited Gerald takes it to school, where his "artifact" is exposed as a fraud, and Gerald returns home in tears. To redeem himself, Jimmie studies old maps and then sneaks out late at night with Gerald to look for real Indian artifacts in a nearby riverbed. They find a buried cache of real Indian pottery, which is authenticated by the local museum. Jimmie lets Gerald take all the credit for the discovery, which makes Gerald a local hero.

When the young attendant brought him the tape transfer, Harvey took it down the hall to a room filled with viewing consoles, sat in one of the upholstered chairs, and inserted the tape in the Sony cassette player built into the desktop. He settled the earphones comfortably over his ears and began watching a cloudy kinescope of Hollywood's version of middle-class suburban life thirty-two years ago.

The show began with a series of shots of the members of the Bolling family tripping gaily down the stairs of their immaculate house. While the theme music effervesced, each smiled into the camera lens as their real names appeared on the screen under their chins. Simon Durley was wearing suspenders, carrying a folded newspaper under one arm, and trying unsuccessfully to light his pipe. Catherine Marcus, wearing a galvanized hairdo, was drying her hands on her apron. Steve Tolson, in a crew-cut and V-neck sweater, bounded down the steps and grinned at the camera with a crowded mouthful of crooked teeth. And finally Roy Ganz, in a striped T-shirt and dungarees, skipped up to the camera, cocked his little blond head slightly to one side, and smiled with tight-lipped mischievousness. It was the expression of someone who was not only about to slip a toad down some girl's dress, but had already devised an alibi for where he was at the time. He was recognizably Roy Ganz under the blond mop of hair: dimpled, small-boned, self-assured, shirt neatly tucked into his pants.

The first scene featured dinner in the Bolling household. Mother asks Jimmie to remove his coonskin cap. Jimmie refuses, saying that Davy Crockett always ate with his hat on. Father says that Davy Crockett didn't eat nice juicy pot roasts for dinner in a civilized suburb like Longdale. Jimmie says that if he had, he'd bet Davy's parents would let him wear his hat at the table. Gerald jerks the tail of his little brother's cap and says, "How do you know, smarty pants?" Father tells his youngest son he's welcome to wear his hat if he wants to take his plate outside and eat his dinner in the woods in the backyard. Jimmie's about to leave the table when he asks if he'll also be able to eat his dessert outside too.

"I'm sorry, Jimmie," Father tells him, "but I remember very clearly from my own schooldays that Davy Crockett hated desserts. You know, Davy never ate a dessert in his entire life. Particularly hot apple pie with a big delicious scoop of vanilla ice cream melting on top. Dear"—he addresses his wife—"you don't remember Davy Crockett ever eating dessert, do you?"

"No," she says, "I distinctly remember that he never, ever ate dessert."

Throughout the exchange, Jimmie is reluctantly taking off his cap. Finally he hangs it on the back of his chair.

"Now, that's better," Father says.

"I do remember one other thing about Davy," Mother says, picking up a serving bowl on the table and holding it toward Jimmie.

"What's that, dear?" Father says.

"Well, I remember that Davy Crockett loved peas. Yes, he just couldn't get enough peas."

Harvey watched intently as the show progressed. Gerald's distress at not having found any arrowheads for the class project. His jealousy of his friend Margaret Rogers, who has. The parents' solicitude. Jimmie's prank. Gerald coming back from school in tears. Jimmie's new scheme, which produces valuable artifacts. Jimmie's refusal to take any credit for the discovery. The lesson made explicit at the end: "Your mother and I were going to punish you, Jimmie, for what you did. We're glad you set things straight on your own. But that doesn't take away the fact that you were responsible for lying and embarrassing your brother at school. Do you understand?"

"I was bad," Jimmie says, "and then I decided to be good."

"Well"—his father smiles—"you weren't all *that* good. We can't have you and Gerald sneaking out of the house in the middle of the night, can we, even if it *is* to find real Indian pottery?"

Jimmie sticks out his lower lip. "This good and bad business is confusing, Dad, isn't it?"

"Yes, it is, Jimmie. And when you figure it all out, guess what?"

"What?"

"You'll be a grown-up."

Jimmie starts to get teary.

"What's wrong, Jimmie?"

"But when I grow up, I won't be able to wear my coonskin cap *anywhere*."

In the episode's last scene the reconciled brothers are getting into bed in the room they share. Soon after they turn off the lights, there's a loud series of cracking sounds.

"Stop it, Gerald," Jimmie says.

"Stop what?"

"Stop making that sound."

"I'm just cracking my knuckles, Jimmie."

"Well, it's too *loud*."

"Oh, all right," Gerald says. "Jimmie?" Harvey shot forward in his seat, studying Gerald's face. The cracking knuckles echoed in his ears.

"Yeah, Gerald?"

"You know, Mom and Dad lie sometimes too."

"Really?"

"Yeah."

"Like how?"

"They fibbed to you about Davy Crockett."

"They did?"

"Yeah."

"What do you mean?"

"I mean," Gerald whispers, "that I happen to know that Davy Crockett loved apple pie, especially with vanilla ice cream."

They both start to giggle in the dark. As their laughter fades, there are more cracking sounds.

"Gerald!"

"What?"

"Gerald," Jimmie says, "I'm gonna get you."

Harvey stared at the screen in disbelief as the last canned laughter bubbled up. He was barely able to focus on the show's writing credits:

Written by

Bill Bruce
Betsy Carmine
Richard Nacke
Alexander Schernecker
Thomas Domberger

Harvey walked out onto Fifty-third Street, where it was thirty-two years later and the sun was shining. So that's who Dickie Nacke is, he thought. Or was. Roy Ganz's "older brother." And that, Harvey calculated, makes his wife, Sally, a woman who uses Dermablend. But who is, or was, Richard Nacke? Harvey walked as far as the corner of Fifth, where he had to lean against the window of the Doubleday bookstore until his legs stopped quivering.

He spent the rest of the morning trying to find out something about Richard Nacke. He called Naomi at the Writers Guild and found out that, of the four other "My Baby Brother" writers, two—Bill Bruce and Alexander Schernecker—were as dead as Nacke. Thomas Domberger hadn't worked in more than twenty years and the Writers Guild had no current address for him. The last writer, Betsy Carmine, had a Venice, California, address and phone number, but her phone rang indefinitely when Harvey tried it.

Marty Beaver, whom Harvey woke up from a nap, had never heard of Richard Nacke.

Harvey could not call the one person, Dickie Nacke, who could tell him the truth about Richard Nacke. If Dickie Nacke heard Harvey's footsteps, Harvey would never catch anything.

19

They were all in Leo's office, the writers and cast members, when Harvey arrived on Monday afternoon. While Leo talked, lumbering up and back behind his desk in a gold-and-brown-checked flannel shirt, the others sat quietly, mostly on the floor, since Leo's office was ill-equipped for meetings, and it went without saying that Ganz's old office next door was undesirable. The scene— all these adults sitting cross-legged or lying on the carpet—struck Harvey as the premise for a sketch about kindergarten children who had been kept after school for thirty years for getting out of hand.

"Come in if you like, Harvey," Leo said.

"If you don't mind, I'll just listen from here," Harvey said, leaning against the doorframe.

"Whatever you like," Leo said. He drew a hand through his rough hair. "Now, Curt."

Geller looked up. "Yes?" He was wearing a black sweatshirt and well-worn running shoes.

"I've got an assignment for you, Dr. Geller."

Was it Harvey's imagination, or had Ganz's death already freed Leo to adopt a higher note of authority?

"I want to open the show this Saturday myself with a short monologue," Leo said, pacing. "A short, sweet, and serious one that acknowledges Roy's death and what his loss means to us. And, Curt, since I think you're the best person here with serious thoughts, I'd

179

like you to draft me about sixty or ninety seconds' worth of sincerity."

"Yeah?" Geller said.

"I'll give you a start," Leo said. "Something like, 'In the two weeks since our friend and mentor Roy Ganz died, we've only begun to mourn him. He not only changed the face of comedy in our time and blah-blah-blah, but with his honesty and intelligence and blah-blah-blah, he deeply touched all who, uh, came to know him and work with him. And then, something like, we're aware that, uh, laughter is not something associated with respect for the dead, but in the case of Roy Ganz, we here at 'Last Laughs' feel that one of the best ways to, uh, honor this man is to continue our work in his tradition. The last thing we at the show want is to feel that Roy is looking down on us tonight and saying what he often said to us when we weren't doing our job, uh, 'Would someone please explain to me why that's funny?' Blah-blah-blah." Leo Rhoades stopped behind his desk, and placed one hand on top of a stack of stapled scripts.

"Gee, Leo, it sounds like you're doing just fine on your own," Geller said. He had been taking notes while Rhoades spoke.

"Well, you take a swing at it, Curt, and see if you can hit it any better than that."

"All right."

"Now," Leo said, "you know what they say about hard work being a good antidote against depression. So let's put together a really good show this week, okay? I'll tell you one thing, it's a hell of a lot more productive than sitting around worrying about what happened to Roy. Okay? I did some work last week, trying to line some pieces up." He turned toward his bulletin board, to which he had transferred the colored index cards formerly in Ganz's office. "The pink cards are the sketches we've got on hand that have a good shot. Karen, whyn't you spend the next twenty-four hours trying to whip your 'Bag Lady for a Day' game show bit into shape. Tweedledumpling, how about the 'Used Cult Salesman' commercial?"

Chuck Causey, who was flat out on the carpet with

his hands behind his head, said, "I think Rick and I can tighten it up."

"Get it down to a minute and a half. Now, Dickie, about puppy-grinding."

Nacke, sitting against the wall with his knees drawn up, lifted his head. "I heard it was going in."

"Yeah," Leo said. "I know there's been a lot of confusion about it, but I think it's safe to do it now. It's been what?—four weeks since we did 'Animal Doctor Malpractice,' which kind of had the same spirit. It's a nice fat part for you, Jimmy," he said, glancing at Lanahan. "But, Dickie, I think the first couple pages need to be brightened up."

"I'll try," Nacke said.

"All right," Leo said. "Now who's working on what?"

Harvey remained in the doorway for another few minutes. Joey Hanes pitched an idea for "Tax Reform School." Causey and Vergaard wanted to do a sketch called "Air Traffic Controller Pajama Party," in which dope-smoking air traffic controllers at LAX airport played loud rock music and ate Oreos while jumbo jets collided in midair. Karen Baldwin recited the first two verses of a song she was working on about Yuppie couples who didn't want to have children because it would interfere with their vacations. Eddie Colasono, the fifteen-year-old, pitched a vague idea about Roy Ganz returning to earth with angel wings and wandering into the middle of sketches to complain that they weren't funny enough. Leo reminded everyone there was going to be a penthouse gathering—staff and spouses only—on Saturday night after the show. Marty Beaver took it all in, massaging his gums with a Stim-u-dent.

Ten minutes later Harvey was in Mike Altiser's office on the thirtieth floor.

"I've just been on the phone with Detective Generra," Altiser said through his pipe smoke. "From several people at the party that night, they've put together a description of some fellow no one seemed to know. Evidently, he went up to a couple of them and demanded to be part of the cast. He later threw an hors d'ouevre plate at Rob Whent. Some kind of nut."

Harvey laced his fingers in his lap. "Mike, I want to ask you to do two favors."

"You don't look well, Harvey. You look a little pale."

"I'm fine."

"Could've fooled me. All right, what do you want me to do?"

"Mike, I want you to let people know I've abandoned the investigation."

"Abandoned it?" He unplugged the pipe from his mouth.

Harvey looked Altiser in the eye. "I want you to let people know that's what I've done."

"Oh," Altiser said. With an index finger he stroked the skin under his right eye. "I think I get it."

"Tell Leo or whoever and let the word get around. Maybe you could even circulate a memo saying that I've discontinued the investigation, but, you know, how much the network has appreciated my efforts."

"You want this done right away."

"Today."

"Correct me if I'm wrong, Harvey, but you wouldn't be asking me to do this unless you were at a total dead end or else you were too close for comfort."

"Yeah." Harvey pulled out a pack of Winstons and tapped one out. "My bill will reflect work performed after today."

"I don't mean to butt in"—he casually knocked his pipe on his cork ashtray, as though the gesture would convince Harvey he really wasn't that interested in what he was about to say—"but I can't help asking—"

"Let's say I know more about the who than the why," Harvey said. "And leave it at that."

"Oh," Altiser said, and resumed the business of refilling his pipe.

"I'm staying at the Crown Hotel on Madison Avenue, and that's between you and me. Tomorrow, or maybe on Wednesday, I'll put in an appearance downstairs and say good-bye to a few people. By then I expect everyone at the show to know that I'm on my way back to Boston."

"I get it."

"Now here's the other favor. I heard about the staff party after the show on Saturday night."

"We just thought it would be good for morale."

Harvey flashed a palm at him. "I think it's a fine idea. In fact, I'd like to come. Incognito."

"As what?"

"Well, you're going to have it catered, aren't you?"

"Naturally."

Harvey reached across Altiser's desk for a pen and pad of paper. He wrote down a name. "This is the name of a caterer that'll be willing to hire me for the night."

Altiser scooped up the pad. "Yummies?"

"Yummies. They're in Harlem."

"Harlem?"

"It's owned by the uncle of a former teammate."

"Oh, yeah? Which one?"

"Les Byers."

"No kidding. Byers. He's getting up there, isn't he?"

"Yeah, Les is a little older than I am," Harvey said.

"And he's still playing."

"That's right, Mike. Les is still playing and I'm not."

"You're a little sensitive about it, aren't you?"

Harvey waved it away. "So we'll use Yummies, all right? It'll probably be the first time cheese grits've been served in this building."

"Soul food?"

"Don't worry about it—I'll handle the menu end with Les's uncle."

"You're sure you know what you're doing, Harvey? There isn't going to be any unpleasantness at this get-together, is there?"

"Well, I should hope not," Harvey said. "But if you like, you can always have Barry Sondell check weapons at the door."

20

In a Harlem storefront on Tuesday morning, in front of a Garland stove on which two salmon were quietly poaching, Harvey asked Les Byers's Uncle Jerome if he would be interested in catering the "Last Laughs" party at twelve-thirty Sunday morning.

"What they want with me, with all their money, up there in that big building?" Byers said, brushing an asparagus spear across the surface of a hollandaise before ramming it into his mouth.

"It's me that wants you," Harvey said. Two employees looked up at him. They were spreading sardine paste on bread rounds before positioning tiny squares of pimiento in the center.

"My nephew put you up to this."

"I haven't talked to Les for months. It's me—I want you to be part of it." He had already explained his one condition to Byers.

"Are you going to get me into trouble, boy?"

"I don't think so, Jerome."

"We've never done a job below Ninety-sixth Street, you know."

"They won't bite."

"They never had much use for us on that show."

"Well, here's your chance to bring it up with the man."

"But the man's dead." Behind Byers, a young man

184

carried a brown paper quiver of French breads into the kitchen.

"There's another guy, a vice-president. You can discuss network comedy and race with *him*." Harvey took a folded piece of paper from his shirt pocket and stuck it in the pocket of Byers's white uniform top. "That's Mike's name and his number at the network. You can talk money with him."

"And I talk menu with you?"

"Make sure you give them a shot at your ribs and chicken."

Byers wiped his blue-black hand across the front of his shirt. "Yeah," he laughed, "ribs and chickens, you got some of my sauce on you, you leave real good fingerprints."

"And a big pot of cheese grits. Les once brought a mess of that shit into the clubhouse in Providence, and I'm assuming he learned it from you."

"Oh, that boy learned a few other things from me."

"No doubt."

"Yeah, like he learned how to keep his butt down on ground balls when he was yay high"—Byers sliced a hand across his thigh, then assumed an infielder's stance, sucked a high hop into his chest, and fired the imaginary ball in the direction of a crate of red leaf lettuce—"and I taught him how to keep his mouth shut too."

"I'm not sure you got through to him."

Byers poked him in the shoulder. "Well, don't you think that boy told me all about you and the trash you talk? Don't you think I *know* he had to keep you in line up there in the bigs?"

Harvey smiled and watched Byers's cooks moving around the kitchen. As a kid, he had spent many hours in the kitchen of his father's Italian restaurant outside of Boston. He would have liked to enter Jerome Byers's world for a few days, possibly longer, until this other business blew over.

"I can't believe you're not playing ball anymore," Byers said, unfolding the piece of paper Harvey had given him, and reading it.

"Jesus Christ. I may have to go back just to shut everyone up."

"Well, you just may have to do that." Byers took a half-step back and studied Harvey's body. "You don't look like you're too far gone there," he muttered. "Although you do have something going on there 'bout halfway down your self that looks like it going to be trouble some day soon." Byers cackled. "No, sir, I don't believe you ought to start tucking into my ribs at this stage. No, sir, I think you ought to be thinking about tucking into some vegetarianism for a while."

"Too bad your nephew's soy bean dairy went under. I'd've been able to get a good price on bulk tofu."

Byers whistled. "Lord, that was a bad investment. I told Lester, he want to do something with his cash, he can buy a piece of this right here, buy me some new stoves, keep it in the family. But no, he had to fuck with soy beans. Nothing like the big leagues to make you forget who you are."

Harvey cabbed down from Harlem to the Crown Hotel and ate halfway through the package of Pepperidge Farm shortbread cookies he'd bought at the Korean grocery on the corner. He opened his spiral notebook and flipped to the leaf that read: *"Esquire:* Max Wiley, baby bro dir, RG's 'father.' " He picked up the phone again and called the Directors Guild of America on Fifty-seventh Street. Please don't have died on me, Maxie, Harvey thought as he listened to the phone ring.

Not only had Max Wiley not died, he had chosen to retire to Sag Harbor, Long Island, and not only had he chosen to live there, he was home.

"My name is Harvey Blissberg, Mr. Wiley, and I've been investigating the death of Roy Ganz a week and a half ago, and—"

"I know, I know," said a bouncy voice at the other end. It brought to mind the theme music playing while all those members of the Bolling family skipped down the stairs in the opening of "My Baby Brother."

"I think we've got some things to talk about, Mr. Wiley."

Max Wiley paused just long enough for Harvey to

wonder if the director had put the phone down and gone off to do something else. "You know, Harvey," he finally said, "I feel like I've been waiting for your call."

"Do you?" Harvey said, walking to the window. "Well, is this a good time for you to talk?"

"Well, I'll tell you, I'm not crazy about the phone. It helps me to see a face, you know how it is."

"I'd be happy to come out there and see you."

"That'd be good."

"Today?"

"Tomorrow'd be a lot better, if you don't mind. We're having some people over later today."

A schoolgirl passing below the window looked like a young Mickey Slavin. Her tawny legs rose out of white ankle socks and disappeared into a kilt, her auburn hair was pulled back and held with a thick plastic barrette. Harvey followed her with his eyes until she disappeared around the corner. The whole thing was a mystery, people clambering out of their cloudy childhoods and vague adolescences to become specific human beings, dragging their poorly remembered lives, heavier by the day, behind them, looking always for pieces of the past in the current litter. He thought of Mickey and him meeting by complex chance. He thought of Roy Ganz's trajectory crossing Dickie Nacke's. "Tomorrow, then," Harvey said. "How do I find you?"

"You're in Manhattan?"

"Yes."

"Well, if you take the Hampton jitney, you'll be here in about two-and-a-half hours. There's one leaves New York around nine-thirty, and I could pick you up at this end. Fair enough?"

"That's fine. But, Mr. Wiley?"

"Yes, and call me Max."

"Fine, Max. I just want to make sure you agree with me, that we've got some things to talk about."

"Oh, I think we've got enough to make a conversation out of."

"You're sure?"

"Mr. Blissberg—"

"Harvey."

"Harvey," Wiley said in his tinkly voice, "you ever have a dog?"

Harvey called Mickey's television station in Boston and had her tracked down in an editing suite.

"Hi, Bliss," she said, and turned away from the phone to say, "No, no, Russ, take the audio right there and L-cut the first few words under the wide shot. I'm back, Bliss. You okay?"

"I'm all right. I won't keep you. I have a big favor to ask you, Mick. I need you to come down this weekend. We're going to a cast party for 'Last Laughs' on Saturday night."

"Oh, yeah?" She paused. "Who'm I going as?"

"Pretty much as yourself, with a slight alteration."

"Russ," she said away from the phone, "now that's a pretty cut, but what do you think about shaving a few frames . . . yeah, off the playback side, thanks. . . . Bliss, I'd better go."

"Okay, I'll call you tonight and fill you in."

"Bye, Bliss."

"Bye, Mick."

Harvey sat on the bed and ate the rest of the shortbread. Mickey was shaving frames in an editing suite in Boston, getting the pictures to join just right, manipulating fractions of seconds, creating out of an incomplete reality an even more incomplete reality, but one with the sleek surface of a dream. Harvey did not have all the pictures of the Ganz story, there was nothing to edit yet, no way of knowing how it would, as Mickey might say, cut together. He noticed that his right leg had been jiggling involuntarily for several minutes.

When he walked into the reception area of "Last Laughs" 's writers' wing Tuesday afternoon, Karen Baldwin, Rick Vergaard, Chuck Causey, and Tom Angel of the cast were sitting around the battered couches, trying to nail down some idea involving, as far as Harvey could make out, a talk show for hypochondriacs, whose host and guests were all hypochondriacs.

"So I say, 'Good evening, I'm Mel Pilton,' " Tom

Angel was saying as Harvey came in, " 'and welcome to another edition of whatever-we're-going-to-call-the-show,' and then I immediately grab the back of my neck?"

"You could think you just broke your neck," Vergaard said.

"Not this early in the sketch," Causey cautioned. "Let's save the real serious stuff for later."

The tall, dark-haired Angel nodded. "Okay, so it's my neck, or maybe my gingivitis could be acting up. Gums usually get a laugh. You know, I could—" He grimaced and bared his gums. "And we can get Candee to do her suburban princess number, so, like, when the host says—"

"You're the host," Vergaard said.

"Okay, so when I say, 'I'm afraid we're going to have to break for a commercial,' Candee whines, 'Do we have to?' "

Karen Baldwin jumped in. "Right, right, and then one of the other guests starts screaming for no apparent reason, 'I just broke my leg!' "

Vergaard said, "Rob says, 'I'm having a heart attack,' and, Tom, you say very knowingly, 'I know exactly what you mean. I get them all the time.' "

"Good," Causey said, taking notes. "And instead of studio technicians, we'll have studio physicians running out all the time to examine everyone."

Vergaard said, "The studio lights, of course, will be blinding someone." He shouted, "I can't see! I'm blinded!"

"And, you know, the little lavaliere mike'll be choking somebody else," Causey added.

Vergaard's hands leaped to his throat. "I'm choking!" he rasped. "I can't get any air!"

Harvey took advantage of the laughter to step forward and cough lightly. "I just wanted to say goodbye," he said.

Baldwin turned his way. "You leaving us?" she said. "We got this memo."

"Yeah, I'm leaving. Good luck to you. I'm sorry I couldn't have hung out here under better circumstances."

The four of them mumbled a chorus of "Take care,"

and "Good luck to you," and "So long." They all looked down, as if admonished by Harvey's presence.

Rick Vergaard raised his head. "You think they're going to—you know, they haven't told us anything."

"I don't know," Harvey said. "I really don't know."

As he moved away, toward the corridor that ran by the writers' offices, he heard Tom Angel say, "Okay, where were we?"

The sound of Harvey's soft knock on Dickie Nacke's door prompted a sharp bark from within, followed by "Sit!" and "Come in."

The springer spaniel was now lying by Nacke's chair, forepaws splayed, rump in the air, her tongue a pink flag draped over one side of her mouth, panting happily beneath her owner's touch. "It's okay," he said to the dog. "It's okay."

Harvey said, "I just wanted to say good-bye, Dickie. I'm heading back to Boston."

"I always liked Boston," he said, glancing quickly at the paper in his typewriter.

"A sketch?" Harvey said.

Nacke hunched his big shoulders. "I figure I've got to turn something in, but who's in the mood?" He was several faces older than the kid who had told Roy Ganz that Davy Crockett loved apple pie with vanilla ice cream.

"Take care of yourself," Harvey said.

They seemed to be talking in code, an impression Nacke reinforced by pulling several times on his ear lobe, then wiping his hand across his mouth—a third base coach's gesture. "You too," he said.

Harvey advanced a step and patted the dog's forehead. "So long, doggie." She thumped the floor once with her tail.

Curt Geller's door was open, and he was standing at the window with his hands plunged inside the back of his blue jeans.

"Searching for that perfect punchline?" Harvey said.

Geller whipped around. "Christ, you scared me."

"Sorry. Didn't mean to sneak up on you."

"It's all right." He dropped into his desk chair. "Hey, Harvey, you look as if you've just seen a ghost."

"Yes." Harvey nodded. He leaned against the wall by the empty bookshelf. One of Geller's file drawers was pulled out, and his desk was piled high with papers. "Hey, looks like you're pulling up stakes too, Curt."

Geller took off his wire-rims and buffed the lenses on his shirt. "Yeah, I'm loading up the old Conestoga. This is my last week. The joke's been on me, I'm afraid."

"Don't take it too hard, Curt."

"I'm not sitting through this movie to the end."

"Where you going?"

Geller settled his glasses back on his nose. "Got me."

"You going to stay in New York?"

"I don't think so."

"What about Mimi?"

He gave a rueful burst of something that was not quite laughter. "That's not my world, either," he said.

"I guess it's good to find these things out."

"I have this theory," Geller said.

Joey Hanes stuck his head in the door and said, "Excuse me, Curt," before holding out his hand to Harvey. "Sorry to lose you."

Harvey took his cold clasp. "Thanks, Joey."

"What can I say?" Hanes shrugged amiably, as if to indicate that no etiquette code he knew of adequately covered the situation at hand.

When Hanes had gone, Geller said, "I have this theory. I call it the Fallacy of the Transferability of Talent. I think it's unique to the media age. When before in history have we had athletes turned TV commentators, TV commercial directors making movies, newspaper journalists becoming TV celebrities? We got a real judge who's become a TV celebrity *playing* a judge, and there're syndicated columnists who'd like to see him on the U.S. Supreme Court. We got an ex–U.S. Congressman in Connecticut who's a TV anchorman. We got corporate presidents writing best-sellers and football players doing rock videos. Everything's interchangeable. Every skill entitles you to some other skill. Everyone thinks if they do one thing well, they can do another."

"We got baseball players looking for guys who toss guys out of windows," Harvey said.

"And not finding them?" Geller smiled. Harvey said nothing, and Geller said: "So, okay, I thought I could transfer my talent for teaching to joke-doctoring, and from the way I was funny in San Francisco to the way they want you to be funny in this place. And I was wrong."

"Well, you know, it's not just what you do. It's also where you do it."

Geller turned slightly to look out the window at Manhattan. "I've got this theory about this show. It's not the best place for me to be. It's second-best. And second-best is the worst of all, Harvey, it's the most dangerous situation, because it's so easily mistaken for what you really want to do."

When Harvey left Geller's office and turned right, he saw Dickie Nacke at the far end of the corridor in the reception area. Nacke was kneeling next to his spaniel, brushing her with short, distracted strokes, while he looked dolefully—an expression not unlike the dog's—straight at Harvey.

21

"So," Max Wiley said, "what kind of dog did you have when you were a kid?"

It had taken them a while to sidle up anywhere near the subject. Only after an hour together did Max Wiley indicate by his abrupt question that he was ready to let his hair—a tight curly white carpet of it—down.

At noon on Wednesday, November 12, when the silver-and-dark-green jitney pulled into Sag Harbor, Wiley had been waiting for him, a small man in an absurdly large quilted parka and sunglasses, with his arm propped up on a blue *New York Times* vending machine. There was an L-shaped tear in the front of his parka, and some of the parka's stitching had worked free, disturbing the diamond pattern.

"No doubt you're Blissberg," Wiley smiled, removing his sunglasses. "You're the only person getting off this jitney who looks remotely like an outfielder."

It was the pleasantry of a man who knew something about establishing character, in this case his own. Wiley had said "who looks remotely like an outfielder," not "like a baseball player," which, for most people, would have been a sufficient phrase. What Wiley's remark told Harvey was that the retired director knew something about Harvey's career, and that he also wished to be known as a man capable of fine distinctions, even if they were frivolous ones, as this one certainly was, since even Harvey, who knew several hundred major league baseball players, and had seen many of them without their clothes on, had no firm ideas about what physically separated pitchers, infielders, and outfielders.

Harvey shook Wiley's soft hand—it felt like a friendly rodent in his palm—and said, "Thanks for coming down to get me."

"Oh, I usually take a walk about this time, anyway." Wiley chuckled. "But I never would have left you stranded here in the middle of this teeming . . . Well, how do you like my little metropolis?"

Harvey squinted down to the end of the street, past a shingled windmill to where a couple of sailboats, their individual colors bleached out by the blinding sunlight, still sparkled in the bay. He turned and looked back toward the business district. There were a couple of videocassette rental stores, two gelato parlors, a custom farmer, and some ugly new mansard-roofed buildings among the older brick buildings. The hardware store had high-priced copper cookware in the window. The village had the form of a fishing village, but the conspicuous contents of Manhattan culture.

"It's always nice to see a horizon," Harvey said.

"I'm partial to low-density living," Wiley mused, taking Harvey by the arm and leading him down the sidewalk toward the water. He had an even-featured, compact face and strong teeth. When he talked, his gold inlays blinked from the back of his mouth. He had managed to carry his mahogany tan into November. Was it a case of self-selection, rapid evolutionary adaptation to Hollywood, or an extraordinary genetic coincidence, that so many show business people had this smooth, nutty appearance? Wiley was the only person in view who looked remotely like a former Hollywood television director.

When, after a ten-minute walk, Wiley finally led Harvey into the rustic den of his shaggy, shingled house, Wiley offered him a cushioned wicker armchair and sat down behind his cluttered desk. Any suspicions Harvey had had about Wiley's financial welfare, based on the torn parka, were allayed by the home's casual prosperity. Wiley immediately began to collect some loose white papers, which Harvey could see from his chair were covered with countless crossed-out phrases.

"Can I ask what all that scribbling is?" Harvey said. "Looks like you've been having a hard time finding the right words."

Wiley rested a hand on the sheaf of papers. "You know what a palindrome is, don't you?"

" 'A man, a plan, a canal,' " Harvey said. " 'Panama.' "

"A very famous one. Trying to come up with palindromes is a diversion of mine. You know how hard it is to make something like that up? The fellow who invented that one spent months on it. For a long time he was stalled with 'A man, a plan, a canal—Honduras.' "

Harvey laughed.

"He knew the last word was a Central American country. He just couldn't figure out which one."

Harvey had the uneasy feeling of being entertained. Wiley kept a straight face, smacking his lips between phrases to milk the timing.

"You know the other famous palindrome 'Able was I ere I saw Elba'?"

"Sure."

"Well, you should've seen some of the early drafts." Wiley worked his mouth for a moment. " 'Capable was I ere I saw elbapac.' "

Harvey shifted in the wicker chair, the smile beginning to ache on his lips.

" 'Poor Dan is in a droop,' " Wiley said. "That's another."

There were a couple of outstanding framed water color harbor scenes on the wall—not the meticulously realistic variety, with strategically placed gulls and too-solid skiffs, that abounded in seaside art galleries. Wiley's bookshelves leaned heavily toward hard-cover fiction. On an end table near the window looking out over the bright bay was a pewter kerosene lamp. Except for a procession of four Emmy awards on a top shelf, the den was devoid of show business mementos.

"Okay, how about this one? I call it the burglar's credo. Ready? 'Fool, a tool, loot, aloof.' "

Harvey smiled.

"See?" Wiley said. "A burglar's got to be a fool to begin with, he has to have the right tools in order to get the loot, and most of all he wants to remain aloof from the law. Fool. A tool. Loot. Aloof. Anyway."

"I don't think you could ask for a better palindrome than that," Harvey said.

"Well"—Wylie consulted his scribbling—"I've been trying to work out something with—well, all I've got so far is 'A nut sat as tuna.' I don't think this one's going to go anywhere. You know, it's like a lot of these television shows on the air."

"What is?"

"Palindromes. Do you watch much TV, Harvey?"

"Some."

"Ah," Wiley said, lips puckered in mock disappointment. "Well, sometimes I watch that thing over there"—he jerked an elbow at the television set in the corner of the den—"and sometimes I think these shows would make just as much sense running backward as forward. There's been a real decline in narrative excellence over the years. What do you think?"

Harvey thought, I think I ought to get Wiley together with Curt Geller and they can exchange theories till the cows come home. "I have to admit, Max, I just don't feel qualified to have an opinion."

It was at this point that Wiley sat forward in his desk chair and said, "So, Blissberg, what kind of dog did you have when you were a kid?"

"Me?" Harvey said. "Oh, I had a Lab until I was twelve. In fact, you'll be interested to know he was named Maxie."

"And what happened to Maxie?"

"We had him put to sleep," Harvey said. "He was only about nine years old, but he had all sorts of problems."

"Where you sad? Did you cry?"

"Yes and yes."

"Well, as bad as I'm sure it was, Harvey, you still don't know how Steve must've felt."

"Steve Tolson," Harvey said. "Also known as Dickie Nacke."

Wiley sat back in his chair. "Yes, I assumed you made that connection or you wouldn't've called."

Harvey sat forward. "So you suspected it was Nacke when you heard about Ganz's death?"

Wiley held up a tanned hand. "Whoa. I don't know if Nacke had anything to do with Jimmie's death."

"Jimmie?"

"I'm sorry. I've always called him Jimmie. It was a little friendly thing we had. I called him Jimmie, even off the set, and he always called me Max. Anyway, I don't know if Nacke had anything to do with it, but I suspected that sooner or later in this thing someone would find out who Dickie Nacke was, and I'd get a call."

It was Harvey's turn to hold up a hand. His thoughts were getting ahead of him. "One thing at a time, Max. You said I didn't know how Dickie—Steve—felt. Do me a favor—can we call them Dickie and Roy?"

"Let's call him Steve, all right? That's how I knew him. His real name. Steve and Roy, okay?"

"All right. What don't I know about how Steve felt?"

Wiley smacked his lips. "Do you remember the show? 'My Baby Brother'?"

"I vaguely remember a rerun or two. But I watched one show at the Museum of Broadcasting."

"You remember the dog?"

Harvey's mind was now only about half a step behind some connection. "Oh, yeah." The dog hadn't been prominently featured, but he had been there; he had been the last to bound down the stairs of the Bolling home during the opening credits. "A Dalmatian?"

"Yes. Her name was Dolly."

"Dolly," Harvey repeated.

"Dolly was Steve's dog."

"His real dog?"

"Yes. When Steve was cast for the part, he asked me if we would audition his dog. The network already wanted a dog in the show, but we didn't have one in mind yet. So we had Steve bring her in. With his parents. And the dog was wonderful, a very good-natured animal. The lights didn't seem to bother her. So we hired Dolly. Steve was elated." Wiley paused, dropping his eyes to his desk.

Harvey swallowed. "We finished with the Dalmatians," the workman had said in the puppy-grinding sketch.

"Well," Max Wiley said, following a long sigh, "Jimmie—I'm sorry—Roy . . . Roy Ganz killed Dolly." Wiley raised his eyes and Harvey met them. "Dolly never did like Roy very much," Wiley said. "There was something about him that animals didn't like. Or other children. Roy was . . . a smart kid, but he was a tough little mother."

"How'd he kill the dog?"

"With a baseball bat."

"Jesus."

"He killed her late in the show's second season. Steve quit the show."

"Well, what happened?"

"Well, I don't know if the dog would've liked Roy more if Roy hadn't treated her pretty badly from the beginning. I guess Roy just didn't like dogs. I think he was mildly allergic. Maybe he was one of those guys who'd been bitten by one as a kid. Anyway, he was always pushing Dolly away, trying to kick her out of scenes, teasing her, pulling her tail, that kind of shit. It got to the point finally where Dolly would growl when she saw him."

"Where was Steve in all this?"

"He tried to reason with Roy, but it was useless. So, naturally, the situation just worsened. To have gotten rid of the dog would've been to acknowledge Roy's power in the situation. And keep in mind now that Roy was already the center of the show. Steve was just a satellite, and a lesser one at that. You know, even Sarah, the girl who played Steve's classmate and friend, had a bigger role in the scheme of things. She was allowed to be smart, have an independent personality of her own. But Steve, he was just the *zhlubby* older brother. The standard by which Roy was always proved to be an exceptional little brat."

"So to get rid of Dolly would've destroyed Steve, right?"

"So we all lived with it. Roy would tease the dog mercilessly—it was such a *thing* with him—and Steve would try to make up for it by doting even more on Dolly. As Roy became a celebrity—'The Miniature Man' and all that—he just naturally became more self-centered and aggressive. It was just sad. All right, so the day Roy killed her, it was the week after Roy had kicked her for barking at him in the middle of a take. You can see the cycle. So one day—we were shooting some scene in the boys' bedroom—Dolly suddenly sank her teeth in Roy's leg. He stopped and glared first at me—remember now we're talking about an angry little man in an eight-year-old boy's clothing —he glared at me, then he glared at Steve, and then he picked up the baseball bat we had propped against the wall in the corner of the room and"—Wiley swallowed—"he beat Dolly's brains out in front of the whole cast and crew."

Harvey looked out one of the den's windows at the corner of the cove.

"I'll spare you the details," Wiley said. "But Steve's first reaction was, he attacked Roy with his fists. Got him down and started pounding the shit out of him. I had to separate them."

"Why did you separate them?"

Wiley's eyes searched the room for a moment. He rubbed the desktop with the fingers of his left hand. He picked at the pilling on his sweater. "Just instinct," he finally said. "To break them up."

"What kind of instinct was it?"

"I don't know," Wiley said after a slight hesitation.

"You've got an eight-year-old who's just murdered another kid's dog in cold blood," Harvey said. "Don't you think Steve had a right to beat up Roy Ganz any way he wanted? I mean, the dog's dead, right, Dolly's bleeding all over the set."

"There wasn't that much blood—" Wiley began, and stopped himself.

Harvey snorted contemptuously.

"All right, I guess it was a director's instinct."

"Protect the star," Harvey said.

"There's that, yes."

"And you were worried about Roy's pretty little face?"

Wiley picked at his sweater, examined the small ball of wool, and flicked it on the floor.

"I asked you if you were worried that Steve would mess up Roy's face, which would give you two big problems, right? It would delay your shooting schedule, and you'd have to explain Roy's bruises to the press?"

"I suppose I was. But I wasn't thinking about it. I just saw a bigger kid jumping on a smaller kid."

"Oh, is that what you saw?"

"Now, just a moment, Blissberg—"

"I'm talking," Harvey said. "Because it seems funny you would so instinctively see a bigger kid jumping on a smaller kid, and be able to act on it, when for over a year you couldn't really see a boy abuse a dog right in front of the dog's master. Now, does that seem funny to you? You were the director."

"Yeah," Wiley said. "I'm not proud of the whole thing."

"Max," Harvey said, "Roy felt you were a surrogate father. He said you kept him in line during those years."

Wiley raised his white eyebrows.

"You call this keeping him in line?"

"Look, Harvey, I don't have any excuse. It was a horrible thing, the whole situation."

"What happened after you pulled the two of them apart?" Harvey lowered his voice. "You tell your writers to get to work on an episode about how the brothers react to their beloved dog getting run over by a car? Some script in which Dad and Mom make it all better with their adult wisdom? Huh? What happened?"

"Steve quit the show. He quit that day."

"How'd you explain it to the viewers? You say that big brother Gerald Bolling, also known as Steve Tolson, later to be known as Dickie Nacke, also got run over by a car, along with his dog Dolly?"

"You really want to know?"

"I'm partial to details."

"As I recall, yes, Dolly got run over, and we explained Steve's absence by saying he'd gone on a long school trip to France."

"A long school trip to France?" Harvey slapped his own forehead and laughed. "Then what?"

"He tried to take Roy to court. To keep it all quiet, the network paid Steve off."

"And, let me see, Steve had to sign an agreement that he would never publicly say what happened to Dolly?"

"That's right," Wiley said.

"What a great deal for everyone! Roy Ganz murders Steve's dog and his punishment is to get to continue being a tyrant and a star, and Steve's half of it is to be out of work and, on top of it, to not be able to tell anyone what happened."

Wiley shrugged. "I know, I know. All because of a dog."

"All because of a dog? What the hell're you talking about, Max? Seems to me it's all because of Roy Ganz!"

"All right, all right."

"Boy, that's just a tremendous bargain for Steve, isn't it? I want you to do me a favor, Max."

"What's that?"

"I want you to watch the show this Saturday night. I think there's going to be a sketch on it that's going to really catch your attention."

"Well, I'll try."

"It's Steve's way of going public with what happened to Dolly, after all these years." Harvey leaned forward. "But, you know, Max, as insane as this is, I don't believe Nacke—Steve—could've thrown Ganz out of a window just because Ganz killed his dog in nineteen fifty-six."

"That would be a little hard to believe," Wiley said.

"Yes, that would be hard to believe." Harvey didn't feel there was any need right now to tell Wiley about the Dermablend. "But, then, Max, there is the whole issue of how it came about that Roy suddenly hired

the long-lost Steve Tolson this fall to be a writer on
'Last Laughs.' "

"The long-lost Steve Tolson?"

There was a soft knock on the den door.

"That's what I said."

"C'mon in," Wiley said in the direction of the door
and turned to Harvey. "Lost, maybe," he said. "But
not long-lost."

"Sorry to disturb you men," a voice behind Harvey
said.

He turned to see a handsome middle-aged woman
in blue jeans, sneakers, and a cable-knit turquoise
sweater. She was carrying a tray.

"Harvey, this is my wife, Charlotte."

Harvey stood. "Nice to meet you."

"Nice to meet you." Her hands were indisposed, so
she bobbed slightly at the waist. "I brought you some
lunch."

"Thanks, honey," Wiley said.

For the next ten minutes Harvey and Max Wiley ate
tuna salad sandwiches on homemade bread. The only
time they spoke was to agree on what a favorable
difference in tuna salad could be made by a little
chopped dill pickle.

22

After lunch Max Wiley unwrapped a Macanudo and lit it with a troubled air. Even after it was burning nicely, he kept frowning at the tip, as if his cigar could be held responsible for the fact that he wasn't enjoying Harvey Blissberg's visit.

"I suppose," Wiley said, "that one of the sad sidebars to the story was that Steve in reality was a baby brother himself. He had, I think, a couple of older brothers and an older sister. He had a stage mother you wouldn't believe—a woman you could see didn't want to let her baby grow up. And the father, Russell Tolson, he'd quit his job somewhere in the Midwest to move to Hollywood with his wife, Steve, and the two other school-age children. Let's see, Russell had been some kind of chemical engineer back home, but he went without work the whole time he was in Hollywood. I remember that he was turned down for a lab job that he was really overqualified for. The employer told him that since his son made so much money, the job ought to go to someone who really needed it."

The ice cubes in Harvey's tall aluminum tumbler of Pepsi had melted.

"Needless to say, Steve's father began to resent the hell out of Steve, and out of his wife, who'd been responsible in a way for getting all of them out to California. Look, when you think of it, it's so—well, here's a nice kid, Steve Tolson, whose mother, in

203

classic fashion, railroaded her son into a show business career, and no one's happy. The husband's unemployed, mortgaged his own future, and the two other school-age kids have been displaced, all so that Steve can play the slow-witted older brother to Jimmie—I mean, Roy. Steve's fate was just made worse by the whim of the show's writers. The role just sort of extended Steve's helplessness. You know, even though the show's name was in Steve's voice—*my* baby brother—he was nowhere near the center of it." He scowled at his cigar and gently laid it in his ashtray. "And the thing is, Harvey, that not only was the family not too pleased—except for the mother, who was elated to be hanging around the set, manipulating her son's career—not only that, but I just don't think Steve really enjoyed acting. I don't think he enjoyed the acting part that much, or the notoriety part—"

"Or the part where his dog gets abused and finally murdered?"

"Yes, or that." The corners of Wiley's thin mouth turned up wearily, as commentary on Harvey's persistence. "I think Steve was probably glad to be out of it finally. But you should've heard his mother—after Dolly was killed, she kept trying to convince me that Steve would be back. She wanted him to go on, for *her* sake. I said to her, 'Millie, your son doesn't want to be on the show anymore, and it would be hard to blame him. I'd be happy to have him back, but we'd both be doing him a favor if we just let him make up his own mind.' 'Oh, no,' she said, 'he'll come to his senses, he's just a little upset about the dog.' I don't even think she could *see* that Roy had killed the dog— even though it happened in front of her too."

"Did Steve ever act again, as far as you know?" As soon as the question was out of his mouth, Harvey remembered Marty Beaver complimenting Nacke on his job filling in for Lanahan on the show a few weeks back.

"No," Wiley said, picking up the cigar and placing it ceremoniously on his tongue, "I don't think so."

"What happened to him after he left 'My Baby Brother'?"

During Wiley's long pause, he stroked the Macanudo with his lips, and Harvey had the strong impression that Wiley was debating whether to stand pat or turn over another card. As he studied Wiley's brown face with its veins trickling down his forehead, Harvey saw the child in it, the bright grammar school student at the other end of his life. Watching Reagan and Gorbachev on television in Iceland for their arms reduction meeting, Harvey had seen two pouting kids in a playground. He did it whenever he saw a group of white men in their official capacity. A group picture of corporate executives would dissolve into a third-grade class photo, a smiling row of astronauts into members of the Science Club. The unforgivably weak scaffolding behind human events. As Wiley toyed with his Macanudo, his bantam face became childlike. A man's life was an imperfect palindrome; it looked nearly the same at either end.

"You said Steve might've been lost," Harvey said, "but not long-lost."

"That's right."

Harvey saw that he was going to have to goose this part of the conversation along. "So you didn't completely lose track of him?"

"Actually, I lost track of him until he was out of college."

"And then?"

Wiley smacked as he withdrew his cigar. "Then I sort of caught up with him a little."

"Well? Did he come see you? Call you?"

"No, not exactly."

"Hey, listen, Max, I've got all afternoon, but why don't we pick up the pace?"

Wiley stretched, arms extended. "Jimmie called me."

"He did?"

"Actually, he'd call me now and then."

"You two've kept in touch over the years?" Harvey said.

"I guess you could say that."

"You kept being his father figure?"

Wiley shook his head, as though rejecting too formidable a role. "Just friends."

"So Roy called you about Steve?"

"Yes, he called me about him . . . let's see, Steve was just out of college, so it must've been about nineteen sixty-six. No, it was probably closer to sixty-eight or -nine. Evidently, Steve had knocked around several community colleges in California and didn't graduate till he was in his mid-twenties." Wiley paused.

"Go on."

"Jimmie—Roy called me. Let's see, Roy was just out of UCLA and working in programming at ABC. He hadn't heard from Steve since he'd walked off the show in fifty-six. Twelve or so years. But Steve called Roy out of the blue one day and said he wanted Roy to help him get a job at ABC. Just like that. Roy called me about it. He was a little worried. He felt that, uh, Steve sounded sort of—sort of entitled to Roy's help."

"Roy thought Steve was using a subtle kind of blackmail on him? Because of the dog?"

"I think Roy felt he could do without hearing from Steve. Apparently, Steve was fairly garrulous on the phone. Roy described it to me as a blue streak, a semipsychotic tirade."

"What'd Steve talk about?"

"This was a long time ago, Harvey."

"I have a feeling you remember some of it. You remembered that Ganz called it a semi-psychotic tirade."

"All right, what I remember is that he, Roy, said that Steve went on about how pretty Roy was sitting, how he owed it to his old friend, that Steve had been having a hard time of it. His mother had become something of a hopeless lush. He had had a hard time in school. He told Roy that he'd gotten a psychiatric deferment from the draft. That he was looking for some work he could get his teeth into, that, you know, Roy was certainly in a position to help him. I got the feeling that Steve was using a combination of flattery and self-pity to get at Roy."

"No mention of the dog?"

"No. In fact, one of the things that frightened Roy a little was that Steve never once brought up the dog.

But the incident just hung there like a cloud. Roy didn't know what to do about the call. He really didn't have any hiring influence at ABC, and even if he had had it, he wouldn't have been too eager to use it to eliminate the distance between him and Steve. He was concerned, so he called me. And I told Roy to send him over to see me."

"What were you doing at the time?"

"I was directing a couple of game shows at CBS."

"Did you see Steve?"

"Not only that, I got him a job. Not a very good one, however. But it wasn't clear if he was qualified for much else at the time."

"What kind of job?"

"A program analyst at CBS."

"Sounds pretty prestigious."

"Well, it's a job," Wiley said.

"What kind of job?"

"When they've got a pilot, you know, they literally pull people off the street and screen the show for them in a theater. They give them a couple of buttons—a 'like' and a 'dislike' button—and ask them to press them if there's something they react strongly to. Then the people fill out a questionnaire. Well, what Steve did was take the graphs generated by the button-pushing and lay it over the plot outline of the show, and then write reports on what people did or didn't like. You know, market research. Steve did this for a few months before he quit."

"I can see where Steve would've thought he deserved more challenging work."

"Yes," Wiley said. "And he still thought it was Roy's job to find it for him."

"He started harassing him again?"

"Yes."

"For a job?"

"And for money. Roy lent him a few thousand dollars in, I would guess, about nineteen seventy or thereabouts. I think he wanted the money to get his mother in an alcoholism program. I don't know if he ever paid it back. Roy used to call me from time to time and say, 'Max, I don't know what to do with him.

I know I did a terrible thing to him years ago, but I don't know what will make it better. He's making my life miserable.' Oh, I forgot—Steve wanted a lot of money from Roy to help bankroll a documentary he hoped to make."

"Let me guess," Harvey said. "About dogs."

"Close. He wanted to make a documentary about what happened to child television stars of the nineteen fifties."

"Jesus." Harvey felt like a window was open in his chest and cold air was blowing through it.

"Don't worry. It never got made."

"Did he lend Steve money for it?"

"No, I think that's when Roy put his foot down. Then Steve started showing up at restaurants where Roy hung out. As I recall, he once tried to pick a fight with him in front of one of Roy's girlfriends. But Roy did make an effort to find him jobs. The problem was, Steve didn't want to act—I think Roy could've helped him get auditions at ABC before he left. Steve wanted something more—he wanted to produce, he wanted power. Basically, he wanted the things that Roy had, and he held Roy responsible for the fact that he didn't have them. Roy did try to help him get an agent when Steve said he wanted to write. In the seventies the whole matter sort of went away. Roy moved to New York, and—"

"Was Steve one of the reasons Roy got out of town?"

"That I couldn't say. Maybe, maybe not. I think, in his own way, Roy was tired of La-La Land. So, anyway, Roy came East, and I think Steve ended up in some Big Sur commune—oh, that's right, shortly before Roy came East, I think, he got a phone call from Steve at this commune. He had some crazy idea he wanted to write a pilot for a television series about commune life, and he wanted Roy to produce it. The only thing I really recall is that he told Roy he had just eaten a peyote button and it had given him something like an instantaneous vision of what the first twenty-six episodes would be like. He had, you know, glimpsed the plots and all the lines of dialogue—in a blinding psychedelic flash."

"Max, did Roy ever go to the police about Steve?"

"No, no. It wasn't like that."

"I suppose Roy didn't want the dog episode to come out, even after all that time."

"Anyway, after he came East, I don't think Roy heard from him for quite a while."

"He must've heard from him when 'Last Laughs' became a success in the mid-seventies."

Wiley's face fell slightly; perhaps he had hoped to withhold this last piece of information. "Well, yes, I believe he called Roy once—or I should say Roy only told me about one time. But Roy said that the tone had changed, that Steve had just called to say he'd really like to work for the show if that ever seemed like a possibility—"

"Well," Harvey said. "That has a certain menacing quality to it."

"I didn't get that feeling. Roy said he sounded better than ever, that he was now married and writing and also working as a salesman of some kind. Or maybe he had a desk job somewhere. In any case, it didn't sound like he was eating peyote buttons anymore. Or eating up his insides."

"He did end up on the show, though."

"And you know something?" Wiley said. "I never even heard from Jimmie—from Roy about that. I only found out about it after the fact, when I heard from Roy a few weeks ago. He called just to chat, and mentioned more or less in passing that he'd hired Steve as a writer. He said that if I'd just come out of retirement and direct 'Last Laughs,' it'd be like old times."

Harvey drew the fingertips of both hands from the bridge of his nose outward over his closed eyelids. "That sounds like it would've been great."

"I imagine the worst of their relationship was finally over," Wiley said.

Harvey said, "Max, if Steve threw Ganz out that window, I'd have to say that the worst was yet to come, wouldn't you?"

Wiley sighed. "If," he said.

"Does this mean that, after everything you've said, you're going to propose to me that someone else did it?"

"You never know."

"You sound to me like all you're doing is desperately trying to avoid the inevitable conclusion."

Wiley broke the cigar ash over the lip of the ashtray. "I suppose. You know, these two guys were like my kids there for a couple years." He rubbed his eyes. "It's like I had this one bright kid and one not-so-bright kid. You try not to play favorites, but I'll admit it was always more pleasant dealing with . . . Roy, but, still, even though I never made much of an effort with Steve all these years, I love him in my own way."

"I'm sure you do. Do you have kids of your own?"

"No, we don't," Wiley said. "Anyway, I've seen what happens to a lot of child-actors—the sadness of those who peak too—I was going to say peak too soon, but that's not really what happened to Steve Tolson. He didn't peak, he was just forced into a very public situation, and it affected so much of what was to follow. But Roy is—was one of the few real successes. He overcame."

Harvey smirked.

"Yes, I know. It's strange, the way it works. The same tenacity or self-interest or whatever you want to call it—the ruthlessness he showed even at that age—that same quality helped to guarantee his success, that he wouldn't be eaten alive in this business. Or any business."

Harvey thought of Curt Geller, whom they had had for breakfast, and he was dumb enough to show up for lunch.

"Harvey," Wiley said, "you asked me before to watch the show this Saturday."

"Yeah, there's a sketch that Steve wrote that Ganz refused to use, but now that he's dead, Leo Rhoades—the producer—is going to put it on, even though he has no idea, I'm afraid, what its real meaning is."

Wiley had held up a hand. "Well, I want *you* to watch something. At the Museum of Broadcasting.

I'm pretty certain they have a cassette of a show we did late in the second year, about Jimmie and Gerald's first airplane flight. It's considered to be one of the classic episodes. Watch it all the way through."

"I'll do that," Harvey said. "Now I haven't asked you why Steve decided to use—"

"Decided to use the name Richard Nacke?"

"Yeah. The sixty-four-thousand-dollar question," Harvey said. "He was a writer on the show. That's all I know."

"Ah," Wiley said slowly, "how can I describe Richard Nacke? He was a very sweet gentleman who took a liking to little Steve."

"So Steve had an ally on the show?"

"You could say that, I guess. So, anyway, I imagine that when Steve embarked on a writing career, this is how he honored him. Beyond that I wouldn't venture to guess."

At five that afternoon, as Wiley was putting Harvey back on the bus, he said, "I hope this was worth your while."

"Very much worth my while. Thanks for taking the time."

"I appreciate this, Harvey. Losing Roy *is* like losing a son."

"And Steve?"

"I hope I don't have to lose him too."

"Oh, Max, I think you lost him a long time ago."

Wiley drew his unzipped parka tighter around him. "Well," he said with contrived finality, "I hope all this makes more sense to you than my palindromes."

Harvey was tired of Wiley. "It scans," he said.

"Take care, Harvey." The bus driver tapped his horn.

"Good luck with your palindromes."

A slow smile broke over Wiley's face. "I'm," he said, "alas, a salami."

"I'm, alas, a salami," Harvey repeated, starting up the steps of the bus. "Very good, Max."

23

The next day, Thursday, began with a dream in which Harvey was surrounded in some unnamed clubhouse by a noisy swarm of sports reporters. "It wasn't a team effort," he was saying into the cluster of microphones. "It was a totally individual effort by me. I deserve the credit because I am responsible for all of it. I made all the hits today, I made all the catches, I scored all the runs. I was able to pitch well today because I was catching my own pitches. As the manager, I made some tough decisions, and I believe that the trades I made earlier in the season as the team's general manager have benefited this club immeasurably. And, no, I think the call I made at second base in the seventh inning was correct, and I stand behind it. . . ."

He had gone on like this until he was awakened by his own unbearable babble, and lay sweating on the blankets. Then he reached for the phone.

The night before, after returning from Sag Harbor, he had called Celeste Temkin, the "Last Laughs" makeup supervisor, and under the guise of being an out-of-town television producer named Michael Slavin, had gotten from her the names of two experienced free-lance makeup people in New York. Now he dialed the first name, Stacy Paultz, a makeup artist with extensive film and theatrical credits. She listened patiently as Harvey outlined what he wanted done, and then said, "Do you want to tell me what this is for?"

"No. I just want to know if you have the time to do it early this Saturday evening."

"It's the weekend," she said. "I'll have to charge you a little more."

"That's fine."

"This isn't for a belated Halloween party, is it?"

"No."

"I didn't think so."

Harvey finished with Stacy Paultz and called Detective Generra.

Generra said, "I heard you jumped ship, rookie."

"Altiser tell you that?"

"Yeah."

"Actually, I'm still aboard."

"What does that make you—a stowaway?"

"What I am is a guy who's about to hand you a collar."

"Are you trying to tell me you've cracked this?"

"Don't sound so indignant, Generra. Listen, I think you should plan to be in your car in front of the network building from about one A.M. on Sunday morning. I think I might be able to deliver the guy who was in Ganz's office with him when he went out the window."

"Is that so? The guy who was with him, or the guy who threw him out?"

Harvey still found it hard to believe that Nacke had actually tossed Roy out the window. "All right," he said. "The guy who threw him out or pushed him out or maybe he just opened the window and said, 'Jump.' "

"Oh, right. The guy who said, 'Jump.' "

"Whatever," Harvey said.

"Where you going to be in the building that you're going to be able to walk out with this guy?"

"Detective, if I told you, you'd want to be there, and if you were there, it would queer the deal."

"You're not going to tell me any more?"

"No," Harvey said. "I've got to do this my own way."

The detective paused for several seconds before

saying, "Yeah, all right. And you expect your man to just climb into the backseat of my car and say, 'Driver, Midtown Precinct North, please. And, oh, yeah, would you mind terribly putting the cuffs on me'?"

"No," Harvey said. "That's not what he's going to do."

What *was* Nacke going to do? And what was Harvey going to do, for that matter? How could he be so sure Nacke had done it? Nacke's lies, the puppy-grinding sketch, the mutual history, the secondhand sibling rivalry—did it have to amount to Ganz's death? While the parts were real enough, the sum of the parts could be taking place only in his own mind. Was that the meaning of the dream? That Harvey only *thought* he was in control of the game?

And yet—Ganz had not only implicated Nacke in the drama of his striving, but carried him forward into the present. Ganz had with his right hand scripted his success, while his left, out of view even from himself, had been scribbling a draft of his undoing. How else to explain the fact that Ganz had brought Nacke back into his life after these years of apparent remission in their disturbed relationship? Harvey thought now that Geller had had it right last week when he suggested that Ganz just might need to invite small disasters into his life to even the moral score. What better agent for the aloof Ganz's comeuppance than Nacke, with his fitful trajectory, peyote buttons, and near crash landings?

"I asked you what he's going to do then," Generra was saying.

"What he's going to do is he's going to come quietly with me," Harvey said.

"Oh, yeah? That's the kind of attitude that could put you on Hot Water Street in a minute. You got some deadly force?"

"Now, look—" Harvey began.

"Other than the deadly force of your special personality?"

"I don't think we're playing cops and robbers."

"No, I don't think you're playing cops and robbers, either. I think it's more like ex-baseball players and innocent suspects."

"If you're not there, then I'll figure something out. I could be wrong about this, anyway."

His show of humility disarmed Generra temporarily. After five seconds of silence he said, "All right. If I don't get any better offers on Saturday night, maybe I'll drive by and see what you're up to. But, frankly, I think there'll be better offers."

By the time Harvey got to the Museum of Broadcasting in the middle of the afternoon, the weather seemed to have turned the corner into winter—something in the air's heaviness, the resolute walk of Midtown pedestrians. In the museum's card catalogue room, he pulled out the *M* drawer and paddled his fingers forward to the "My Baby Brother" cards. There were six. The last one listed an episode from December 1955, called "First Flight."

Harvey had to wait ten minutes for a viewing console to free up. He slipped the videocassette in, punched PLAY, and sat back. This time he didn't miss it when Dolly the Dalmatian clattered down the steps of the Bolling household in the opening sequence. She came down the stairs right behind Nacke. He was a sturdy twelve-year-old with short brown hair severely parted on the side. He was wearing a smile that looked like he had borrowed it from another child-actor. His features somehow seemed much more interesting at twelve than they were at forty-three. At the bottom of the stairs Dolly raised her spotted head and barked once, poking at Nacke's side with her nose.

The episode unfolded with a familiar rhythm. Mr. Bolling announced at the dinner table that they were all going to take a plane to see his own mommy and daddy the following weekend. Nacke was troubled by the prospect, but Ganz was excited; in fact, it just so happened that Ganz's third-grade class was studying the Wright brothers, and the students had been asked to make reports on the subject of flight. As the day of the flight approached, the parents tried to allay Nacke's fears—Father's stories about flying in the Army during the war, Mother's sappy, daffy reassurances. She told Nacke about Dramamine. Today Dramamine, Harvey thought, tomorrow peyote buttons. The script arranged for Ganz to taunt Nacke about his trepidation. The subplot revolved around Ganz's top-secret class report, which he insisted on preparing behind the locked bedroom door. Since he shared the room with his older brother, this created yet another layer of fraternal friction.

In the end, the trip to Grandma and Grandpa's goes off with only a single hitch—that it's baby brother, of course, who gets temporary cold feet at the last moment. Safely back home, everyone is still wondering what Ganz's secret school project is. At last, it's ready and Ganz goes upstairs to get it after dinner. He comes down wearing a ludicrous pair of wings on his arms. Ganz's contraption has been crudely fashioned from bamboo tomato plant sticks, construction paper, old bed sheets, electrical tape, and his older brother's shoulder pads, for which Nacke has been looking. On the top face of the wings Ganz has lettered the words "AIR BOLLING."

Allan and Midge Bolling are delighted with their son's ingenuity. "You're a regular Orville Wright," Mrs. Bolling beams.

"Actually," Ganz replies with a tight-fisted smirk, "I've always identified more with Wilbur." It was the episode's biggest laugh line.

Harvey looked at his watch. The show was almost over and he still didn't know why Max Wiley had asked him to watch the episode. There were a few seconds of black on the tape, where the final commercial went, and then the final scene.

Nacke is knocking on the bedroom door. "Open up, Jimmie," he says.

From behind the closed door, Ganz's voice calls out, "It's open, Gerald. Stop yelling."

Nacke opens the door. The camera angle shifts to show him entering the bedroom and stopping, eyes wide. "What're you doing?" Nacke shrieks.

Cut to Roy Ganz poised on the sill of the bedroom's open window, flapping his enormous wings slowly. He looks over his shoulder at Nacke and says, "I'm getting ready to fly. That's what I'm doing."

Harvey reached out and stopped the machine. His

mouth was dry. Why had Wiley waited till the end of their long afternoon together to mention this episode? He pushed PLAY.

"You're crazy," Nacke says. "You can't fly!"

"Sure I can."

"Don't be an idiot, Jimmie. People can't fly."

"You never know until you try," Ganz says.

"You'll kill yourself. It's a long drop."

"You're just a scaredy-cat."

As Nacke approaches the window, Ganz starts bending at the knees and flapping his wings more vigorously.

"Better a live scaredy-cat than a dead Orville Wright," Nacke says.

"That's what *you* say. Here I go."

"Jimmie!"

"Bye, Gerald. Flight three fifty-nine cleared for takeoff."

As Ganz starts flapping harder, he begins to lose his balance, threatening to fall out of the window into the suburban night.

Cut to Nacke, watching in shock for a moment.

Cut to Ganz, flapping. "Help me, Gerald!" he yells. In the process of trying to regain his balance he breaks one of his wings against the window casing. "Help!" he screams in dead earnest as he starts to fall.

Cut to Nacke rushing toward him.

Cut to Ganz losing his balance.

Ganz, as seen from the yard. He is dangling from the windowsill by his ankles.

Nacke, hanging on for dear life to Ganz's ankles, slowly pulling his brother back into the bedroom.

Standing finally in front of his brother, Ganz, a pint-size Icarus with a broken wing, looks as if he's about to say something to Nacke. But the bedroom door opens and both parents burst into the room.

"*What* is all the ruckus about?" Dad says sternly.

Mom: "Are you boys all right?"

Dad: "Gee, your mother and I thought you two must've been fighting!"

Nacke puts his arm around Ganz. "It's nothing, Mom, Dad. Right, Jimmie?"

Ganz: "That's right, Mom, Dad. I—I just—I just . . ."

Mom, kneeling: "Well, what is it, Jimmie? And look what's happened to your wings! And your pants are all dirty!"

Ganz glances first at Nacke, then at his mother. "I was—I was just showing Gerald how my wings work, I was standing on the chair over there, and it slipped, and I fell down, and . . ." He starts to cry, badly.

Mom braces his little shoulders with her hands. "Oh, I'm so sorry, Jimmie."

Dad: "You didn't hurt yourself, Tiger, didja?"

Ganz: "I'm okay, Dad."

Dad, patting him on the head: "That's my boy. But, you know, you should be careful with those wings."

Mom: "The next thing you know, you'll be trying to fly out the window!"

Ganz wipes his tears away with a shirt-sleeve. "Don't be silly, Mom."

They all start to laugh, a chorus of good-natured television chuckles.

Dad, suddenly looking off to one side, hands on hips: "Hey, boys, now what's the window doing open?"

Cut to the open bedroom window. The camera dollies forward through the window toward the branches of a tree, then tilts up into the night sky as the theme music bubbles up and the first credit—"DIRECTOR MAX WILEY"—rolls.

══ 24 ══

Harvey, wearing a white shirt and short black waiter's jacket, stirred the scrambled eggs with a spoon. He stood behind the long table of chafing dishes— barbecued ribs, chicken livers wrapped in bacon, hash browns, sausages, biscuits, shrimp Creole, tortellini. At his back, the floor-to-ceiling windows of the network's penthouse showed a clear view of lower Manhattan. The Empire State Building's upper levels were lit an uncommemorative yellow tonight. Farther south, at the far end of the dark architectural sea, rose the bland, light-speckled towers of the World Trade Center. Harvey ran a spoon through Jerome Byers's creamy mass of cheese grits and glanced at Mickey Slavin across the room. She was standing by the door with Mike Altiser. It was almost one in the morning on Sunday, and the staff and cast of "Last Laughs" was beginning to get out of their makeup and filter into the vast penthouse.

Three hours earlier, in Stacy Paultz's apartment, the makeup artist had highlighted Harvey's hair, broadened his nose with foam rubber and Rubber Mask Grease, slightly discolored his teeth, and glued on a blond brush mustache. Even Jerome Byers, who had been forewarned of Harvey's disguise, had failed to recognize him when Harvey showed up in the small kitchen off the penthouse. Forty feet away, Mickey was wearing, courtesy of Stacy Paultz, a purplish-red birthmark on her temple, roughly the shape of California.

Between 11:30 and 12:30, Harvey had watched snatches of the show on the closed-circuit television in the kitchen. Leo Rhoades had successfully snared Alex Rind as the guest host. Candee, Nancy, and Brenda played three high school cheerleaders hired by a manufacturer of prophylactics to promote their product in the high schools. Harvey watched it until Jerome called him out to move some chairs.

Some time after midnight he returned from a trip setting up the buffet table to discover the puppy-grinding sketch in progress. Nancy Pildone, wearing a blazer with a "National Puppy-Grinding Company" emblem on the breast, had just poked her head in the door of Jimmy Lanahan's office and said over a lot of grinding and barking noises, "Excuse me, Mr. Crockett, but the first batch of German shepherd puppies just arrived. You want to take a look at them?"

Lanahan had to wait until the studio audience laughter died down before delivering his next line.

Now Harvey stood behind the buffet table, watching Candee Wersch stick her finger into the cheese grits.

"Hey, this is good," she said to him. "What is it?"

"Cheese grits," Harvey said. In trying to disguise his voice, he sounded like a cartoon character.

The penthouse was really a glorified function room, a high wide space with heavy green-and-white candy-striped draperies and upholstered Federal square-back sofas. Jimmy Lanahan wove his way between two of the sofas to the table. He had his arm around a woman. "Candee," he said, "have you met my friend Lucy?"

"Hi, again," she said to Lucy, then turned to Lanahan. "Remember? You already introduced me to her."

"Well, meet her again." Lanahan smiled.

"He's drunk," Lanahan's new girlfriend said with a sequined shrug.

"Hey," Wersch said, "I won't hold your choice of boyfriends against you."

"You were good in the show tonight," Lucy said.

"Thanks."

"Hey, give me a plate of those ribs, will you?" Lanahan suddenly said to Harvey, although it was evident that people were expected to help themselves.

"What's good here?" a voice on his right said. Leo Rhoades was swinging his head back and forth over the chafing dishes.

"Everything," Harvey said, lowering his voice.

"Huh?"

"All good."

As Rhoades helped himself, Celeste Temkin, the makeup supervisor, came up to him.

Oh, Jesus, Harvey thought, as if the fact that she had recommended Stacy Paultz entitled her to penetrate his disguise. He bent over and began polishing a serving fork with the cloth tucked in his belt.

"Leo," Temkin said, "will you please tell me what kind of party this is? It's just us. There's no fresh blood." There were, it was true, too few people for the size of the room. "I was hoping to meet the love of my life here tonight." She popped a chicken liver into her mouth. "There isn't even any music." There was, but nothing you could dance to.

Rhoades beeped and dropped a fistful of pork sausages onto his plate. "By the way, I thought you did a great job on Ron tonight. Excellent wattles."

"Nothing to it." But she was beaming. Harvey had caught a little bit of "Turkey Man," a Thanksgiving-inspired sketch in which Ron Fellows had been transformed by a failed biogenetics experiment into a creature with the body of a man and the head of a self-basting turkey. "Although I had a hell of a time getting his beak to stay on," she added.

Harvey glimpsed Mickey in conversation with Marty Beaver. He had never seen Beaver so animated. Microphone in her hand or not, Mickey had some power that enabled her to melt the resistance of most strangers, solder their attention to hers. He suspected that Mickey was asking Beaver some eccentric question about his work. In a world of people who didn't listen, her ability to find wonder in the commonplace was irresistible. The first time she had interviewed Harvey, her initial question had not been about the batting slump he was then experiencing, but whether his eating habits changed depending on his performance on the field.

Fifteen feet from Mickey, Dickie Nacke and his wife suddenly emerged from the shadowy perimeter into the better-lit center of the penthouse. They had had no choice but to come. They paused for a moment on the edge of the id"_ dance floor, Nacke with his hands shoved deeply in his pants pockets, she tentatively touching her short blond perm. Harvey could see how hard they were struggling with the painful charade of sociability. He remembered Sally better now, the angelic blonde who had come into the offices during the week of Kasick's show, asking for her husband. "Cornfed," the waiter at Saletra's had described her.

Mickey turned away briefly from Marty Beaver and caught Harvey's eye. She tilted her head in the direction of Nacke and his wife, flexing her brow. Harvey nodded, and she resumed her conversation with the Grand Old Man of Gags.

Jerome Byers himself had come out of the kitchen with a fresh tray of sausages. "How's it going, Harvey?" he said.

Harvey glowered. "The name's . . . Charles."

"Oh, yeah," Byers said, aggravating the situation by swiveling to see who might have overheard. "Got you, Charles, my man."

"But you can call me Chuck," Harvey said, "and the cheese grits are moving extremely well."

"I brought you more sausages." He emptied his tray into the chafing dish.

"Thank you."

"This is not a very funny crowd."

"You know," Harvey whispered, "when you're funny for a living, you—" He broke off. Nacke and his wife were coming toward the buffet table with drinks in their hands. "Jerome, don't you have something to do in the kitchen?"

"You trying to get rid of me, Chuck?"

"I got some business here."

Byers picked up his empty tray. "Just don't forget who signs your paycheck."

As Nacke and his wife approached, the downbeat jazz music gave way to some early Jackson 5. A few cast members, plus Karen Baldwin, took to the dance floor. Young Eddie Colasono did a modified breakdance. Nancy Pildone placed her hands on the padded shoulders of Rob Whent's outsize Italian sports coat and began to bounce distractedly.

"Hi." Nacke nodded to Harvey, causing his stomach to contract. "Could I have some eggs, please?"

Harvey had no choice but to throw a dollop of scrambled eggs on Nacke's plate.

Nacke reached for his own sausages. "Sally," he said, "you want something?"

She sipped her white wine. "I'm not hungry."

"You sure?"

"I said I'm not hungry."

"Those ribs over there look good," he said to her.

"Sweetheart," she said brittlely, crushing a crumb off his lip with a little too much force, "if *you'd* like some ribs, why don't you just help yourself?"

After Nacke and his wife had moved away to join Curt Geller, who had arrived alone, without Mimi Weiss, a small dapper man with a lush mustache and beard came up to survey the food. As his eyes met each dish, he hmmm'ed a different note. No one Harvey knew.

He looked up at Harvey quizzically. "Do you know what I think are the two finest phrases in the English language?" he said in a British accent.

Harvey stirred the scrambled eggs again. Joey Hanes and Ralph Morello, the show's director, had joined Nacke, Sally, and Geller. On the sound system, Elvis Costello had supplanted the Jackson 5.

"I say," the man said. "The two finest phrases in the language." He sucked wetly on a corner of his mustache.

Harvey didn't need this. He shook his head.

"Well, sport, I think the two finest phrases in the English language are 'A hint of mint' and 'The great smell of musk.' Don't you agree? I might also include 'Weak, neglected antifreeze.' "

Harvey couldn't turn his attention elsewhere because the man was his only customer at the moment.

The man leaned over the buffet table and whispered, "Let me recommend a new makeup person for you, Harvey."

Harvey looked him in the eye and said, "Sondell?"

"It takes one to know one, Harvey," he said, dropping the accent. "Nice try, but the nose doesn't fool me."

Harvey looked around him. "Would you do me a favor, Sondell?"

"Like don't make a public announcement that Harvey Blissberg, the allegedly erstwhile pursuer of Roy Ganz's killer, is now manning the buffet table, disguised as a Presbyterian Yuppie management consultant with a very bad dentist?"

"You ever hear of obstruction of justice?" Harvey whispered.

"That is the disguise, right?" Sondell selected a rib from the dish and gnawed it. "You *are* a Presbyterian Yuppie management consultant, right?"

"Barry, please behave yourself for once." Harvey was breaking into an immense sweat.

A giggle trickled out of Sondell's mouth. "Behave myself? Really, Harvey—you cheap blond. The least you could've done is get a decent disguise."

"It was working well enough till you showed up."

"But, of course, I'm the real test." He scraped the bare rib bone clean against his upper teeth. "Honestly, you're obviously here to close in for the kill. To nab your man. Sew it up. Who's the lucky suspect?"

Harvey rearranged the pork sausages—he'd just as soon they were Sondell's features—with a serving fork.

"Am I still in the running?"

"This isn't a game now, Sondell."

"Oh, it's all a game when you look at it from the right angle."

Geller was walking toward the buffet table.

"Please don't blow it, Barry. What will it take to shut you up?"

"This whole party was your idea, wasn't it? You're gonna smoke out your man tonight, right?"

Harvey looked past Sondell's shoulder. "Barry—"
Sondell turned around. "Well, hello, Curt."

"Hello," Geller said. "Do I know you?"

"Yes."

"Who are you?"

"C'mon, Geller. It's your old friend Barry Sondell."

"Nice to see you, Barry," Geller said, uninterested in Sondell's masquerade. He looked at Harvey. "Pretty eclectic spread—grits, steak tartare."

Harvey smiled beneath his false mustache, watching Sondell.

"How'd the show go tonight, Curt?" Sondell asked. "Did it have the appropriate tone of mourning?"

Geller refused to look at Sondell. "You don't even watch the show, do you?"

"If you've seen one bad sketch, you've seen them all."

Geller loaded some shrimp Creole and biscuits on his plate. "You're the only one who's funny, right, Barry?"

Sondell looked to Harvey. "This is a bitter guy, isn't it?" he said, indicating Geller.

Geller said, "Barry, there're a lot of people who could use all that money you make by not writing for the show. Whyn't you do something good for the economy? Like die."

"Now, that's funny," Sondell said. "That's very funny. Have you had anything on the show yet? Huh? What's your batting average? Although I admit you've been at a disadvantage. I want to be fair, Curt. They hired you to take Beaver's place, and they never got rid of Beaver. But that's just like Ganz, isn't it? Welcome to show biz. Why shouldn't I take their money? If I didn't, it'd just go up some network executive's nose, or help pay for more limousines, or pay some half-ass private detective to clean up their mess."

"I guess that's a reference to Blissberg," Geller said, turning to walk away.

"Well, what the hell do you expect from a mediocre former outfielder? Huh, Curt?"

"Take a walk," Geller said over his shoulder.

"A walk's as good as a hit," Sondell called out.

"Thanks," Harvey said to Sondell under his breath when Geller was gone.

Sondell ripped the meat off another rib. "Don't mention it." He had barbecue sauce all over his phony beard.

When Sondell was gone, Harvey looked up for Mickey and couldn't find her. He didn't see Sally, either, or her husband, Dickie.

25

Harvey came from behind the buffet table and walked briskly across the floor toward the double doors. People stood talking in twos and threes. It was not, by any reasonable social standard, much of a party. A nondescript instrumental had cleared the dance floor. In the foyer by the elevators, Marty Beaver was talking to Tweedledumpling and Tweedledee. "We tried that once, oh, twenty years ago on a Jay Reynolds special," was all Harvey caught.

He spun, slipped back into the penthouse, and turned into the kitchen. He told Jerome that he had to leave the buffet table, and Jerome sent a man named Juan to replace him. As he came out of the kitchen, Mickey appeared in front of him.

"I was just—" she began.

"What's happening?" he whispered breathlessly. "Where are they?"

"I don't know, I came out of—"

He took her by the arm and pulled her back out of sight into a corner of the kitchen. "Where are they?"

"Calm down, Bliss."

"Where *are* they?"

"Well, give me a chance."

"All right." Harvey took a deep breath.

"Here," she said, pressing a small object into his hand.

Harvey looked down at his hand. Mickey had slipped a small white jar of Dermablend into his palm.

"It worked like a charm," she said.

"She gave it to you?"

"I came up to her at the next sink and said, 'I wish I knew of a good makeup to cover this damn birthmark. I've tried everything.' "

"Yeah?" he panted. Where the hell was Dickie?

"And she said, 'Boy, did u ever say that in front of the right person! Would yo i believe I've got the ugliest damn scar tissue on my chin?' I said, 'You do?' 'Yeah,' she said, 'car crash. I hate it. It's a mean little thing that never healed properly.' I said, 'You'd never know.' "

"Yeah?" Harvey said impatiently.

"And she said, 'You need some of this,' and she pulled the jar out of her purse. 'It's the best thing I've found.' And, Bliss, she just gave it to me. She said, 'There's not much left in here, but take it.' "

"You're a genius, Mick. So where'd Sally go?"

"She left the bathroom before I did. When I came out, I saw her talking to Dickie. About, I don't know, ten minutes ago."

"Oh, Jesus."

"What? What, Bliss?"

"I'll bet Sally very innocently told Dickie about giving you the cream, and Nacke, who's got to be freaking out anyway, saw that something was up, and he took off. Our little ruse is working too well, Mick." He looked nervously around him. "Mick—I want you to stand guard by the elevators and make sure that Nacke, if he's still up here, doesn't leave this floor. Watch the stairs too. I'm going downstairs to see if he's already left the building."

She left the kitchen, but immediately wheeled back around and pushed Harvey away from the door. "Sally's standing out there talking to some other woman."

Harvey looked through the round window in the door and saw Sally talking with Karen Baldwin. Both of them were laughing. "Go," he said to Mickey.

Harvey rode down in the elevator alone. The security guard hadn't seen Nacke. Harvey ran through the high lobby with its dark muscular WPA murals and onto the sidewalk. Opposite the entrance he saw a Plymouth Fury of indeterminate color and ran up to the passenger window. Generra was sitting behind the wheel smoking a cigar. Harvey knocked on the glass. Generra waved him away. He knocked furiously, and Generra leaned over, rolled down the window a crack, and said, "Go on, get out of here, get lost."

"It's me, for God's sake."

"Blissberg?"

"Yeah, it's me. Open up." Across the street a busload of tourists was passing into the budget hotel.

Generra broke into a gray laugh. "You look like a fucking diseased Troy Donahue," he said.

"Did you see Nacke come out?"

"No."

"You're sure?"

"Yeah, I'm sure. What's with the nose and your goddamn hair?"

"I'll explain later. Nacke knows he's being set up, and I can't find him now. Watch for him, will you?"

"And what do you want me to do with him if I see him?"

"I don't know. Detain him. How's that?"

"On what grounds?"

Harvey looked over his shoulder at the entrance. "I don't know, come up with some grounds. Tell him— just tell him you know all about Dolly the dog, okay?"

"Who's Dolly the dog?"

"Just do it. Please? Okay? I'm going back upstairs."

Generra rolled up the window, laughing. "Dolly the dog, huh? What breed?"

Harvey took the elevator up to the twenty-fourth and rampaged through the halls, surprising no one but a cleaning woman vacuuming Leo Rhoades's office.

He punched the elevator button and had to wait a good minute and a half, slamming his open hand against the marble façade. When he got off at the fortieth floor, Mickey was leaning against the wall opposite the elevator bank. She shook her head slowly.

Harvey swept through the penthouse without luck. In the men's room the stalls were all empty—there must have been a time when you couldn't take a shit for all the cokeheads monopolizing the toilets. The only person in the bathroom was little Eddie Colasono, who glanced up at him from a urinal with his hairless wedge face. Fifteen going on forty.

"You seen Dickie Nacke?" he said. Colasono shook his head.

In the hallway outside the men's room, Harvey opened the door under the red EXIT sign and stood on the landing looking down forty stories of stairwell. He could hear no footsteps, only his own heart.

When he came back into the carpeted hall, Mickey was there. "I even asked Sally if she'd introduce me to her husband," she said. "She hasn't seen him."

"I've screwed up, Mick."

"What do you want me to do?"

"Go back and watch the elevators. I already checked the offices downstairs. No sign of him."

Harvey watched her turn the corner. Colasono came out of the bathroom and disappeared back into the party. An old Steely Dan song drifted through the double doors.

"Harvey?" a voice said behind him.

It was Sondell, leaning on a pretentious cane with one hand, pointing with the other to the fire door across from the men's room. "Try that door," he said.

Harvey pushed open the door and crept up a half flight of darkened stairs to a second metal door. Harvey reached under his white caterer's coat and from his belt pulled out the revolver that he had spirited out of Props. The simple sliding bolt lock on the door had been thrown open. With his left hand Harvey pushed the door open and took a single step onto the tar and gravel roof. He heard the muffled sound of a city below him. It sounded as if the taxis were honking in a jar. In the cold his first breath stuck in his throat. He opened the door farther, stepped completely onto the roof, and pressed his body against the wall of the small free-standing brick house that enclosed the exit.

To his right rose the carved granite tower that crowned the network building. Two-thirds of the way up the tower, blackened gargoyles guarded the turret. To Harvey's left was the girded cylindrical wood water tank on its metal stanchions, a frenzy of antennas, and the sooty scaffolded back of the huge neon ANC sign that looked out over Broadway. The unfinished face of a thirty-foot-tall woman wearing designer sunglasses looked back from a brick building two blocks away. Her sign painters had left her at the end of the last workday with half a mouth and no chin. Broadway cast a hot cloud of light upward, but it didn't reach the roof of ANC's building, which remained a world of dark, quiet shapes, as if it were standing in Manhattan's wings.

It was a minute before Harvey even noticed that Dickie Nacke was standing twenty feet in front of him. He stood with his back to Harvey, facing Broadway, on the two-foot-wide ledge that ran around the roof. It was the same side of the building that Roy Ganz had traveled two weeks before. In his sports coat and tailored slacks, gold I.D. bracelet picking up Broadway's light, Nacke peered over the edge. He looked as if he were trying to find a safe place to land.

Harvey took a slow step toward him and stopped, afraid that the sound of his feet crunching gravel might startle Nacke, with unforgivable results. But Nacke gave no indication that he knew he was no longer alone. After a moment Nacke raised his right hand and ran his palm over his face.

"Don't be an idiot, Dickie," Harvey said. He spoke just loud enough to be heard over the hum of the city. "People can't fly."

With a series of tiny shuffling steps, Nacke turned around on the ledge and said, "Roy proved that, didn't he?"

"Yeah, I think so, Steve."

"You can take your mustache off now, Harvey." He squinted in the furry darkness. He was trying desperately to be casual. "And put your gun away while you're at it. You look silly. And that looks like a prop gun."

Harvey threw it on the gravel.

"It is a prop gun, isn't it?"

"Does it matter?" Harvey said.

"If it were real and I could convince you to use it on me, it *would* matter. I'd rather be shot than jump."

"Those aren't the only options." Harvey took a step toward Nacke.

"Don't come any closer or I'll show you they are."

Harvey stopped. "You're not going to jump."

"Oh, yes, eventually I'm going to jump." He shuffled a quarter turn. The fall was on his right side, Harvey on his left. "Did you watch the show tonight?"

"Snatches."

"Did you catch the thing I wrote?" Nacke looked to his right and down.

"A little bit. But I've read it."

"You read it?" A little wind had picked up.

"I happened to pick up a copy. Maybe if I hadn't, you wouldn't be in this situation right now. You'd still be a free man."

"Harvey, this situation's fine with me. This is the best I've felt in years. I'd almost say that I kind of like it up here. These past two weeks, now *that* was hell. Not being able to run away, not being able to do anything."

Harvey's eyes were fastened on Nacke's feet, the narrow loafers standing on the ledge.

"I feel pretty damned good right now," Nacke said. "So what did you think of my sketch?"

"I liked it more than Ganz did."

"Ha!" Nacke fell silent. The two of them stood there in the cold. After about five seconds there was an instant when Harvey thought Nacke was going over. Instead, Nacke said, "What happened after that—after you read the sketch?"

"One thing led to another." Harvey kept his voice even and smooth.

"How'd you know about Steve Tolson? I don't imagine you recognized me, did you?"

"I recognized you at the Museum of Broadcasting."

He laughed lightly. " 'Don't be an idiot—people can't fly.' How could you tell it was me?"

"The knuckle-cracking gave you away."

"Huh." Nacke lifted his chin into the wind and exhaled forcefully. "I guess you've been in touch with Max."

Harvey pulled his white jacket around him tighter and crossed his arms.

"I mean Dolly and all that."

"I've talked to Max," Harvey said.

"Of course you have. Who's the woman who asked Sally about the birthmark? You know, in the bathroom before."

"Her name's Mickey. That's what tipped you off, wasn't it?"

"Yeah," Nacke said, "it was too odd to be incidental. But, you know, I don't get it. How'd you know about Sally's scar and the makeup?"

"Someone left a jar of her makeup in Ganz's apartment—"

"And once you'd figured out what Roy's and my relationship was in the past . . ." Nacke filled in.

"I guessed that the makeup was Sally's. And I sent Mickey in to confirm it."

"You didn't have to make such a production of it," Nacke said. "The theatricality of this place must be rubbing off on you."

"I wanted to be sure about Sally's makeup. I needed to be sure about what pushed you over the edge in the present."

Nacke ignored Harvey's unfortunate choice of metaphor. "You know, I've known that you knew for a few days."

"I know," Harvey said.

"Kind of a variation on two shy people who like each other but are afraid to say anything."

"Yeah."

"And that," Nacke said, "makes this our first date." He paused a long time. "I have to give you credit, Harvey, but there's a lot you don't know."

"Uh-huh," Harvey said. He shifted his weight from one foot to the other. "Steve, why don't you sit down on the ledge? Facing me. I'm not going to move."

"I think I'll stand. You want to know something funny?"

"Sure."

"I want to tell you something funny, because the show isn't very funny. Do you think the show's funny?"

"Sometimes."

"Oh, now that's a very polite way to put it. Anyway, here's what's funny. Sally didn't want to leave L.A. She didn't want me to take this job at all. She didn't even know that 'Last Laughs' was still on the air. She doesn't watch much television. I had to drag her here. And then she fell in love with Roy. You've heard of identifying with the aggressor, right? Well, this is called *fucking* the aggressor. Once I got her out here, just about the first thing she did was fall for Roy. She got the hots for the embodiment of the show that she didn't know was still on the air, the embodiment of the show that dragged her away from home." He blew a "Ha!" into the night. "Now *that's* funny."

"She fell in love with Ganz even without knowing about you and him?"

"That's right. Of course, it takes two to tango. And old Roy could tango with the best of them. You know he *had* to go for her, don't you?"

"Uh-huh," Harvey said.

"You know he had to do these things to me."

"Seems so."

"Yeah."

"Sally doesn't know about Gerald Bolling, does she? Let alone that you were born Steve Tolson."

"She *didn't* know about either of them. She knows now. We've done a lot of talking the past week."

"It's hard to believe she never knew before."

"Not that hard. You remember 'Leave It to Beaver,' don't you?"

"Sure."

"Well," Nacke said, gazing out over the rooftops toward Broadway. Harvey had to strain to hear him when he faced the other way. "I read just a few months ago that Jerry Mathers, the Beaver himself, said he tried to organize a reunion of the show's cast and he couldn't find the guy who played the Beaver's friend, Larry Mondello. A guy named Rusty Stevens.

So he hired a private detective, who found Rusty selling insurance in Atlantic City. But when they called Rusty's house, Rusty's wife kept saying they had the wrong number. Later they learned that he had simply never told her that he'd been on the show. And when she asked Rusty finally why he never said anything, he told her, 'It never came up.' Ha! It never came up. And old Rusty never even bothered to change his name. So you can imagine how easy it's been for me to keep it a secret. No, I'm afraid it just . . . never came up."

Harvey wondered if he should yell for help.

"It's an occupational hazard of being a child-actor—that later on, you wish to dear God that you'd never been one. I can't tell you. And I can't tell you what hell it was to hear Sally tell me"—he spat over the edge—"about her plans."

"Her plans?"

It was Nacke's turn to say nothing.

Harvey said, "She told you she was leaving you for Ganz, right? The last straw."

"When I had him in his office that night . . . two weeks ago—" His voice drifted.

"What happened, Steve?"

"I told him I wanted to discuss Sally with him, man to man, just clear the air. It took me two hours to pry him away from his celebrity friends. I don't think he knew that Sally had told me about the two of them. But I got him in his office and then I closed the door behind us, and I only thought I was going to kick the shit out of him."

"And complete the job you started thirty years ago? When Wiley pulled you off of him?"

Nacke looked through Harvey for a moment, then said, "Yeah, but then I thought—then suddenly all I could see was Jimmie and Gerald, not Roy and Steve or Roy and Dickie, or anything. I'd had a few, you know, but I just thought I was going to kick the living shit out of him, and quit the show, and—and—and I don't know what—"

"Please get off the ledge."

"No!" Nacke shouted. "I *will not move!* I opened

the fucking window and I picked Roy up and I put him on the window sill—he doesn't weigh any more than a fucking child—and I said to him, I said—I said—I said, 'Let's try it this time without the wings, Jimmie, shall we?' " He turned away from Harvey and screamed into the night, *"LET'S TRY IT THIS TIME WITH-OUT THE FUCKING WINGS, JIMMIE, SHALL WE?"*

Against the lights of Broadway, Harvey could see the beads of Nacke's spittle fly like a handful of small jewels. He took advantage of Nacke's turn to advance two more steps. He was now no more than ten feet from the ledge.

Nacke swiveled sharply and said, "I've got to tell you—if you come one step closer I'll jump right now, and you'll never know the rest of it."

"All right. I've stopped now."

"Kill my dog," Nacke said, "woo my wife while I have to stay late every night, keeping these college hours. I don't know." He sucked in some air. "So—Max told you how Roy killed Dolly." He changed the subject as if throwing Ganz out the window had been a digression from the real story, the one way back there about the dog.

"Yeah, he told me."

"And did he tell you about Richard Nacke?"

"He just said he thought you might've taken his name later on because he was an important person to you."

Nacke coughed up a shrill laugh. "Ha! Well, what do you expect? Max is the original slimeball. I tell you, Harvey—Mr. Roy Ganz, my baby brother, he died of . . . you know how they should've listed his official cause of death? They should've said he died as a result of inflicting a long series of insults on Steve, Gerald, and Dickie. With Max's help, of course." He was trembling.

Where was everybody? "So who was the real Richard Nacke?"

"Oh, yes, the *real* Richard Nacke. When I was . . . about ten years ago, when I decided to try to become a writer and make something of my life, I . . . I"—he shot a glance over the edge into the alley, as if to make sure that it hadn't moved—"I called just about everyone I could think of who might help me or teach me something . . . I wanted to make something . . . so I called the writers of 'My Baby Brother,' there were five in all, 'cause you know, they'd remember me, even though it had been twenty years. Of course, I'd only met one of them when I was with the show, because out there, in Hollywood, I mean, it's not like 'Last Laughs,' where the writers and the actors work together. Out there the actors hardly ever see the writers. So that's how it was."

His voice trailed off, stopped, and he looked up at the sky. Harvey wondered if he'd forgotten the rest of the story, or was too tired to go on.

"Then what, Steve?" Harvey said. "What happened then?"

"I think I'd like it if you called me Dickie."

"Of course."

"So some of them talked to me, gave me the names of agents, things like that. One of them had died. Then I tried to find Richard Nacke. I called the Writers Guild to try to find this guy Richard Nacke, and the only address they had for him was in care of guess who?"

"I don't know," Harvey said. "Who?"

"Max Wiley."

"Wiley?" Harvey was at a loss.

"Wiley was his mailing address. But Wiley was already living back East and I had bigger fish to fry, I didn't need to be asking favors from someone three thousand miles away. There were enough writers I knew in L.A. that I could hit on for help. So I didn't think anything about it. And then one night about five years ago, I guess I must've been reading about some Hollywood creative bookkeeping scandal or something, and I woke up in the middle of the night thinking about Max Wiley and Richard Nacke. I woke up and I realized that Richard Nacke didn't exist."

Harvey shifted his weight on the gravel. The huge neon ANC sign shed watery rose-colored light on the roof to his left.

"So I called old Max and he picked up the phone and I said, 'Hello, Max, this is Richard Nacke. How are you?' And there was this long pause, and then I said, 'I was wondering about my last residual check, Max. I haven't received it.' And there was a long pause again. And I cornered him.''

"I think I get it."

"He wasn't anybody!" Nacke yelled. "He was nobody. But Max Wiley had sure been cashing his checks for years."

No wonder Wiley had insisted that Harvey refer to Dickie Nacke as Steve; to call him Nacke cut too close to the truth Wiley was concealing. "And so you decided to take his name," Harvey interrupted.

"Nobody else was using it. Changing your name—easiest damn thing in the world if you haven't committed a felony. Ha! Anyway, I was pretty damned tired of my own. And using it had a—well, it had a certain justice to it. I changed 'Richard' to 'Dickie' when I joined the Writers Guild for 'Last Laughs' in September, 'cause I knew they already had a 'Richard Nacke' on their rolls. But I was saying that old Max had been getting Nacke's salary checks, and then his residual checks for years. But of course he had to share the money.''

"With Ganz?" Harvey said.

"Roy?" Nacke wiped his nose with the back of his hand. "When the scam started, Roy was only seven years old. No, not Roy." He turned a faint smile toward Harvey.

His secret knowledge had momentarily distracted him from the edge. Everyone loves a game, and Harvey was beginning to understand how much Nacke had enjoyed this one for the past few years. "So who was it?" Harvey asked.

"*Celia,*" Nacke said. "Celia Ganz. Roy's charming mother. Who else?"

Harvey had the impression of peeling away the last layer of muscle to expose the beating heart of the thing. Nacke was saying, "Hey, in Hollywood, you can always use a little more money. Celia wore hers in the form of furs. She was the real businessman in that family, not Roy's dad. For all I know, it was her idea."

"Did Max try to stop you from using what you knew?" he said.

"No, because I told him I had better uses for it."

"Like getting a job on 'Last Laughs'?"

The corners of Nacke's mouth flicked upward. "Well, hell, Roy didn't need any bad publicity while he was trying to mount, you know, a major comeback, now did he?" Nacke's breathing accelerated. "Well, of course, I *can* write, you know. It wasn't just what I knew. Was it?" He said the last two words so softly that Harvey almost didn't catch them.

"And he knew? About his mother's deal with Wiley?"

"She told him finally. I guess the prospect of old age and dying had, you know, galvanized what was left of her conscience. What her character hadn't eaten away."

Harvey wasn't sure how to proceed. He didn't want Nacke to stop telling stories, but he also didn't want the conversation to take the wrong turn.

"You'd think," Nacke said, "that Roy would've wanted to watch his step around me. Given what I knew."

Max and Celia's scam, Harvey thought, implicated Roy Ganz only by familial association. He would have survived its revelation. Unless his devotion to his mother made Nacke's knowledge too threatening. It was possible —Roy needed to protect not only his mother, but his surrogate father as well. In any case, Harvey saw that Nacke's simple presence on the premises of "Last Laughs" would have to have been a constant rebuke to Ganz.

"I once slugged him in a restaurant while he was having dinner with a woman," Nacke said.

"Max told me."

"The woman was my girlfriend."

Bound by something worse than blood. To be bad brothers would have been a thousand times better.

"Roy's mother was buying furs with money paid to someone who didn't exist, who was supposed to be writing for 'My Baby Brother.'"

"I understand," Harvey said. A phantom writer, just like Barry Sondell.

"Supposed to be writing scripts where Roy would look good at my expense." The pain got caught in Nacke's throat and he coughed to cover it. "Roy's mother was buying furs and mine was dying of alcoholism. You know, I had a fucking mother too!"

"Whyn't you come down now?"

"I don't see why."

"Because you're going to be all right."

"Yeah, if you like jail."

"Don't worry about jail."

"Oh, c'mon!"

"You didn't go into Ganz's office intending to kill him."

"No, maybe not."

"Okay then."

"I've been fucked up in my life."

"Okay. So you've been fucked up in your life. It's behind you now."

"Yeah, everything's behind me. My whole fucked-up life's behind me." His voice rose. "No, I want to jump! I swear to God, I'm going to jump!"

"No you're not." He took a cautious step toward Nacke. All that Dickie Nacke had to swallow, all the indigestible, gristly material of his life. "You're not going to jump, Dickie. Everything's going to be taken care of."

"You said it. Everything's going to be taken care of now. Why don't I just save everybody a lot of trouble?"

"Listen to me now. You're not jumping. There're a lot of people who care about you. You have to believe me now, I'm serious." Just keep talking, keep talking. "Are you listening to me? You want to do the smart thing now. You just want to keep your head. The worst is over now." He wished he had the power to acquit Nacke right then and there on grounds of temporary insanity. "You weren't thinking when you did what you did. That wasn't you, was it? Ganz was quite a load to carry around for your whole life." Keep the words coming. "You've got the strength to go on. I know you do. C'mon, give me your hand now."

Nacke ignored his hand. "I'm fucked, Harvey." He was swinging his head back and forth, from Harvey to the abyss, over and over again. He was losing it again.

"Listen to me now," Harvey said. "Are you listening to me?"

Nacke kept swinging his head, saying, "I'm fucked," over and over.

"Are you listening? Say yes. Say yes, you're listening, goddamn it!"

Nacke stopped swinging his head long enough to look at Harvey, to look at him with some queer fire in his eyes, as if he had never seen Harvey before in his life.

"I won't let you jump," Harvey said. "You hear me? I . . . won't . . . let . . . you . . . fall. Are you with me? Are you with me now?"

Nacke was staring at him, saying nothing. Harvey thought, I've got to keep his eyes on me. "Listen to me now, because it's me talking to you. It's Harvey Blissberg. If you don't come down from the ledge now, I won't be able to forgive you, Dickie. I like you. Are you listening? You didn't know what you were doing. It's that simple. Things like this happen, and it happened to you. But you are not a killer. Are you with me on that?"

"I—" Nacke began.

"You what?"

"I—I didn't really push him out . . . the window."

"Okay, then."

"I know—you know—I did put him up there—I opened the window—and I put him up there—even though he didn't want to go—I remember that part—"

"Listen to me. I can't come over and get you. You have to do it yourself. You have to climb down from the ledge on your own. I'm not going to move until you've come down. This is something you have to do yourself." Please be the right thing, Harvey prayed. If you jump now, I won't be able to forgive myself. Ever. But I think that if I move, you'll jump. Be the right thing. "Listen to me. I'm going to step back." Harvey retreated a few steps. "I want to give you plenty of room. You're going to step down and come over to me, and we're going to go on talking about this. You're going to live. Do you understand? You're going to live. That's all there is to it. Can I have your promise now?"

Nacke turned to look over the edge. Please, Harvey thought, please be saying good-bye to that jump.

"I think I have to jump."

Nacke lost his balance slightly. The soles of his loafers made scraping sounds, unbearably loud, on the stone. Harvey's guts lurched up. He felt as if he was going to pass out. He lunged forward.

Nacke regained his balance by bending over, palms flat on the ledge. He steadied himself on all fours.

"There you go," Harvey said, letting his breath out in stages. He was still several feet away from him. "Now just let your knees down slowly on the ledge. Then you'll feel much safer."

"I can still jump." What sadness and defiance there were in that. In the show Ganz flapped his wings on the bedroom windowsill, but in real life it was Nacke who needed desperately to escape.

"Please put your knees down now."

Very slowly, Nacke lowered his knees, and then his whole body, until he was lying flat on the ledge, gripping the sides with his hands. He laid his right cheek on the stone, looking away from the edge. Tears glittered in his eyes, picking up the red neon from the sign.

"Now just roll this way onto the roof. There you go."

Nacke didn't budge. Harvey was about to grab him when Nacke said, "Would—"

"Yes?"

"Would you come get me?"

When Harvey had rolled him off and they were sitting side by side against the inside of the ledge, Nacke began to sob. For the first time in several minutes Harvey was aware of the sounds of the city going about its business forty stories beneath them.

For many minutes they said nothing. Once or twice

Nacke looked up at Harvey, but Harvey kept his own face turned away.

"Poor Steve," Nacke said after a while. "Poor Steve, poor Dickie, poor Gerald."

"Yeah," Harvey said. "All those different lives, and none of them yours."

26

Harvey packed on Monday afternoon. On the bed of his room at the Crown, he carefully folded his olive-green fashion trenchcoat with the leather collar. He wadded up his dirty underwear and socks and shoved them in the plastic bag in which the Korean market had put his Pepperidge Farm shortbread cookies. As he collected his spiral notebook and other belongings from the table by the window, he checked his illegally parked rental car down below on Madison. On the table, underneath a yellow cardboard Double Duck Deli coffee cup and pecked-at peach Danish, his image glowered at him from the front page of the *New York Daily News*. While he and Generra had led Dickie Nacke into Roosevelt–St. Luke's Hospital early Sunday morning, a photographer had snapped the three of them. Harvey wore a violated expression. He had let Generra and Altiser handle most of the questions at the press conference later in the day.

Harvey had had little trouble persuading Mickey to spend a day or two cooling out at an inn on the southern coast of Rhode Island that had the distinction of having installed, on its widow's walk, a hot tub with a view of Block Island. At the moment, she was out on Madison shopping for a new miracle cream for the skin around her eyes, the ointment she mail-ordered from New Jersey having failed to reverse completely the progress of her wrinkles.

They made one stop on their way out of town. The Pavilion Park Nursing Home occupied a sturdy prewar building on Manhattan's Upper West Side, its once red brick deep burgundy with dirt and age. In the solarium on the fourteenth floor Harvey sat next to Mickey on a laminated chair and contemplated New Jersey across the Hudson. The very old, some with assistance, others on their laborious own, scraped softly in and out of the bright room. The nurse Harvey had spoken with over the phone, and again ten minutes earlier on his arrival, pushed Celia Ganz toward them in a wheelchair.

Harvey and Mickey stood and said hello as the nurse took Mrs. Ganz's skeletal hand and announced in a rather loud voice, "Celia, dear, this is Harvey and this is Mickey. They're doing some research about your son, and they'd like to talk to you."

Celia Ganz raised her right hand—the arm revealed by the falling sleeve of her pastel housedress looked like a dowel rod loosely wrapped in white muslin—and brought her hand to her chin. She had painted a small, bow-shaped, coral-colored mouth in the middle of her thin lips. Clouds of rouge wandered across her cheeks. "My son," she said in a tiny voice.

"That's right, dear," the nurse said, releasing her other hand and laying it in her charge's lap. "Your son, Roy." She turned her head and winked knowingly at Harvey.

With some effort Celia Ganz slowly lifted her right leg and crossed it over her left one. With three sweeps of both hands, she smoothed the housedress over her knees. This done, she smiled proudly at Harvey and Mickey and said, "See how nice I cross my legs?"

"Very nice," Harvey said.

"I'll leave you alone with these nice people now, dear." The nurse leaned over and whispered in Harvey's ear, "Remember our agreement."

"Don't worry," Harvey said.

"I'll be back in ten minutes. You mustn't tire her."

In response to Harvey's small talk—about Roy's brilliance, the significance of "Last Laughs" for his generation, the solarium's incomparable view of New

Jersey—Celia Ganz dispensed a variety of smiles. Some
were silly grins, others childlike smirks that suggested
a powerful and largely vanished vanity, but none of
her expressions indicated she cared about—or understood a single word of—what Harvey was saying. Only
when he worked around to the subject of "My Baby
Brother" did something in her eyes ignite.

"What a lovely show!" she said. "Is it still on?"

"Now, Mrs. Ganz, I think you know it's been off
the air for almost thirty years."

She tilted her head slightly and smiled the remnants
of a dazzling smile.

"Yes, 'My Baby Brother' *was* a long time ago, wasn't
it?"

"A long time," Harvey said. "But isn't it funny how
we can remember things that happened a long time
ago so much easier sometimes than we can remember
what happened this morning?"

Mickey reached out between the chairs, took Harvey's hand, and gave it a squeeze.

Celia Ganz puckered her mouth, the painted mouth
forming a coral oval, offering this expression to one,
then to the other. In her entitled bearing it was easy to
see the son.

"You're such a nice young couple," she said.

"Well," Mickey said, "thank you *so* much."

"Lovely, dear. Just lovely."

Harvey took a breath and said, "You know, Mrs.
Ganz, we're especially interested in the director of
'My Baby Brother.' Max Wiley."

She blinked at him, altered her smile slightly, folded
her knotty hands in her lap, and looked at them with
pleasure.

"Now I know you know Max Wiley," Harvey said
with a light laugh. "Max Wi-ley."

She tugged at the hem of her housedress, managing
to pull it a quarter of an inch over her alabaster knees.
"Well, I believe I do know him," she said. "He's quite
a gentleman. *Quite* the gentleman."

"You and he were pals in those days, weren't you?"

"My, yes. I think we were." She began very subtly
to rock her hips forward and back, bracing her hands

on the wheelchair grips. "Lovely gentleman. Very generous."

Mickey turned to Harvey, delight dancing in her eyes. He returned a quizzical look. She nodded in the direction of Celia Ganz, whose rocking was now more pronounced, leaned toward Harvey, and whispered, "Don't be dumb, Bliss."

He shrugged and was about to ask Celia his next question when the slight figure in the wheelchair beckoned both of them closer.

"In all my years on this planet"—eyes flashing right and left—"in all my years on this planet," she repeated, then stopped, her secret too precious.

Harvey leaned closer. "Yes?"

"You're such a lovely couple," Celia whispered.

"Please go ahead."

"But," she said, "in all my years on this planet, Max Wiley . . . was . . . by far . . . the . . ." A little giggle chirped in her throat.

"Yes?" Harvey said.

"In all my years he was . . . the single . . . best . . . *screw* . . . I ever had." Her clenched hands flew open and she fell back in her wheelchair. "There! I said it! But it's true!"

Mickey coughed quietly into her fist.

Celia Ganz beckoned them again with a finger. "Let me tell you," she whispered, "it's true! You, my dear"—she tapped Mickey's knee—"you should be so lucky!" She bore scant resemblance to the wraith who had been wheeled in ten minutes before.

Harvey wiped a hand down his face. "Mrs. Ganz," he said, "quite apart from your romantic dealings with Max Wiley—"

"If only you'd been there, young man—"

"Isn't it true that you and Max played a little game back in the fifties?"

"Yes, we played quite a bit, a lovely man, that Max—"

"No, Mrs. Ganz. What I'm referring to is that apparently you and Max Wiley invented a writer who didn't exist, and you opened a bank account for him, and split the money between the two of you."

For the last few seconds she had been making smacking noises and wagging her index finger back and
forth. "Now, I don't believe you're supposed to know
about that," she whispered. "Now *that* is a secret."
Either some neurological deficit had transformed her
long-term memory into a coquette's game, or else
Harvey was talking to a woman whose conscience had
been on a very long coffee break.

"Then you remember what I'm talking about?"

"Shhh." She winked at both of them. "They never
caught us."

"It's not a joke," Harvey said, although he was well
aware that his opinion, or anybody else's, was lost on
her.

She batted her pale lashes. "It was—well, it was just
one of those silly things that lovers do."

"Do you remember the name of the writer you and
Max made up?"

"Well, if you just give me a moment." She drew
down her translucent eyelids. "It will come to me
because I picked the name myself. Yes, I picked the
name of one of my first loves. A lovely young boy
named"—she opened her eyes—"Nacke. Dick Nacke.
A funny little name. Yes, I remember, I used to call
him Snick Snack. Oh, he was very precious. Dick
Nacke Snick Snack. He was a year younger than I
was, he had the most lovely hairline, and sometimes I
think I should have married him."

Five minutes later, when they said good-bye to Celia Ganz in the corridor outside the solarium, she
reached out and held Harvey's wrist. "Tell me," she
said. "How *is* Roy? He's such a lovely boy." She
frowned theatrically. "But he hasn't come to see me
lately."

They had been on the Long Island Expressway for
two or three miles when Mickey said, "Bliss, about
Celia Ganz and this guy Max—do you get the feeling
that Roy had some subliminal sense of what was going
on and, you know, maybe he was taking some of it out
on Nacke and his dog? I mean, if Max was like Roy's
father, and he sensed on some level that his mom was

schtupping Max, well, I don't know, it must've been very confusing for him."

A cold November drizzle started, and Harvey flicked on the wipers. "Yeah, Mick, I get that feeling."

After another mile she said, "Bliss, it hasn't escaped my notice that we're on the Long Island Expressway. Do you sometimes get the feeling that if we're going to Rhode Island we ought to be on the New England Thruway rather than the Long Island Expressway?"

"I've got another errand to run. In Sag Harbor. Then we'll take the ferry over to New London."

"Max Wiley?"

"Yeah."

"What for? I thought Detective What's-his-name was going to question Wiley."

"He is. I wonder if they're going to prosecute him. I wonder if there's a statute-of-limitations on this sort of thing."

"So what's your errand?"

"I don't know."

"Bliss, it seems to me that the quickest route from Roy Ganz's death to the rest of your life doesn't pass through Max Wiley. Maybe we should just kind of move on."

"I've got to talk to Wiley."

"Why?"

After half a mile he said, "You know, after we lost a game, I was often the last one to leave the locker room. It was like there might be something I could do to change things if I stayed long enough."

"Well, there's nothing you can do to change things. And I don't see how you can call this a loss."

He set the wipers at the faster speed. "I don't know," he said. "Just don't tell me this is what winning feels like."

When they arrived in Sag Harbor, it was still cold and wet, and now it was very dark. Harvey called Max Wiley from a phone booth outside the Sand Bar on Main Street while Mickey stayed in the car scanning the Rhode Island section in a guide to New England eateries that purported to elevate turkey club sandwiches to the ranks of America's great culinary contributions. Harvey punched in Wiley's home number, wondering after all if Mickey didn't have a point, if he was just hanging around the clubhouse in his underwear long after everyone else had gone home.

Wiley answered, saying, "Hello?" in his crinkly voice.

"Max, it's Harvey Blissberg."

"Oh." There was a pause. "You know, Harvey, I feel like I've also been waiting for *this* phone call."

"I'll bet you have."

"I got the *Times* right here. So Roy was about to steal Steve's wife. Figures. Roy was always sort of frisky. A sad business. Did you go watch that episode I told you about? Pretty chilling, huh? Talk about life imitating art. I'm getting the chills right now. That's if you want to call 'My Baby Brother' art." He was talking a mile a minute. "Some people treat these old shows as if they were high art, you know. Symposiums and graduate theses and all that. But to me it was just a job. You know, there was nothing in the *Times* about the flying episode. I was wondering—"

"Shut up, Max. I saw Celia Ganz today."

"Celia Ganz? I'm not sure what you're talking about."

"Then read between the fucking lines, Max."

After a long pause Wiley said, "So I guess you want to come out here again and have a little talk."

"I'm already here, Max."

"Where?"

"I'm practically in your front yard."

"Oh."

"So I wouldn't take that long-awaited vacation just yet, Max."

"I'm too old to leave town."

"But not too old to cash Richard Nacke's checks, right?"

Wiley didn't respond for many seconds, and Harvey couldn't tell whether his silence indicated contempt for the question or was just the wordless recognition that nothing now, certainly not ripping up Nacke's next residual check, would make the slightest bit of difference. "Nacke's deceased."

"Right. I forgot," Harvey said. "What'd you do?

Notify the Writers Guild of his death right after you found out that Steve Tolson was onto you?"

"That's right."

"Brilliant, Max."

"Well, Harvey," Wiley said after a pause, "as long as you're here, you're welcome to stop in. If you think it'll do some good."

Harvey hesitated. He was going four hours and three ferry rides out of his way to talk to Wiley, and now it seemed pointless. The rain ticked against the glass of the telephone booth. In the yellow interior light of the Buick rental, Mickey slowly turned the pages of the guide.

"Max?"

"Yes?"

"Why the hell didn't you tell me everything the last time I was out here? How the hell could you lie to me?"

There was a pause. "Lie to *you?* Harvey, in all the years I've lied about this, now don't you think I lied to many more important people than you? I mean, with all due respect. And I didn't lie—I simply gave you part of the truth. Look"—he sighed—"okay, I plead guilty. I plead guilty to falling in love with a married woman many years ago. And I plead guilty to stealing money from the network. I'll pay it back, I'll make a deal, whatever. After a while I didn't need the dough, but what was I going to do? If I'd tried to put a stop to it—I only could've stopped getting the money by confessing that this guy never existed, that I was a first-class schmuck, and it would've killed my career."

"What, are you crazy? You could've killed Nacke off years ago if you'd wanted to! But you waited till Tolson found out."

"I was sending the dough to Celia."

"So your hands are clean, right?"

"You know, Harvey, maybe even you—maybe even you've done something dumb that'll reach up out of the deep in twenty or thirty years and take a huge bite out of your balls. You hurt the ones you love, and all that bullshit."

"We were talking about you, Max."

Wiley paused. "So you saw Celia?"

"Yeah. This afternoon."

"Hmmm. How, uh . . . how was she?"

"She was fine, Max. Very forthcoming."

"She talked about me?"

"She was at her best when she was talking about you. You know, that was a hell of a way to be Roy's surrogate daddy. Did you have to fuck his mother?"

"Roy's real daddy sure as hell wasn't fucking her. Look, Harvey—"

"Look, Max." Harvey was tired. "A detective named Generra's going to be in touch with you."

"Well, I'm not going anywhere. You know, you're welcome to come over. Maybe you want to know the details."

"I think I know enough details."

"Charlotte's making some kind of Mediterranean fish stew. There's plenty."

"I've got a better invitation."

"You sure?"

"Good-bye, Max." He hung up quickly, got back in the Buick, started the engine, and said, "All right, let's go." Mickey assessed his mood with a glance and said nothing. Harvey waited for a pickup to barrel by, and backed out of the space. Neither of them spoke until they were on the little ferry from North Haven to Shelter Island, when she said, "The guidebook says there's a nice place not far from the inn. The clear clam chowder comes highly recommended."

The ferry was a minimalist barge, functional to a fault, nothing more than a way of getting from one place to another, very nearby. Theirs was the only car on the boat. They cracked the windows to let in some of the cold black air.

"Chowder sounds fine," Harvey said, watching the thin necklace of lights strung across the shore of Noyack Bay.

"Hey, you got to look ahead. Even if it's only to a bowl of clear clam chowder."

Harvey turned to her. He felt like he hadn't really seen her in months. "Hi, Mick," he said.

"Hey, Bliss." She smiled.

He reached out and took her hand across the carpeted chasm between the bucket seats. He opened the driver's window farther and sucked in some sea air. An original grievance between two boys, he thought—or was it between a boy and his mother?—or between a mother and her husband?—whatever it was, it had grown, radiated, been passed on from one to the other, and passed back again. It was a telephone game, history, each whisper more unreliable than the last, ending in a disastrous distortion. When the game was over, you could no longer tell what the original message was.

About the Author

RICHARD ROSEN is the author of the 1985
Edgar Award–winning *Strike Three You're
Dead*, as well as *Fadeaway*, both of which
feature Harvey Blissberg. Both novels are
available in Signet editions. Rosen's award-
winning work as a television commentator
and humorist includes the 1983 PBS comedy special "The Generic News." He has
also worked as a writer for a late-night network comedy show. He lives with his wife,
Diane McWhorter, in New York City.

JAMES MAXFIELD MALLORY IS ON A
CHASE THROUGH BOSTON'S
UPPERCRUST TO FIND A MURDERER
WITH A SENSE OF STYLE

A Secret Singing
A Mystery by
Richard C. Smith

One thing Boston private investigator James
Maxfield Mallory learned in his business was
that the rich are different, they even kill with
that touch of class. When the aging Caleb
Johnson was propelled to the hereafter with
a dash of cyanide in a $2,000 gift bottle of
scotch, he left behind a young blonde bride
and a suspicious stepdaughter with a few
skeletons of her own beside the minks in her
closet. With all trails leading from a sleazy
underworld gambling syndicate straight to the
city's biggest law firm, Mallory's chase un-
covers some revealing secrets about the
uppercrust—secrets someone wanted him to
die for. . . .